"Listen, Trent, I should be honest with you."

She pierced him with a look so earnest, he held his breath.

"Please."

"I don't want you to think I'm...well...a maiden in distress. I can take care of myself. One of the things I've realized is that I'm a magnet for guys who...are inappropriate for me."

"That's diplomatic." He frowned.

"I can't stand losing control. You have to know that, and right now I can't let you take over my life—"

"I wasn't trying to do that."

"Sure you were. Our situation gives you a control over me and Danny that isn't healthy...in the long run, I mean."

He let her continue.

"Listen, I think it's best I take a step back."

She was right and ░░░░░░░░░░░

Dear Reader,

For those of you who have followed the loves and lives of my friends in Indian Lake, you may remember I introduced Cate Sullivan in my first book of the series, *Love Shadows*. In that book, she was the Realtor who sold Luke Bosworth's house when he couldn't pay his deceased wife Jenny's medical bills.

As I wrote other books, Cate kept niggling at me, but her words were strange. "You don't know me. Nobody does. I won't let them. I'm in disguise." The night I heard that in my head, that did it. I had to delve into Cate and find out who she was.

Then, when I wanted to write a miniseries within the Indian Lake series on the issue of illegal drugs in our modern lives and how all of us feel those wretched effects, Cate's story slapped me in the face. I really had to pay attention to her, because she wasn't about to leave me alone.

I have always found silver linings in the worst circumstances. To find the love of one's life while pitched into the center ring of death and terror not only makes for an edge-of-your-seat story but, to me, proves that love does conquer all. Happily-ever-after is that much sweeter after a high-stakes battle, and Cate and Trent have earned their joy.

Please share your thoughts with me—I'd love to hear from you. Write to me at cathlanigan1@gmail.com and connect with me on Twitter (@cathlanigan), Facebook, LinkedIn and Wattpad, and at www.catherinelanigan.com and www.heartwarmingauthors.blogspot.com.

All my best,

Catherine

HEARTWARMING

Protecting the Single Mom

—

Catherine Lanigan

HARLEQUIN® HEARTWARMING™

Recycling programs for this product may not exist in your area.

ISBN-13: 978-0-373-36834-1

Protecting the Single Mom

Copyright © 2017 by Catherine Lanigan

Printed in U.S.A.

Catherine Lanigan knew she was born to storytelling at a very young age when she told stories to her younger brothers and sister to entertain them. After years of encouragement from family and high school teachers, Catherine was shocked and brokenhearted when her freshman college creative-writing professor told her that she had "no writing talent whatsoever" and that she would never earn a dime as a writer. He promised her that he would be her crutches and get her through his demanding class with a B grade so as not to destroy her high grade point average too much, *if* Catherine would promise never to write again. Catherine assumed he was the voice of authority and gave in to the bargain.

For fourteen years she did not write until she was encouraged by a television journalist to give her dream a shot. She wrote a six-hundred-page historical romantic spy thriller set against World War I. The journalist sent the manuscript to his agent, who then garnered bids from two publishers. That was nearly forty published novels, nonfiction books and anthologies ago.

Books by Catherine Lanigan

Harlequin Heartwarming

Sophie's Path
Fear of Falling
Katia's Promise
A Fine Year for Love
Heart's Desire
Love Shadows

MIRA Books

Dangerous Love
Elusive Love

Harlequin Desire

The Texan

Visit the Author Profile page
at Harlequin.com for more titles.

This book is dedicated to my son, Ryan Pieszchala, whose sense of honor, responsibility and unconditional love for his family was the inspiration for my hero, Trent Davis.

And to all the men and women in blue who Serve and Protect our lives across rural farmlands and sprawling cities: your sacrifices do not go unnoticed. God bless you all. You are true heroes and heroines.

To my late husband, Jed Nolan, my hero, my best friend. I will love you to the moon and back, throughout all galaxies and all the universes.

Acknowledgments

Passions and causes have rumbled through my life and my writings since I wrote my first poems at the age of ten. I wish I was powerful enough to eradicate heroin from the streets and the playgrounds. I wish I could stop every man from beating his wife and children. I wish I could eradicate harsh and hateful words and actions from all humans.

I can't.

My blessings are the trust and belief that my editors, Claire Caldwell, Megan Long, Dianne Moggy and Victoria Curran have in my ability to deliver a romance that has wide wings and deep, moral roots. It is your intelligence, commitment and heartfelt compassion for my story and me, that gave me the courage to delve into Cate's fears about loving and her unrelenting devotion to her son, her friends and her town.

I can't change the world, but as a writer, I can change a reader's perspective. Even if one person who is being abused physically, mentally or verbally, reads this story and finds the courage to make changes in her life, then I have succeeded.

Thank you to everyone at Heartwarming for giving me the voice to help others..

CHAPTER ONE

TRENT DAVIS GRIPPED his fully loaded Smith & Wesson M&P 45 semiautomatic pistol and motioned to his fellow officers who had approached the abandoned brick building with as much stealth and expertise as his Special Forces team had used in Afghanistan. They plastered their backs against the outside walls. All wore Kevlar vests and navy windbreakers with yellow ILPD patches on the back. Trent tried the rickety door. It was locked. He gave a hand signal that said he would bust it down.

"Police!" Trent bellowed with a voice that used to thunder down rocky mountains and desert terrain, as he kicked the door in.

The heroin dealers were sitting at a table counting money, just as the two undercover officers had planned. Both Sal Paluzzi and Bob Paxton had been Green Beret just as he was. They'd been to Iraq while Trent had been all over the Middle East. The three of them had worked closely on this sting for two months.

Trent knew a lift of an eyebrow, sidelong glance or nod of recognition could blow future efforts if this bust didn't go well. Trent had worked undercover a few times and never liked it. He didn't like living amid criminals even for a single day. He wanted them behind bars where they couldn't sell dope to a kid or pull the trigger on an innocent bystander.

Trent worked best as the leader. The first guy in. The one who might have to take a bullet for his men, but who knew he could take down any obstacles in his path.

Trent was not just good at his work, he was excellent. He knew it. The United States Army had plastered ribbons and stars on his chest because they knew it, and now the Indian Lake Police Force knew it.

He was prepared for anything. Even to die.

Instantly, Trent recognized Sal and Bob slouched in their metal folding chairs watching the gang leader count money. Behind the table was a stack of plastic-wrapped heroin. Five-pound bags, Trent assumed. All of it looking like innocent sugar.

There has to be half a million dollars of dope in that pile.

Sal and Bob shot to their feet, whipping their guns out from under their shirts.

In a nanosecond, the tall, lean Asian dealer whisked his semiautomatic off the table, spun around and away from the table, making himself a tougher target to hit. Immediately he fired, spewing bullets at Sal and Bob.

Trent fired and winged the perp. Right shoulder. It didn't faze the creep, who kept firing. Trent dropped to the floor, belly down flat, aimed and shot the perp's gun out of his right hand. Blood sprayed the man's face. He screamed and hugged his hand to his chest.

Another gang member, as rotund as he was tall, spilled off his chair, hit the floor and rolled, spraying bullets randomly from his black .40-caliber Smith & Wesson. Bullets pierced the tin ceiling, pinged off pipes, but, mercifully, didn't hit anyone. Trent guessed the guy was a wheelman.

Trent shot the jerk in the foot. He squealed like a pig.

More bullets from the third gang member zinged through the air as he spun the table on its side, sending money fanning in all directions. The guy was quick. He moved like the wind toward a far wall where a window was covered by a sheet. The man was tall, dark haired and stared at Trent with black, cunning, evil eyes.

Eyes Trent had seen once before. Eyes on a terrorist in Afghanistan who'd held Trent dead in his sights. He'd thought he'd been a dead man for sure. But he'd been too fast for the poorly trained al-Qaeda shooter. Trent tried to shake off the memory, but it held him like a prisoner. The flashback of the sound of his gun firing reverberated in his ears. His aim had been deadly. Trent had lived.

The present slammed back at Trent as the sound of his men shouting broke through his PTSD terrors. He looked up to see the gang leader getting away.

"Le Grande," Trent shouted, and the hair on his neck prickled as he stared down the leader. Trent wanted this one—bad.

Le Grande scrambled toward the far wall and was out the window. He bolted down the alley.

Trent cursed and leaped across the over-turned table in pursuit. He swung through the window.

A black SUV started, and Le Grande jumped in the passenger's seat. It sped down the alley, out on to the street.

Trent shot at the tires and missed. He ran as fast as he could, trying to catch up to the ve-hicle. As the SUV raced through a red light, dodging one oncoming car and swerving around another, Trent realized that the license plate had been muddied enough he couldn't get an accurate read.

Out of breath, he stopped in the middle of the empty side street, bent at the waist and placed his hands on his knees to catch his breath. What he wouldn't give to be nineteen again. At thirty-one, he felt like an old man.

Trent hustled back to the building and heard obscenities fill the air, but the sound of bullets had died. Then he heard the rattle of handcuffs being latched to wrists. Miranda rights were recited. More curses.

But Trent's hands shook as he finally holstered his gun. He shoved them in his pants pockets and let his eyes scan the melee.

The interior was exactly as his undercover investigation team had described, but that wasn't what Trent saw. Suddenly, he was inside a bombed-out building in Kandahar where his special ops team had rappelled in to extract an American marine who'd been taken prisoner by al-Qaeda terrorists. He smelled rotted food, urine, sweat and blood. He heard voices hammering curses in Pashto and Dari like rattlesnakes. The images slithered across his memory, reminding him of horrors.

Trent knew one thing—evil was everywhere. Even in Indian Lake.

And right now, Trent's home was under fire. Drug lords thought they'd found an easy target here. Little kids, ripe for the picking. Citizens so naive and trusting they couldn't believe that drug lords would set up shop in their town.

Yes, they were at war in Indian Lake—just like he'd been in Afghanistan.

Sal Paluzzi was talking to him, but he couldn't make out the words.

Instructions.

Sal wanted instructions, and Trent was their leader.

Trent tried to remember. Yes. The chopper. There was always a chopper, and it would be here in seconds. Hoist them out as if they'd never been here.

"…back to the station?" Sal said. "Sir?"

Trent blinked. Only once. He was here. He never stayed back there too long. Couldn't afford to.

"Copy that. Get these creeps out of here," Trent ordered, as his eyes scoped the interior. He touched the radio phone Velcroed to his shoulder. "Coming out. Send in Forensics."

Trent turned and led the way for his men— as was expected of him.

TRENT POURED COFFEE from the glass pot into a foam cup, sipped the stale, nearly cold brew, then dumped the rest down the drain. He looked around. The break area was vacant. Dead as a tomb. It was nearly midnight. Everyone had gone home. He stared at the stained coffeepot. He guessed the last batch had been made around suppertime—when he'd been bringing in the perps. Booking them. Filling out paperwork. Doing his job.

He shoved the pot onto the warming plate. "Too late for coffee."

He went to the nearly empty vending machine and bought a pack of jalapeño potato chips. He hated them. But the Doritos were long gone. He knew. He was probably the only guy eating them.

He went to the refrigerator and grabbed a bottle of water. It was the only thing that the department provided free. That and the coffee.

Trent went to his desk and stared at the computer screen. He'd nearly finished his report. He felt as if he'd written a book.

Trent had been assigned to this sting for three months, but it had been ongoing long before his promotion to detective. The Indian Lake police chief told Trent that the Chicago Police Department had been hunting Le Grande for two years. The man was like a shadow. No one knew his real name, but he was a vicious drug lord, and his gang had tentacles from Houston to Chicago to Detroit. Le Grande's network went straight through Indian Lake. Thanks to geography and unpatrolled country highways and roads, drugs moved from Mexico through Texas all the way to Toronto.

In Trent's background report on Le Grande, he discovered that Le Grande was the name of the gang, though the members called this man Le Grande, too. His largest contingent gang was based in Chicago. His minions sold drugs on the first floor of the John Hancock Building, the Merchandise Mart and even in the lobby of the luxe Drake Hotel. These were scores of a thousand dollars each. Sometimes more.

There was nothing small-time about Le Grande, and whenever the CPD closed down his dealers, they were replaced within hours. Le Grande grew dealers like an amoeba replicated.

But the one thing that Trent knew was that evil could exist only so long. Sooner or later, Le Grande would be apprehended. Trent had hoped to be the man who took him down. But not tonight.

Just as Trent downed a slug of water, a new email popped onto his screen. It was from

Richard Schmitz, a lieutenant with the Chicago Bureau of Organized Crime, with whom Trent had been working for months. Richard wanted to nab Le Grande as much as, or more than, Trent did.

Trent respected Richard's ability to sift clues out of a mass of information, and he always came up with gold. Richard's analytical skills were the very reason Trent and the Indian Lake PD had been brought into the investigation. Richard and his superiors at CBOC strategized with Trent and Stan Williams, Indian Lake's chief of police, about the plan for this sting. They'd all been so certain that *this* time they would lure Le Grande into their trap.

But Trent had bungled it. He felt guilty. And angry with himself. He was better than this. It had been that split second. That tiny falter where his mind had tripped there. To Afghanistan.

The military said he had PTSD. He hadn't believed them at first. He'd thought it was just an adjustment to civilian life, but it had been over five years now. He'd tried counseling until he felt he was counseling the counselor. He'd meditated. He took medications guaranteed to stop the flashbacks. He'd been to the mountain of Zen and back. Nothing worked.

Finally, he faced the fact that like the memories, the flashbacks would never go away.

They just were.

And that could get him killed. He couldn't and wouldn't tell a soul about his flashback today. It had been a blip. Two seconds. Maybe less. But that's all it had taken. If Le Grande had been firing his gun, Trent or someone else could have been killed.

Trent had to find a way to push through his demons. He'd learned to focus more on the moment, and that had helped. But it wasn't perfect yet. He wasn't perfect.

The email pinged again.

Trent shook off his dour thoughts and read Richard's note.

Trent—

I can't believe we've been on this guy's case so long and missed this one. Get this. He's been married before. Even has a kid. And yes, you guessed it, she's right there in Indian Lake. My team is all over the news. No wonder the creep is in your backyard.

Keep this on the down low. Except for your COP, I'd play it close to the vest for now. We don't need anyone alerting her to our knowledge about Le Grande. She could be in on his gang activity. We're checking that out.

Trent, I have a man on the inside. Undercover cop. Not just an informant, which I don't trust completely. He's feeding me intel.

There's not much on her. We tracked down a divorce decree. No particulars other than that. And there was no mention of a kid in the decree. It was six years ago. So maybe he didn't know about the kid.

Le Grande chose Indian Lake initially as a transfer station for drug trafficking. This new intel is a game changer. Because of the ex-wife, we believe he's not lost to you.

Was it possible that he was getting a second chance? Maybe his luck had turned. He and his men had rounded up every man in the building. They'd only missed Le Grande.

So, Le Grande had a family.

Now that was an anchor for any man.

Trent had never had a family of his own and didn't think he ever would. Not with his PTSD. But even his two undercover agents had wives and kids. Lives. They didn't seem to have any problems after Iraq. At least none they talked about.

Trent finished reading Richard's note.

The woman's name is Susan Kramer. We believe Raoul Le Grande is actually Brad Kramer. They lived on Chicago's South Side.

She's living in Indian Lake under an alias. You'll find her as Cate Sullivan.

Trent slammed back against his chair. "Cate Sullivan? The real-estate agent?"

Cate Sullivan had her photograph plastered on huge agency billboards at the main entrances to town. She was that pretty brunette he'd seen at the Indian Lake Deli from time to time with one of the deli owners, Olivia Melton, who'd just got engaged to Rafe Barzonni. Trent knew the four Barzonni brothers—Gabe, Rafe, Mica and Nate—as well as their mother, Gina, a recent widow, because they donated heavily to the policemen's widows and orphans fund as well as the City Playground Fund, which Trent spearheaded. He'd even seen Cate with Sarah Bosworth, the wife of his workout buddy, Luke.

Luke was a former navy SEAL and, along with Scott Abbott, a journalist for the local newspaper and owner of the Book Stop and Coffee Shop; they all tested their skills at the shooting range south of town twice a month. Just yesterday morning, Trent had bumped into Cate at Cupcakes and Cappuccino, Maddie Barzonni's café.

Trent swiped his face. So while he didn't know Cate Sullivan personally, he definitely knew *of* her.

This was ludicrous. She seemed like a nice person. A sweet woman, always smiling and polite.

She was mixed up with one of the biggest drug dealers in the Midwest?

Trent stared at the email. The longer he was a cop, the more humanity shocked him. He'd thought he'd seen it all in Afghanistan.

But the thought that Cate Sullivan was part of Le Grande's heroin trafficking gang—Trent's heart grew weary with the idea. God help them all.

CHAPTER TWO

CATE WALKED INTO the living room during the baby shower for Liz and Gabe Barzonni in time to see her six-year-old son, Danny, holding Liz's baby, Angelo Ezekiel. Sarah and Luke Bosworth's children, Timmy and Annie, sat on either side of him. On the floor surrounding the kids was a sea of tissue, boxes and glittery gift bags that Liz and Gabe had clearly opened earlier. The children were oblivious to the mess or the pile of presents to the side of the sofa.

"Danny, be careful," Cate said as she deposited a silver tray of petits fours on the linen-covered dining-room table. She'd never been to a couple's shower like this. Nearly every light in Sarah's house had been turned on, not to mention dozens of taper candles and votives flickering on the tables, mantel and along the windowsills. The house was so illuminated it could probably be seen from outer space, Cate thought. And everywhere laughter suffused the air with joy.

"I'm doing good, Mom!" Danny assured her, tilting the baby into the crook of his arm. He looked so grown-up and sure of himself at that moment, her little man. It seemed only a blink ago that Danny was a baby, and here he was already in kindergarten and making new friends.

Cate looked around. The entire Barzonni family was present, and not one of Cate's girlfriends was missing. Mrs. Bcabots, an clcgant eighty-year-old wearing a black vintage Chanel suit with a half dozen ropes of pearls, gold links and colored gems, held court with the newly engaged Olivia Melton and Rafe Barzonni.

Luke walked through the room with an open bottle of sparkling wine. "Gabe's vineyard is very proud of their first sparkling crop." He smiled at Cate.

"Oh, Luke, wine isn't a crop," Cate joked.

"Why not?" He foisted a wounded look onto the bottle with its gold foil label.

"It's a batch," handsome, black-haired Gabe said, breezing through the clusters of guests with empty glasses and another bottle.

Luke winked at Cate. "You watch the kids for me? I have to help pour."

"Sure."

Cate had known Luke when he was married to his first wife, Jenny. She'd sold them their lovely bungalow house. She'd also resold it for him after Jenny died. It all seemed impossible to her that Jenny could be dead. And now, Luke was as happy—or happier—with Sarah, who'd been one of the first friends Cate had met in Indian Lake.

"Mom!" Danny called as he looked up from the sleeping baby. "Come here. Don't you think Zeke is cute?"

"He is," Cate replied, approaching to look at the baby. "Is his name Zeke? I thought it was Angelo. After his grandfather."

"Oh, no," Annie and Timmy chimed together.

"It's definitely Zeke," Annie stated.

"Definitely." Danny and Timmy nodded.

"He's got a lot of black hair." Danny grinned proudly. "Like me."

Gabe walked up, put his arm around Cate's shoulder and said, "You get yours from your mother, Danny. Zeke's hair is like mine. I'm told a baby's hair can fall out and grow back another color."

Danny's blue eyes widened. "No way. Is that true, Mom?"

Cate nodded. "Actually, yes. When you were a baby, you were a towhead. Er, blond."

Danny shook his head. "That's just crazy. Why would I do that?"

Cate shrugged. "I don't know. Must have been someone in the family."

"Well," Gabe said as he scooped up baby Zeke, "I have to take him to his momma."

Cate was aware Danny appeared slightly reluctant to release the baby. "She probably needs to change him."

"Yeah, I know," Danny said. "Mom, when can we get a brother for me?"

Before Cate could answer, Annie chimed in. "Good luck with that," she groaned. "We've been asking our mom that for months."

"Yeah," Timmy said. "She's not listening to us at all."

"But you guys have each other," Danny replied. "I don't have anybody to play with."

"Sure you do. Sarah said you can come play with Timmy and Annie after school anytime you want." Cate held out her hand. "C'mon, sweetheart, don't you want a cupcake or a petit four?"

Timmy jumped off the sofa. "Maddie made them special for us! Let's get Beau."

Danny took his mother's hand as Annie scrambled off the sofa as well and raced away.

"Mom, do you think that's a good idea letting the dog have cake?"

Cate stifled a laugh. "I think if Sarah says it's okay, it's fine. Just take one cupcake."

Danny grinned. "Sure, Mom."

Cate knew that mischievous look on her son's face. He was up to something. "Only one treat. No cookie. No petits fours. Just the cupcake."

"Aw, Mom!" Danny stomped away as if his shoes were lined with lead.

Sarah stood next to Cate. "He's adorable, Cate. The kids love him to pieces, and they all play so well together. Honestly, anytime you have to show a house or do an open house, we'd love to have him stay with us."

Cate felt her smile of gratitude bloom. "Sarah, you don't know what this means. Ever since his regular babysitter moved, I've been in a quandary. He hates day care, because all the kids are younger than he is. He's only six, but he thinks he's fifteen. He's growing up so fast."

Sarah smiled wistfully. "I know what you mean. Annie is so much the young lady now, it scares me. Her piano playing is astounding and her voice… Last week she asked me if she could enter the Indiana Junior Miss Pageant."

Cate's jaw dropped. "For real?"

"Uh-huh. You know? I think she'd win."

"But that's…so much, er, notoriety. I mean her photo would be everywhere. She'd be on television," Cate replied, trying to suppress a wave of niggling fear.

"Facebook. Twitter. Instagram. Oh, absolutely," Sarah said.

"So what are you going to do?" Cate put her fingers to her lips as if to stifle her fearful words. Cate hated that her buried demons crept up on her at times like this. Sarah's decisions had nothing to do with her—or Danny. She and her son were safe. Secure. She'd made certain of that.

"We'll go for it. The one thing that Luke and I agree on is that we don't want to hold the kids back from anything within reason. Too many people go through life trying to do the sensible thing. When it's all said and done, they wish they'd taken more risks. If the kids fail, at least they tried."

Cate kept her gaze on Danny as he and Timmy sat on the floor with Beau, petting him. Danny was the happiest, most well-adjusted little boy she'd ever seen. She loved him beyond measure and would do anything for him.

Cate knew all about risks. She could write volumes about the determination that came from terror. Half the people in this room didn't have the first clue about life-and-death risks. Except Luke, possibly.

He never talked about his time as a navy SEAL, but Cate had always been curious.

She supposed her caution was because she'd taken a lot of risks for Danny. Risked her life. She still risked her life for him. Daily.

No one knew that. And they never would.

"Mom! If I can't have a baby brother, can I get a dog like Beau?" Danny asked, getting up from the floor.

He had white icing on his lips. Cate wiped his mouth with the napkin she held. "A dog? I'm not sure. But, I will think about it."

"Promise?" Danny asked excitedly.

"Yes." It might be time he started learning some responsibilities. "You could help out by feeding and walking it."

Timmy patted Beau's head. "Don't forget cleaning up the poop. Mom wouldn't let me do that till I was seven. I have to wear plastic gloves," he said matter-of-factly.

Danny nodded seriously. "I could do that."

Cate laughed. "Yes, you could." She ruffled his hair. "We better get our things. Tomorrow is a school day."

"I know," Danny said dejectedly as he gave Beau one last pet.

"I have to say my goodbyes, Danny. You stay there," Cate said, going into the kitchen where Sam Crenshaw and Gina Barzonni were pouring coffee. Ever since Gina's husband, Angelo, had died of a sudden heart attack, Cate had noticed that Liz's grandfather, Sam, always seemed to be at Gina's side. Cate wouldn't be surprised if there was something romantic brewing between the two.

Sarah was at the sink washing dishes.

"Sarah, I have to take Danny home," Cate said. "It was a wonderful party. I think Danny would be happier if Liz let him take the baby with us."

Gina laughed. "He'll have to stand in line. That baby has got half the town wrapped around his tiny fingers."

"You can say that again." Sam smiled, pulling Gina closer to him and giving her a look that was so loving and intimate, Cate nearly winced. No one had ever looked at her like that.

She knew she'd never give anyone the chance to, either.

Sarah dried her hands. "Let me give you some cookies to take home. Luke will go nuts if I keep all this sugar in the house."

"Thank you, Sarah. That's so kind. Assure

Luke that I'll dole them out carefully. No sugar overload at my house."

Sarah placed six oatmeal-and-raisin cookies inside a plastic container and snapped the lid shut. "Actually, they're fairly healthy. I made them myself."

Cate went to the living room and hugged her friends one by one.

Mrs. Beabots tugged on Cate's hand and whispered, "Anytime you want to bring Danny over, I wouldn't mind watching him. He's such a good boy."

"What a nice thing to say, Mrs. Beabots. I'll do that."

"See that you do," Mrs. Beabots replied. "Being around the little ones keeps me young."

Cate squeezed her hand and went to get her purse. Though she and Danny were the first ones to leave, she noticed that others were starting to say their goodnights, as well.

Cate buckled Danny in and reversed out of the drive.

Her house was on the west side of Indian Lake, though not on the lake itself. They were close enough so that she and Danny could walk to the beach, but she didn't have the sky-high property taxes.

The 1930s Craftsman-style bungalow was

Cate's third house in town. The same week that she'd landed her first real-estate commission, she bought her first house. It had been a matchbox, but she didn't care. It had been a start, and they hadn't needed much since Danny was a baby then. She'd traded up until she'd finally bought this house. It was sturdy, in a good neighborhood and shouted *respectability*. The house was the antithesis of what Cate felt in her soul.

She would do everything in her power to make certain her son had a good life. A happy home, security and friends.

So far, Cate had provided all that.

But Danny was getting older and asking a lot of questions. Ones that she couldn't answer or didn't dare to.

As was her custom, she parked in the detached garage. Waiting until the automatic garage door lowered, they got out of the car. She locked it and they exited the garage through the side door, which Cate also locked, double-checking the handle to make sure it was secure. They walked the short sidewalk and up the back steps. Cate unlocked the door and they entered the kitchen.

She turned on the light, reengaged the lock

and threw the inside bolt. Again, she tried the handle to make sure the door was tightly shut.

"So, Mom. Can we talk about what I was talking about?" Danny asked as he took off his jacket.

Cate glanced out the window. "What? I'm sorry, sweetheart. What did you ask?"

"A baby brother? Remember? When can we get one?" Danny stood with his hands on his little hips, his face earnest and concerned.

"Sweetie, in order to do that, I have to have a husband. And that could take a long time. Then he and I would have to decide if we want anyone besides you. Honestly, I'm very happy with the current arrangement."

Danny shook his head. "That's not how it works."

"It's not?" She couldn't wait to hear his take on this one.

"No. You go to the attorney's office. I saw a sign for one on Main Street. You get the baby there."

"Who told you this?"

"Jessica. She's in my class. Her mom can't have any more babies. So they went to the attorney. Now she's got a sister. I don't want a sister. I really want a brother. Can you tell the attorney that?"

The laughter that threatened to explode from Cate was next to impossible to choke back, but she had to. Danny was so serious. This was a complication she hadn't ever calculated. Cate knew Jessica Anderson's parents. She'd sold them their house six months ago. She'd wondered why they'd wanted so much extra room. Now she knew.

"Sweetie, I'm pretty sure that getting a baby like Jessica's parents did would be very expensive. Right now I can't afford a baby that way. Plus, I also believe because they had a mommy and a daddy, the adoption went fairly well for them."

"Hmm. Yeah. Jessica has a daddy."

"A father is an important ingredient for an adoption."

"But not for a family, right? Because we're a family. Even if my daddy died. And he never got to see me."

Cate's heart went out to her little boy. There was so much he was missing because he didn't have a father. Sure, there were thousands of boys without a father, but she'd never planned to be a single mother. She'd wanted the dream. A knight in shining armor. Happily-ever-after. Still, she'd been granted the most perfect child a mother could ever want.

Danny was her blessing. She'd take that.

"Yes. He never got to see you, but I know he sees you from heaven. Don't you think?"

Danny smiled, as he always did when they talked about his father. "Yeah."

"Okay," she said, kissing his cheek. "Time for your bath and pajamas. I'll run the water. You pick out a book for me to read to you."

"Okay!" Danny rushed off to his bedroom as Cate went to the bathroom.

She turned on the water, testing the temperature. She could feel fingers of gloom pulling at her. She always felt this way when Danny mentioned his father.

Brad Kramer could be dead. Should be dead if there was justice in the world, but she didn't know for certain. She didn't want to know.

"Mom! I found my raptor! He was under my pillow all this time!" Danny raced to the bathroom stark naked and jumped in the tub before she had a chance to slow him down.

Using a plastic tumbler, Cate doused his thick dark hair and built a foamy lather with tearless shampoo. Danny pretended his dinosaur was diving into the sea while she scrubbed his back, arms and legs. She rinsed his hair and took a towel from the wicker stand.

Danny hummed one of the songs he'd learned

at school while she dried his hair and helped him into his pajamas. He was the sweetest thing, and it took a great deal of self-control to keep her kisses to less than a dozen every night.

He raced to his bedroom and scrambled between the covers. "Here," he said, handing her a Shel Silverstein book. "You like this one."

"My mother read that to me when I was a little girl."

"Uh-huh. And she's with Daddy in heaven."

Cate felt a twinge of sorrow as she always did when she thought of her mother, who had died when Cate was seventeen. That was the year she'd met Brad.

Brad couldn't have been more perfect if he'd walked out of a dream. He was dark haired, tall and handsome. He worked as a lifeguard at the public pool where she and her two girlfriends hung out on weekends. He was twenty-one years old and tanned, wearing the regulation black bathing trunks and aviator sunglasses. He looked like a mysterious, rock-hard model. When he asked her out for a burger one Saturday, she'd felt as if she'd walked on air. Even now, she could remember the heady rush of excitement and the thrumming of her heart when he got off his shiny chrome motorcycle at Smitty's Hamburger Diner holding a single rose.

He worked two jobs, driving a truck during the week and working as a lifeguard on weekends—to keep up his tan.

Brad told her he'd watched her for two weeks before getting up the courage to ask her out. He told her he didn't date much. He had to watch his expenses.

He told her she was the most beautiful girl he'd ever seen. He played old Johnny Mathis love songs on every jukebox in every diner they went to over that first month. And each time he did, he sang along, as if serenading her. He held her hand when they walked to his bike.

And he kissed her with so much passion she thought she would melt to the pavement.

Despite the fact that Cate was struggling with grief, trying to adjust to the foster home where the state forced her to live until graduation, she believed she was in love with Brad from that first night.

Cate didn't understand the nuances of grief. She didn't know that what she was feeling wasn't love. She didn't recognize that Brad was simply the force that filled the void left by her mother's death. Cate didn't know how to combat grief.

Over that summer, Brad offered her excitement and recklessness. She'd ridden on the back of his motorcycle, wondering if she could find her mother in the wind. They'd sped across downstate Illinois highways, through country towns, drinking beer and eating mini-mart food because they had so little money. He was wild, and she wanted to be wild, hoping the pain and grief would go away.

Brad pleaded with her to marry him. She'd been flattered. She'd felt special, even important, after months of feeling small and insignificant. Brad wanted her, and when he kissed her with so much fire and abandon, her reasoning turned to ash.

Because Cate had promised her mother she would finish high school, she kept Brad at arm's length until she graduated. He'd been angry about that. Very angry. Cate had translated his outbursts as desire and passion. She was convinced she'd bewitched him.

The night they were married by a justice of the peace, Brad got drunk, started an argument and hit her. He swore it would never happen again. He begged her forgiveness.

He'd treated her like a queen—for five days. He bought her roses, ran her bath and brought her breakfast in bed. He said odd things that, at the time, she thought were endearments.

"You belong to me now," he'd said. "You're

mine. All mine now that we're married. You have my name, and I like that very much."

A month later, it happened again. This time he was more than just drunk. His pupils were dilated, and he looked as if he had a fever. He'd told her that because they were married, he could do whatever he liked. He wanted her to be submissive. When Cate refused, he hit her and threw her against the wall. She'd hit her head and was stunned, momentarily unconscious.

The incident must have frightened him, because Brad apologized again. This time he brought home an expensive bottle of champagne and a silver bracelet she knew they couldn't afford. When she asked him where he got the money, he told her that he'd started a "side business" to cover "extras."

Cate didn't trust a thing he told her.

Of all the things she was, stupid wasn't one of them. It was as if the minute she'd agreed to marry, he changed. The challenge of winning her was gone.

She had to admit that she'd changed, too. She'd dreamed of a little house with children someday. Brad had argued that he didn't have the kind of income to afford a house. Their very small apartment in a complex filled with people she didn't know—who appeared to sleep all day and party by the pool all night—was not enough. She wanted more.

Each time she tried to discuss her dreams with Brad, he yelled that he would never be able to afford the things she wanted. Cate realized if she brought in a paycheck, she could make her dreams a reality. She applied for a data entry job at a nearby pool equipment company and was hired on the spot. Brad was furious. He'd stormed out of the apartment to meet his friends.

That night, Brad came home drunk, though now she realized he was high on some drug that his friends had sold him. He marched toward her with menacing eyes and balled fists. He screamed obscenities at her. Then he said, "I own you!" Before he took the first swing, Cate took action.

She ran out of the house with her wallet containing forty-two dollars. She ran. And ran.

She kept to the state highways and eventually a middle-aged woman who said she was driving from Chicago to Detroit stopped to pick her up. By the time they reached Indian Lake, they needed gas. Cate appreciated the ride, but the woman asked too many questions. It was to that woman that she'd first given her alias. Cate

Sullivan. The name had come to her quickly. She'd had a classmate in grade school whose parents were Irish, and the real Cate had competed in Irish dance competitions. Cate envied her those lessons and had wanted to be that girl with both parents still alive.

In an instant, she altered her life drastically.

She'd covered over a hundred miles that night. That's when Cate knew she was a survivor.

"Mom? The story?" Danny nudged the book toward her.

"Sorry." She kissed the top of his head and hugged him close.

No, she thought. She was more than surviving. She was living the dream she'd wanted for herself. She had Danny, her pretty house and wonderful friends who loved her. Indian Lake was no accident in her life. It was the pot of gold at the end of the rainbow, and she cherished every moment.

CHAPTER THREE

TRENT MADE A fresh pot of coffee and delivered a cup to Ned Quigley, the dispatcher, just as a 911 call came in. With only a skeleton crew on duty, Trent waited until Ned had written down the particulars.

"What is it?" Trent asked, sipping his coffee and thinking that one of these days he had to learn how to make decent coffee. It couldn't be all that tough, could it?

"Home invasion. Wife's on the phone. Appleton is a block away." Ned patched through to the cop on duty and gave him the address. Then Ned sent two more patrols as backup. He looked at Trent.

"Where is it?" Trent asked.

"By the skating rink."

That was only half a mile from Cate's address. Trent knew Le Grande was too smart to draw attention to himself on the same night as a shootout with cops. So where would Le Grande have gone after the bust? To Chicago where the CPD practically had him in their sights? The guy had to know that all of Indian Lake PD was on alert for him. Most of the drug dealers coming into small towns across the Illinois border tended to underestimate local law enforcement. They thought they were dealing with hicks and idiots. Granted, the citizenry might not be as astute about drugs and dealers as Chicagoans, but the police investigators were savvy and well-informed. What men like Le Grande didn't know was that because the number of active cases with a small-town force was much less than in a city, the investigators had time to spend on each one until it was solved.

Trent listened as Ned gave instructions to the patrol cop. Trent's neck hairs prickled. An intruder, Ned had said.

What if Le Grande had discovered Cate's— or Susan's or whatever her name was—existence here in Indian Lake just as he had? Would he go to her? There was a possibility that Trent had shot him. Winged him, maybe. If Le Grande knew about Cate, he might have gone to her for help. Even if she was resistant, Le Grande might think he could get money from her. Steal a car or coerce her to drive him out of town.

Then there was the question of Cate-Susan

herself. Was she a cover for Le Grande? Part of his gang? Had she scoped the town for him, pretending to be someone she wasn't?

There was no criminal record on her or any reason for Trent to suspect that she was dealing drugs. She had a kid, after all. Not that a kid would stop an addict mother from using or dealing.

She didn't strike him as anything but a model citizen.

But she'd been married to Le Grande.

If Le Grande went to her and needed help, would she do it?

As usual when new information on a case came to light, it posed a myriad of new questions. Trent knew exactly what to do.

Investigate.

Following Richard's advice, Trent would keep this new info quiet. There were too many leaks in any organization. "The chief at home tonight?"

"Should be. You need him?"

"Nah. Just curious. I didn't finish my report."

"Slacker," Ned joked.

"I'm going out for a sandwich. You want anything?" Trent took out his car keys.

"No, but thanks," Ned replied as another call came in.

Trent decided to call the chief from his car and fill him in about Cate.

He exited the station and went to his unmarked car. As he climbed in, he had the eerie feeling that Le Grande was close. Trent had looked the man straight in the face. It was the blink of an eye, but they'd exchanged that look—the one between foes—the hunter and the prey. In Le Grande's case, his look communicated the steely belief that he, Le Grande, was the hunter and Trent was the prey.

He's here. He never left, Trent thought as he turned the key. The engine roared. He smiled. Two years ago, Trent had bought a high-performance Mercedes-Benz engine at a Chicago junkyard. Being an amateur wrencher, he installed the engine into his unmarked car—at his own expense. He'd had some help from Kenny at Indian Lake Service Garage, but he'd gotten the job done. When the day came that he was in pursuit of a drug dealer in a Porsche, Trent would be well-equipped for the task.

Trent patted his shoulder holster as was his habit every time he left the station. He'd cleaned his gun and filled the magazine at the station after the shoot-out. If, by any chance, he came up against Le Grande, Trent didn't want to be short. He checked to make sure his cell phone was on, the dispatch radio was tuned into the station and he checked to make certain he had a full tank of gas.

Still, he felt very unprepared.

TRENT HAD PUNCHED Cate's address into his GPS. He drove up the street and parked three houses away. There were few cars on the street. The houses were all bungalow types, Craftsman style, built in the 1930s and well maintained. They were over a third of a mile from Indian Lake, and the residents took great pride in ownership. The hedges were clipped, the weeds pulled and late-summer flowers and lush potato vines filled planters and window boxes. It was the kind of area Trent would have liked to live—if a normal life could ever be his.

He turned off his lights and got out. It was dark, with only a quarter moon. *Good night for intruders.* It was the kind of night that someone like Le Grande would prefer to skulk around an ex-wife's house. Or, if Cate was a willing participant in Le Grande's schemes, an evening the neighbors probably wouldn't notice him coming or going.

The lights in Cate's house were on. She was up. Probably the kid, too.

Trent turned to the right and saw the drive led to the detached single-car garage. Her car.

If the car was gone, then he had to find out if she was part of Le Grande's gang or if he'd threatened her. Trent was walking a fine line by coming here tonight.

Protocol stated he should knock on the door and conduct a proper investigation. Regulations demanded he show his badge, offer his card.

But protocol didn't consider that Le Grande could be hiding in that garage at this very minute, armed with his 9 mm gun. Ready to blow Trent away and think nothing of it.

Trent crept closer, taking out his gun. He picked up sounds—the scurry of a small animal over the garden mulch; the chirping of a cricket near the garage door. He felt the breeze as it slipped around the house, chilling the night.

A night-light burned in a socket near the entry door. Not only was it a smart idea so she could easily see to lock and unlock the door, but it also illuminated the car.

"Not here," he whispered to himself and instantly spun toward the house. "But are you closer? Inside?"

Trent stuck his gun in his holster. No need to get anxious. Still, he needed to make sure his instincts were simply being overly alert before going to the front door to announce himself.

He moved toward the back porch, checking the boxwood hedges for any signs of footprints, lost items. Anything Le Grande might have dropped in his haste.

CATE HAD JUST finished the story for Danny.

"Mom, can I have some water?" Danny asked.

"Sure, pumpkin. I'll be right back."

In the kitchen, she took a glass from the upper cabinet next to the kitchen window. She glanced into the yard as she turned on the tap, thinking that she needed to plant more daffodil bulbs. Maybe those Casa Blanca lily bulbs she'd seen in the catalog.

Suddenly, a man's face was framed by her kitchen window.

She dropped the glass in the sink, and the sound of shattering glass and her scream stung the air.

The man put his palms against the windowpane. He shook his head.

"Mom!" Danny shot into the kitchen carrying his baseball bat. "What is it? I'm here!"

Cate felt as if she'd been socked in the chest.

She couldn't breathe. She was light-headed. She was dying.

She held on to the edge of the sink with one hand and pointed toward the window. "You go away! Get out of here or I'm calling the police. Right now! Go away!" she screamed at the figure on her porch, unsure of the man's identity. She was so terrified, she could be seeing things.

The man stepped back and disappeared into the darkness. Cate sucked in a breath, holding her hand over her heart. This wasn't happening. It couldn't be happening, could it?

Then she heard Danny talking. He held her cell phone to his ear. "Hello, 911? Help!"

Cate looked out the window, but the man was gone. Suddenly, the front doorbell rang.

Danny stared at the phone. "Wow. That was fast!" He raced into the living room.

"Don't open that door!" Cate shouted anxiously as she rushed up behind Danny and shoved him behind her. "You don't know who it is. What if it's him?"

"The bad guy?" Danny asked, wide-eyed.

"Absolutely." She peered through the peephole. He didn't look like a bad guy. He was dressed in a sport jacket, white shirt and tie. His hair was dark, groomed and he was handsome. But there was no mistaking it. It was the Peeping Tom.

"Go away!" she shouted through the door. "We've called the police."

"Ma'am, I know. I am the police."

"I don't believe you."

"Here's my badge. My name is Trent Davis. I'm very sorry to have frightened you."

Cate looked at the badge through the peephole. "You're really a cop?"

"Yes, ma'am. Detective."

Detective. The man had barely gotten the word out and already Cate's hands were shaking and her mouth had gone dry. Her next words felt as if they were tumbling out over sand. "What do you want with us?"

"I'm investigating a break-in a few houses away. Again, I'm very sorry to have frightened you. I thought I'd seen someone in your backyard. I'd like to ask you some questions. May I come in?"

"Questions," she said to herself as she backed up and bumped into Danny.

"Mom, let him in. He's a policeman."

"I'm not sure." She chewed her thumbnail. Cate had woven a perfect cocoon around Danny and herself. No one had invaded their privacy because she hadn't given anyone a reason to look past the face she presented to the town. When she'd first arrived in Indian Lake on that frightening night, the owners of the mini-mart and the adjacent marina and docks—Captain Redbeard, Redmond Wilkerson Taylor and his wife, Julie—realized her plight, without her saying much at all. They didn't care that Cate didn't have a penny to her name. They saw through her anxiety to the honest person she was.

They asked her if she had a place to live. When she'd hemmed and hawed, they insisted she stay with them.

Cate had never seen such unquestioning trust.

They'd offered her a job working the register in the mini-mart and she took it. During the course of one long night, her life spun on that thin dime of fate—and all for the better.

Yet, even they didn't know the whole truth. She'd never told anyone about the abuse. She'd only said she'd run away.

Questions.

As if someone had thrown a breaker, electricity ignited every cell in her body. She reasoned it was adrenaline. It felt like terror.

Danny circled her and put his hand on the knob. "Talk to him, Mom."

Cate turned the dead bolt and opened the door. The man was still holding his badge for her to inspect. Gingerly, she took it from him and read the specifics. She returned it, noticing how big his hands were and how his shoulders seemed to fill the doorway. He looked strong and buff under his jacket. She supposed his looks and strength would probably put some people at ease. Instead, her nerves were erratic.

He was a cop. Poking around in her backyard. What if he was one of those cops who'd snapped? What if he'd had some kind of meltdown and was now exactly what she'd thought earlier: a Peeping Tom? Or worse.

"May I come in?"

"No," she replied with more force than she'd intended.

Danny was looking at him like he'd hung the moon. "Can I see your badge, too?"

"Sure." Detective Davis handed the badge to Danny.

"Wow. Cool." Danny traced the brass edges and lettering with his fingers as if memorizing every carving.

"Danny, give the man his badge," she ordered, folding her arms over her chest, feeling as defiant as she probably looked.

"Thanks," Danny said.

The detective closed the door behind him, leaving it slightly ajar. "I should explain that I'd come to your front porch initially, but I was certain I'd seen someone in your backyard. You should get some motion lights."

"I have them," she replied.

"But, Mom," Danny said. "That light burned out. Remember? We got the new one."

"Right," she said sheepishly, and dropped her arms. "I haven't had time to put the replacement in."

"I could do that for you," Trent offered.

"That's not necessary," she said curtly. "I'm quite capable of changing a light bulb."

The detective scratched the back of his head and smiled. "Boy. We've really gotten off on the wrong foot. Not only am I trying to apologize for frightening you, but I want to warn you about home invasion."

"You said there was a break-in."

"There was. About half a mile from here, there was the report of a home invasion." He looked at Danny, then at Cate. "Anyway, what I wanted to know was if you'd seen anything unusual. Anyone on the street you've never seen before? Strange cars?"

"No," she said, shaking her head.

He handed her his card. "I'd appreciate you

letting me know if you do see anything. Maybe ask your neighbors to do the same. That's my cell," he said, pointing to the last number on the list of contact information.

"Okay," she said, realizing that her hand was still shaking.

"Look, Mrs. Sullivan. I'm very sorry to have frightened you."

"I'll live," she quipped, and forced a smile. She'd be fine after he left. Detectives were gifted with keen curiosity, laser eyesight and brains that put puzzles together. At least that's how she saw him. He was the kind of detector who could unmask her. Expose her. Ruin her life. "Well, if I see anything, I'll be sure to call."

She reached around him and pulled the door open.

He didn't move.

What was with this guy? He wasn't taking the hint to leave.

Goose bumps skipped across her arms. She'd bet a hundred bucks he knew something about her past. He was smooth and polished, formal and courteous as he talked to Danny. Still, Trent didn't take a single step to leave. She didn't trust him in the least.

"So, what school do you go to?"

"St. Mark's. I'm in kindergarten."

"That's cool. Your school is only a block from the police station."

"Yeah," Danny said with a big grin. "I watch the cop cars go in and out of the parking lot."

Cate could see that Danny's eyes were filled with admiration. She glanced at the detective and realized that he had picked up on it, too.

"You know, Danny, next weekend is the Sunflower Festival, and our station has a booth to raise money for widows and orphans of other cops. If you stop by, I'll save a brownie for you."

"We go to the Sunflower Festival every year." Danny looked at his mother. "Don't we, Mom?"

"Uh, yes." Cate was perplexed as she raised her eyes to Trent.

He pushed on. "Mrs. Beabots makes the brownies for us as her donation. They're the best in town." Trent smiled broadly.

"She gave me a brownie tonight at the party," Danny said.

"Party?" Trent cocked his head toward Cate.

Cate paused, her eyes locked on Trent. "It was a baby shower."

"Oh," he said, and turned to Danny. "So, I'll see you at the Sunflower Festival?"

"Sure," Danny replied quickly.

Cate noticed that Danny didn't look to her

for approval. He was too busy smiling at the detective.

"I'll be going," Trent said as he opened the door fully. "Make sure all the doors are locked, and double-check your windows, too."

Cate's eyes widened. "The windows."

"They are locked, right? You always check them, right?" he asked warily.

"Uh. No."

"What about the basement windows where someone can crawl in?"

"Those I had boarded up and sealed when we moved in. I try never to go down there if I can help it."

"Yeah," Danny chimed in. "It's spooky."

She nodded. "It is."

"Do you want me to check the windows for you?"

"No, I can do it. There aren't that many," she said.

"Okay." Trent stepped out. "Lock up behind me."

"Goodbye… Detective Davis." She closed the door and locked it.

Cate felt as if she'd run a gauntlet through swinging knife blades. Police. The last thing she needed in her life right now was a cop. Now or ever.

TRENT WENT TO his car. As he drove away, he noticed that Cate and Danny were watching him leave from the living-room window.

Purposefully, he drove down two blocks, then doubled back, turning off his headlights so she wouldn't see him returning. He parked four doors away.

As his eyes tracked over to the house, he noticed as each of the lights was turned off. The last one was at the far right end of the house. Presumably, Cate's bedroom.

Cate.

He'd never paid much attention to her when he'd seen her around town. Thinking about it, he realized she was the kind of woman who didn't meet a man's eyes. She didn't flirt. Didn't smile much, either. Now he knew why.

She was pretty enough. Soft peachy skin. Thick brunette hair that hung in a straight cut just past her chin.

Trent flung even the hint of Cate out of his head. With his PTSD, he wasn't relationship material—for anybody. To save everyone heartache, it was best for him to bury romantic emotions.

Cate was simply part of his investigation. That was all.

Trent's life worked best with him alone. No

one to hear his screams in the night. No one to talk him down from another nightmare. No one to whom he'd have to describe what it was like to have his best buddy blown to pieces right before his eyes. The IED should have been detected. It would have been better if Trent had been the one to die. Trent didn't have a wife and kids. But Parker had.

The vision of Parker's bloody body pieces strewed over the sand was burned on his soul. It was part of him. He couldn't right click and delete it. Shoot it or kill it. It lived deep in his psyche where it haunted him.

Trent dropped his face to his hands. Sweat had sprung out on his forehead and ran down his temples. It was always like this. He'd heat up and then when the memory faded, he'd cool off. His mouth was dry.

It was always the same. Predictable. But the onset was like a rogue wave. He never knew when it was coming. Only that it would be back again and again. That was the hell of it.

Because no treatment worked. Cognitive processing therapy and prolonged exposure therapy didn't help. He'd tried a selective serotonin reuptake inhibitor, but it hadn't made a dent.

He drank deeply from his water bottle and looked at Cate's bedroom window.

The light had gone out.

"Time for some shut-eye," he mumbled as he stared at the house.

Trent sat up in his seat as he remembered Cate's brown eyes.

That was it. There was something wrong with her eyes. Tonight, in the harsh overhead foyer light, she'd looked straight at him.

That's when he'd noticed it. She wore colored contacts. The kind that muted the eye. Made it difficult, if not impossible, to read someone's thoughts. Trent was usually spot-on with deciphering expressions, voice tones, nuances that disclosed valuable information.

He'd frightened her tonight. He'd blundered and hoped he'd smoothed it over. He needed her to trust him. It was a bonus that her son had taken a liking to him. He might need some support in the days to come. Cate was wary and suspicious, as well she should be. He couldn't imagine what life had been like for her all this time—living this lie.

Looking at the situation from Cate's side, he imagined that to her, he was just about the worst thing that could happen to her. His investigation would blow her story to pieces.

Cate was right not to trust him.

In order to throw the snare on Le Grande, he might hurt Cate.

CHAPTER FOUR

CATE THREW BACK the last precious drops of the cappuccino that Maddie Barzonni had made especially for her. Maddie had drawn a little house with a "sold" sign over the door because Cate had a showing with a new buyer today. Maddie was a firm believer in manifesting one's destiny. So was Cate. In fact, she'd been manifesting and creating her life so expertly and for so many years, she felt she should give fiction writing a shot.

"Maybe a screenplay," she mumbled to herself as she drove up to 415 Park Street.

She looked at the computer printout she'd brought with her. The house had been on the market for nearly a year, and Cate could see why. The grass was ankle-high, all the landscaping was in need of watering and trimming. The windows were dirty, and there were flyers and free newspapers flung around the door.

"Definitely no curb appeal," she grumbled as she unhooked her seat belt. She gathered her purse, briefcase and the code she'd need to unlock the key lock. Cate had seen this situation before. The house was part of an estate, and the remaining family lived thousands of miles from Indian Lake. There was no one to oversee the house, and the listing agent realized early on that the place was a hard sell and, quite obviously, didn't bother to mow the yard or have any work done. Efforts like those were paid for by the agent in hopes of a large commission. Even Cate would have given up on this house.

As she approached, she could see that the house needed paint, repairs to the gutters and a new storm door. Cate tried to tuck the piece of screen that had come loose into the metal groove along the inside of the frame, but the screen was so old and rusty, she was afraid she'd need a tetanus shot.

She was just about to punch in the security code when she heard a thundering rumble as a massive black Toyota Tacoma truck pulled up. The tires were so huge, the vehicle looked more like a military tank than a flatbed truck.

The door opened, and a man dressed in blue jeans, work boots and a black T-shirt that looked spray-painted over his broad chest, shoulders and bulging biceps swung out of the truck. This was Rand Nelson. On the phone, he'd told her he was a fire jumper who'd just moved back to town. Rand was tall, she thought, but not as tall as Trent Davis.

Fleetingly, she wondered what a black T-shirt would look like on Trent.

What was the matter with her?

She hadn't thought about a man or his physique in years. And why on earth would Trent Davis come to mind?

She felt the hairs on her arm stand on end as she put logic to her reactions. Trent was a lawman. Rand was a firefighter, but his job also skirted too close to those kinds of individuals who asked a lot of questions. *How did the fire start? Were you anywhere near the house when it was set ablaze? When did you move to Indian Lake? What's your real name?*

Questions like that. Though she'd legally changed her name before she enrolled in real-estate school—which also made Danny's legal name Sullivan—she didn't like probing questions. Of any kind.

Rand stared at the house, feet sturdily apart, hands on his hips. Gnawing his bottom lip. Contemplating.

Cate swallowed hard. Buyers had a way of keeping a check on their emotions when they looked at houses. She'd seen clients who could go through a house, even on a third walk-through, and still not register a single speck of desire or dislike. Some people didn't want to get their hopes up. Others somehow believed they could keep the price down by appearing ambivalent.

This guy was the best at stoicism she'd ever seen. He was stone. But she would still bet he wasn't interested, and she didn't blame him. She let the computerized lock dangle on the door latch. She wouldn't need the code after all.

"Hi." She waved, starting toward him. "I'm Cate Sullivan. You must be Rand Nelson."

"I am," he replied, still surveying the house and not once glancing at her.

"After we talked on the phone and you told me your price range, I thought I'd start here. Clearly, the photo and specs I sent you are out-of-date."

"How long has it been on the market?" he asked, his ink-dark eyes tracking up to the roof.

"Eleven months and a couple days. It needs a landscape crew to—"

"No sprinkler system. That's why the bushes died. The trees might make it."

"Uh-huh." She flipped through the other printouts in the manila folder she carried. "I have a house over on Sutton Court, just off Lily

Avenue, that you might like. It's closer to town, and I could call the owner—"

"Not yet. I like this one."

Cate's eyes widened. "You do? Why?" Her gaze locked on him. He was unreadable.

Rand pressed his lips together thoughtfully. "It needs me."

"It—"

"Can we go inside? I need to see the kitchen. From the photographs, it looked awesome."

"Uh, yeah. Sure," Cate replied, taking the key code out of her purse and walking to the house.

While she pressed the buttons, Rand continued assessing the front yard.

"Yep. I can put in the sprinkler system myself. Paint the house. It's not that large a place, which is what I want. Shouldn't take long. Fix that gutter up there. Some redbud trees would be nice along that side there, don't you think? They're pretty in the spring. Or flowering almond. I have to think about that."

Cate opened the door. She couldn't believe it. Rand was sold before she'd made a pitch about the house only being four blocks from the lake or shown him the interior. Was this her lucky day or what?

Cate walked into the living room and went

to the white French doors that opened onto a small patio. She frowned at the weeds sticking up between the old bricks. "The backyard is fenced," she said as she turned around.

Rand had gone to the right and into the kitchen. "Would you look at this?"

Cate entered the kitchen as Rand opened the stainless-steel refrigerator door. The kitchen had been remodeled three years prior. The owner had apparently died before using it much.

"This stove looks like it's never been turned on. Six gas burners. A dream. And did you see?" He pulled out a stainless-steel drawer. "A warming oven. The wall oven is convection. A microwave." He ran a hand over the charcoal-gray, slate-looking countertop. "What is this?"

"Soapstone," Cate said. "Impervious to everything, I'm told. I've never had one, but one of the women in my office has it. She loves it."

"I never heard of it." He frowned.

This was one of those times that Cate was glad she'd done her homework. Showing a house was not the same as selling a house. She was not one of those agents who opened the door then went to her car to text her friends. She stayed on the job.

"Soapstone is a natural quarried stone like

granite. It just comes in shorter sheets. It's metamorphic rock and feels a bit soft or soapy because of the talc in the stone. I believe this stone comes from the Appalachian Mountains. The owner who did the remodel was adamant that all the products be made in the USA."

"Hmm. I like this guy." Rand grinned brightly.

"I'll show you the rest of the house." Cate started toward the hall.

"I suppose I should see it," he replied. "But I'm sold. I'll take it."

Cate whirled around, surprised and a bit shocked. She'd never sold any house this easily, especially without having shown every nook and cranny. "Just like that?"

"Look, Cate. There's just me. I'm a fire jumper. They fly me wherever I'm needed. I'm here because my mom is sick and she's too much for my siblings to handle. Other than some family dinners, which this kitchen can handle like a dream, I'm pretty much a homebody. When I'm off duty, I cook for relaxation. My father was a carpenter, plumber, handyman, you name it. I learned a lot about houses from him. We used to remodel houses on the side to make ends meet. There's nothing I can't do here myself…within reason, of course. But I didn't want to live through a kitchen remodel."

Cate smiled. "Then I suggest we breeze through the rest of the house, see the garage and check the plumbing. We should talk about what kind of offer you want to make."

"That's your area of expertise. I'll take any direction you suggest."

"You could pay their asking price but make it a stipulation that they pay for some of the yard cleanup, including removal of the dead shrubs."

"That sounds fair," he said.

"Good," she replied with a satisfied smile. "I'll go to the office, call the owners and then write up the papers. Can I reach you on your cell?"

"Yes, and if I don't answer, try the fire station number I gave you. I'm working there in between forest fire assignments. Just to help out. My brother is a firefighter, as well. He talked me into it."

"Sounds like a great family, Rand. I'd like to meet them all some time. So, can I bring the papers there for you to sign?"

"Absolutely," Rand said, and quickly walked through the master bedroom, which was larger than he'd expected. The other rooms were smaller than he'd hoped. Still, he was happy.

As Rand rumbled down the street in his

truck, Cate couldn't help thinking that it suited him perfectly.

Cate called Sarah. "Hi. I finished much earlier than I'd thought. I have to run by the office, but I shouldn't be more than an hour."

Sarah explained she and Miss Milse were making dinner for the kids, and there was no rush. Danny and Timmy were playing with Beau, and Annie was practicing the piano.

Cate pulled away from the curb and drove to the first stop sign. She glanced in her rearview mirror, saw only a black Mercury sedan behind her, then checked right and left before proceeding across the intersection. She stopped at the red light at Indian Lake Avenue, turned on the stereo and punched in a new classical station she'd found.

Cruising toward the real-estate office on Indian Lake Avenue, Cate looked in the rearview mirror, checking the traffic.

She nearly froze. Was that the same black Mercury she'd seen on Park Street?

"No." She refused to believe that anyone could be following her. This was a coincidence. Lots of people would travel to town taking the same route she was.

But after the visit from Trent Davis and his warnings about home invaders and watching for anything that was out of the ordinary, she had to admit to being slightly spooked.

Each time she came to a red light, even though the Mercury was directly behind her, it stayed back far enough that she couldn't see the driver. That, in itself, seemed strange. And she didn't like it.

Because of Cate's work as a real-estate agent, showing houses, sitting in vacant houses on weekends, she'd taught herself to be aware of her surroundings. Maybe her ultrasensitivity or flat-out paranoia was due to the fact that she'd been living in disguise for over six years. Whatever it was, she knew when things didn't feel right.

Like now.

There was only one way to find out if she was imagining things or if she should call the cops. She hit her turn signal and slipped to the right lane. Then she made a right turn onto Cove Beach Lane, which circled the entire lake.

The Mercury followed.

Cate's blood pounded in her temples, heating her veins despite the fact her fingers were cold. She gripped the steering wheel. There was only one person who'd ever speared her with so much fear that she turned off all human emotion.

Brad.

That was impossible, wasn't it? How could Brad be here? When she'd changed her name, it had needed to be published in the Indiana newspaper, but she still felt fairly safe since Brad had never looked at a newspaper that she remembered and he lived in Illinois. Still, she wondered how he could have found her. These days, there were ways. There were internet sites notorious for finding lost family and friends. Cate had been ridiculous in her distrust of providing any online information. She never paid her bills online. In fact, she hand-delivered her utilities checks. She paid cash at the grocery store, and she always paid the mortgage in person. Once she secured her first mortgage, she cancelled her credit card. Cate kept her money in a floor safe in her house. If she ever had to run again, even in the middle of the night, she was prepared.

There was the matter of her face being on not one, but three roadside real-estate billboards at the primary entrances to town. These billboards were a major part of her agency's advertising campaign. Cate had tried to ditch the photography session, but her boss had been insistent. Cate had no choice but to agree to the photo.

This same photo of her was plastered on the company website, free neighborhood newspapers, the *Indian Lake Argus* newspaper and on flyers on a corkboard at the Indian Lake Grocery.

For years she'd told herself that the chances of Brad driving through Indian Lake were one in a billion.

He would never find her.

But what if he had stumbled upon her little town?

What if he had seen the billboard? Being supercritical now, she realized that, except for the hair and eye color, she really hadn't changed much in the past seven years. Brad had always been sharp—it was one of the things she'd been attracted to. She liked smart people.

Her nerves jangled. Logically, there was no reason for her to think for one millisecond that the Mercury following her was driven by Brad.

But her intuition had never betrayed her. Never.

Cate tilted her head to the rearview mirror and looked hard and long at the man driving the Mercury. Though terrified at what she might see, she eased off the gas and let him approach.

He had dark hair, but that was all she could see.

If it was Brad, he had to want something.

But what?

She didn't have any real money, just a few thousand in her safe. If Brad had found her, and knew anything at all, he most certainly knew about Danny.

Cate felt her stomach twist. She ground her jaw, already feeling massively protective toward her son. Late at night when dread drew mental pictures of Brad confronting her, she felt the kind of aggression that wouldn't stop until she'd eliminated him from their lives completely. Brad's need to possess was toxic. Cate believed that if Brad found out Danny was his son, he would try to take him away from her. Not because he loved Danny. Not because he wanted Cate back. He would take because that's what Brad Kramer did. He took. He sucked energy from people. He stole lives.

It stupefied her that she'd once been so gullible, so naive as to fall into his trap. And it had been a trap—hard steel and metal teeth. Like the wolf that would bite off its own paw to escape from a hunter's snare, Cate did the same thing. She'd thrown away everything she'd ever known to be rid of him.

Cate followed the curving road around the north side of the lake. The Mercury pursued.

She didn't dare drive to her house. She wasn't safe there.

If this was Brad, he would follow her and break down the door once he knew she was home alone. Then what would he do? Beat her like before? Kill her for leaving him?

Cate's hands trembled as she wiped a tear from her cheek. She wasn't crying—was she? She'd never cried before over Brad and she scolded herself for doing it now. She had to think.

The Mercury pulled closer. Was he going to run her off the road? Slam into the back of her? Or just damage her car to punish her?

Cate pressed the gas and lurched out of his way. She was speeding, but she didn't care. She'd circle the lake and then head into town. If he followed her, she'd drive straight to the police station.

Are you crazy? And tell them what? That you've been living here in disguise for over six years? That all your friends don't even know who you really are?

Just then, Cate's eyes shot to the right to check her side mirror. She saw Sophie Mattuchi pulling a garden cart filled with yellow and bronze mums into the front yard of Jack

Carter's condo. Automatically, Cate waved and Sophie waved back, signaling for her to pull in.

Cate quickly made her decision. The mysterious Mercury was enough to give her arrhythmia. She needed help. Now.

She turned into the drive, but didn't get out. She watched her rearview mirror while pretending to put on some lip gloss.

The Mercury drove past. Slowly.

Cate choked on her breath. There was no mistaking the handsome face, the strong jaw and wide shoulders. She had no idea how or why Brad was in Indian Lake.

Was Brad's presence here a fluke? A random trip? Was he a tourist like so many people from Chicago?

She wouldn't know until she talked to him and that wasn't an option.

Every muscle in her body had tightened, causing pain to shoot from her neck to her tailbone. She was as rigid as steel when Brad looked directly at her and lifted his forefinger like it was a gun barrel. He blew on his fingertip, stepped on the gas and sped away.

Brad. After all this time. He's found me.

For more than six years, Cate's new identity had worked to keep her invisible. Now he'd seen her. And that pointed finger. That was a promise—of bad things to come.

In those days when she'd been shackled to him, he used to point his finger like a gun then ball his fists. She knew precisely what Brad meant to do.

She dropped the lip gloss. She felt as if a vacuum had sucked her up a portal to an alien ship. All reality altered. She was in terror land. Pain, loss and danger circled her, harping at her like screaming banshees. She covered her ears.

"Hi, Cate!" Sophie called as she walked toward the car. "It's nice to see you."

Cate opened her eyes.

Not banshees.

Sophie. What is she saying? Get it together, Cate.

She forced her shaking, frigid hands to open the door, forced herself to climb out. "Hi, Sophie." Cate tried to smile, but her lips felt like they'd been dragged through concrete. Brad had that effect on her. She walked toward Sophie, and when Sophie stretched open her arms for a hug, Cate hugged her back. "What are you doing?" She managed to cough out the words. She put her fist to her mouth and coughed again. "Sorry. Dry mouth. Allergies."

She was back on earth. Talking to her friend.

Brad was gone. At least for the moment. She had to calm the whirlwind of emotions inside her.

"Can I get you some water?" Sophie asked sweetly.

"I'm fine." Cate thought she was smiling. She couldn't tell. "So, what's all this?" Cate asked walking toward the wagon.

"Oh, I'm planting my fall mums. I thought some yellow against the green Japanese yews and the white house would be pretty. What do you think?"

Though Cate's mind was still disabled from the encounter with her ex-husband, she had enough presence of mind to act curious. "Your mums?" Cate looked at Jack's condo—the one she'd sold him nearly a year ago. But Sophie lived in Mrs. Beabots's upstairs apartment. Cate turned to Sophie. "*Your* mums, you said." Cate was certain her hearing had been impaired by the shock she'd just endured.

"Er, uh," Sophie stammered.

Cate's eyes narrowed. Sophie was a cardiac nurse, a smart, career-oriented woman. Cate had never seen her at a loss for words. "Is something wrong?"

Sophie smiled sheepishly. Then she blushed. Cate had run into Sophie over the years at various social events. They weren't close friends the way Cate was with Sarah, Liz or Maddie. But they knew each other. Cate knew Sophie to be serious-minded nearly all the time. Sophie was a take-charge woman. There was nothing sheepish about her.

Then it hit Cate. "You and Jack?"

Sophie nodded like a bobblehead doll and chuckled. "Can you keep a secret?"

Could she? No one in the world could keep secrets as well as Cate. Her entire life was a secret. "I certainly can."

Sophie thrust up her left hand. A diamond solitaire twinkled in the sunlight. "We're engaged!" She blurted and covered her mouth as she started laughing. "Isn't it amazing?"

Cate's reaction was to be filled with dread. Marriage meant entrapment. Danger zone. Everything dire in life. Other people believed in happiness, love and forever. Cate wanted none of that.

She'd never shared her innermost thoughts with any of her friends. She didn't dare start now. "I'm so happy for you," Cate lied.

"Oh, thanks, Cate. Hardly anyone knows. Mrs. Beabots does, of course. Jack and I are starting to talk about the wedding and set a date. But it's just crazy. My family would go nuts if we did it at city hall, but I can't wait for my new life to begin. I never thought that I…"

"…would get married," Cate murmured.

Sophie sighed dreamily. "Uh-huh."

"I had no idea you were seeing him. I mean, that he was seeing you. Or that you two were together."

"Nobody does, really. I mean, I took him to meet my parents just last weekend. They adore him already and he loves them, too, which is a very good thing. Don't you think?"

"Oh, I do. I do." Cate suddenly spied a black sedan drive past. He was stalking her. And there wasn't a thing she could do about it.

She glanced at the car.

A Cadillac. Not Brad.

Cate exhaled. She planted a particularly sweet smile on her lips. Acting. Cate had been doing it for years. She was good at it. "I'm sure your parents will want a wedding with all the trimmings for their only daughter."

"You've got that right. But I don't want it to be too nuts, you know. We're having the reception at their farm. Plenty of Italian food and lots of flowers from my grandmother's sunflower garden, of course." Sophie gushed. "It'll be beautiful. You're invited, of course. And please bring Danny. We definitely want kids there."

"So," Cate said. "You'll be moving in here after the wedding."

"Yes. But you know, Jack says he wants to look for a proper house. Still on the lake and one with a pier so he can have a little fishing boat. I don't know what he's thinking. This condo is wonderful."

Cate shook her head. "Sophie. Please. He's smart. He's thinking of the future. You can't put little kids in a house like this."

Sophie's brown eyes rounded. "Oh, my gosh, that *is* what he's thinking, isn't it? He'd said he wanted to talk to you so that you could be on the lookout if anything came up."

Cate took out a business card from her jacket pocket. She'd meant to give it to Rand Nelson, but with the instant sale she'd forgotten. "Here. My new cell number is on the card. Tell Jack not to worry. I'll ask around. I know a few houses where the couples want to downsize. And I won't tell a soul anything about your engagement until after you make the announcement."

"Thanks, Cate. I'll be sure to tell him." Sophie hugged Cate. "We're lucky to have a good friend like you!"

Cate smiled at Sophie. She'd never seen Sophie so effusive. She'd always been standoffish and distant. Her relationship with Jack had certainly brought out a new and more affectionate side that Cate liked. "I have to run. You take care."

"Bye, Cate." Sophie waved and returned to the wagon of flowers.

Cate backed out of the driveway and drove away. *Sophie and Jack.* Cate thought Jack would be a good mate for any woman. She'd thought he was handsome when she first met him. Liked the way he did business. He treated people with kindness and fairness.

It would be nice if Cate had found a man like that. But she hadn't. She'd chosen the worst kind of person a woman could pick.

Cate shook the visions of weddings and engagements and happily-ever-afters out of her head. Those things were fine for other women.

Just not for Cate Sullivan. Susan Kramer. Or whoever else she had to become in order to keep away from Brad—and stay alive.

CHAPTER FIVE

TRENT FINISHED TIGHTENING the heavy ropes that held the blue-and-gold-striped tent in place and shaded the Indian Lake Police booth from the noon sun. There were four officers working with him not counting Max, their one and only K-9 officer. Max was a highly trained narcotics detection canine and could be invaluable in helping Trent ramp up his investigation to bring down the Le Grande gang.

As much as Trent wanted to focus on the assorted donated items the men had gathered to sell—baked goods fragrant with sugar and butter, jars of homemade jellies, salsa, barbecue marinades, as well as jewelry made by some of the police widows and wives, and potted herbs the children had been growing all summer—his mind was on Le Grande.

Last night's telephone conversation with Richard Schmitz had been enlightening.

"I met with my inside man and here's what I know. Le Grande's wife isn't part of the gang.

She's clean. He didn't know she was in Indian Lake when he set up operations there. He wanted your town because those country roads of yours are not well-patrolled. His Detroit connection has been using Indian Lake for years. That's how Le Grande heard of it."

"Does he know she's here?"

"Yeah. My man was with him at a mini-mart buying cigarettes. There was a photo of her on a real-estate flyer under the glass at the checkout counter."

"I've seen that flyer."

"Apparently Le Grande goes off his nut when my guy brings up the subject of his wife. Le Grande told our guy that once he owns a person—family or gang member—that person is his for life."

"So, Le Grande has objectified her."

"Affirmative," Richard replied dourly. "That fact has its good points. For one, it makes his actions predictable. People who see other humans as objects have a relentless need to possess and control. Le Grande's mental issues could be to our advantage."

"In his mind his business, drugs, gang members and ex-wife are all in the same category."

"Exactly. It's all his property," Richard agreed.

"So he's going to want her back."

"I'm hoping so. If he concentrates on Indian Lake, where he hasn't set up safe houses, hideaways and escape routes, we just might catch him in the act."

"Is CPD thinking to set up another sting?"

"Think *we*, buddy. Both Chicago PD and Indian Lake need to plan this carefully. By the way, my inside guy says that Le Grande thinks the wife will want him back now that he's wealthy."

"I don't see that at all," Trent countered.

"Well, you'd know that from your end. I'm giving you a heads-up. We have to work out a lot of details. I'll be in touch."

Trent had a great deal to consider. He'd been relieved to know that Cate had no part of Le Grande or his drug trafficking business. Her sweet persona had not been put on, and she was the caring mother he'd gauged her to be. For a brief moment, he felt his tension lift. However, the focus of the CPD and ILPD was now on Cate. Trent knew that Richard was dedicated to ending Le Grande's reign in Chicago. Trent wanted the drug lord out of Indian Lake for good.

Trent felt his nerves jangle. Utilizing an untrained citizen for a police sting was precarious, but often effective. Already he could think of a dozen reasons not to move forward and one reason they should.

With Trent and his military skill set as a Green Beret at the helm, it should work.

Drake Parsons, Max's handler, bumped him with his elbow. "Help me with this poster, would ya, Trent?"

"Yeah, sure." Trent cleared his mind of thoughts about Cate and Le Grande. He tacked the poster to a wooden framework he'd put together to display snapshots of the annual policemen's picnic in City Park, and the police baseball team in their winning game at the city championship in late August. Trent had pitched after the regular pitcher had torn a ligament in his shoulder. Trent had surprised himself since he hadn't pitched much since high school and a few impromptu games in the military.

In Afghanistan.

Just the thought of a baseball, its stitches fitting familiarly in his palm, skin against skin, brought back horrors. He dropped his arms and felt a spring of perspiration on his forehead. Nerves. Not heat. Would he ever get past the past?

"Trent, is that you?" He heard a woman's voice behind him. He whirled, holding the hammer like a weapon.

He shook away the sticky cobweb of memories, peering through it to see Mrs. Beabots holding a huge apple pie.

She had the bluest eyes he'd ever seen. Approaching her was Cate Sullivan, whose eyes were dull—due to the brown contacts she wore. He wondered what color her eyes were. Blue? Green? Hazel? He'd probably never find out. Strangely, he wanted to know. It mattered to him, but he didn't know why. It was probably because of his overactive detective antennae.

"Wow." Trent reached to take the spectacular-looking pie from Mrs. Beabots. "This should bring a good price. Maybe we should auction it."

Mrs. Beabots winked at him. "That's the ticket. I like that idea."

"Hi, Cate," Trent said, noticing her eyes were focused on him. She stood still, holding a tray with two pies.

"Hi," Cate replied with a faint smile. She continued to look at him, as though she were inspecting him. Taking stock. Her behavior was odd based on their meeting the night of the intruder.

But then she'd been frightened.

Terror twisted things. He should know.

Danny wiggled in between both women and

shoved a canvas bag at Trent. "We have more in the car," the boy said. "I'm going back."

"Not without me you aren't, young man," Cate said instantly.

Trent could have sworn the little shake of her head was to break her focus on him. He wasn't sure why she took such close inventory. Did cops make her nervous? He had to believe that was partly true since she'd been lying to everyone in town.

Fascinating, when he thought about it. He wondered exactly how she had picked Indian Lake. It could have been as simple as the fact that she didn't know anyone here. No relatives to blow the whistle on her. No former friends. Anonymity. That had to be it.

He'd seen the scenario a million times over. Fresh starts. New vistas. And no past to think about. But even he knew that no matter how focused one was on the future, the past never left. His past crept around like slinky varmints with sharp teeth ready to gnaw at his Achilles' heel.

"Do you have a lot of stuff?" Trent asked Cate as she started to walk away.

"Enough to fill all four of these tables," Mrs. Beabots said. "Cate and Danny were kind enough to help me."

Trent turned to Drake, who was placing price

stickers on jars of green pepper jelly. "I'm going with Cate. Be back in a few."

Drake's eyes shot over to the pretty brunette. "Sure, Trent." He chuckled with a playful lift to his grin. "You go right ahead."

He was no more interested in Cate romantically than he was in pigs flying. He followed her, noticing the tight fit to the skinny jeans she wore and the feminine, aqua-and-blue print blouse. There were silver hoops in her ears that hung below the precision-cut edge of her chin-length dark hair. She wore some kind of open-toed canvas shoes that revealed brightly painted aqua toes.

The toes matched her blouse. She liked fashion? Or was she meticulous about her appearance? He remembered that her house was very clean—and she had a six-year-old son. The way he remembered being six, he'd been constantly in and out of dirt, and almost never walked into the house without grass stains from playing baseball at the nearby park. Was she overprotective? Paranoid? Or both?

They reached the SUV, and Cate opened the hatch. Trent noticed that the vehicle, too, was immaculate. The windows didn't have a speck of dirt or grime, and it would take him half a Saturday to get a wax gleam this perfect.

Cate lifted a tray of cupcakes. "You take these. I'll bring the pies. Danny, sweetheart, you take the pan of brownies."

"Yes, ma'am!" Danny replied, staring wide-eyed at the chocolate confections.

Trent couldn't help it; he had to ask. "You just have your car detailed?"

"Huh?" She looked at the tan leather seats. "Not really. I keep it up myself. An agent's car is practically the office, you know. First impressions to clients are crucial."

"I've heard that," Trent replied with a smile.

Cate didn't return the smile, only scanned him with laser-like scrutiny.

Had he revealed too much too soon? He had to win her confidence if he was to get any information about Le Grande. He continued smiling as they walked to the booth.

Keeping up with small talk was important. As an investigator, he never knew when an important piece of information would drop in his lap. "Well, you must be doing something right because you've built a good business here in town. How long have you been in real estate?"

"A little over five years. The minute I had my license, I went right to work. I swear, I haven't had a day off since. It's been good to me, and I enjoy every minute. My clients have become friends, as well." There was a slight stiffness to her response.

Trent had the impression she'd given this same explanation many times before. She was treating him like a prospective client.

At the booth, Mrs. Beabots had rearranged half the goods on the tables and made room—in the very front, of course—for her pastries. Trent couldn't hide his smile. Mrs. Beabots was the take-charge woman he'd heard so much about. This proved it.

"I'll take those blueberry pies, Cate." Mrs. Beabots put them on the table. "Then the brownies next to them. I brought some paper plates so we could arrange them in groups of half a dozen. After all, no one eats just one."

"Don't say that," Cate said, putting her hands over Danny's ears in mock fashion. "I tell him one is plenty."

Danny pulled her hands away. "She's right, Mom. One for each hand. Right, Mrs. Beabots?"

Trent crossed his arms over his chest and shot a stern look at Danny. "I'm pretty sure your mother knows what's best for you, Danny."

Mrs. Beabots nodded. "I said a cookie for each hand, Danny. And those were my small Snickerdoodles. My brownies are very rich."

Danny hung his head. "Aw, gee."

Cate's gaze again clamped on Trent. He wished he was a mind reader. Or that she would drop her guard. He had to hand it to her. She'd learned how to mask her emotions like a highly trained actress. He couldn't tell if she was angry, concerned, curious or pleased. He had to wait for her comments, but unfortunately, she thought long and hard before speaking.

Looking away from Cate, Trent saw Sarah and Luke Bosworth, Annie and Timmy.

"Mrs. Beabots!" Sarah called and waved. "We got here just in time. I want that apple pie before anyone else buys it."

Mrs. Beabots looked over Sarah's shoulder at Luke. "Really? No objections from you, Luke?"

"Me? Object to you? Never."

"How goes it, Luke?" Trent asked, placing his left hand on Luke's strong shoulder and shaking his right hand with a firm grip.

"Great. You working out tomorrow?"

"I was planning on it," Trent replied. "I'll meet you at the Y. One o'clock?"

"Great," Luke replied and looked at Timmy, who was trying to get his father's attention by grabbing his belt. "What is it?"

"Dad. Mrs. Beabots made brownies. The really good ones. Can I buy some? I have my allowance."

Luke rolled his eyes.

Trent laughed. "Think of the kids he's helping. It's a good cause."

"Okay."

Timmy's jaw dropped. "You mean it?"

Sarah's eyes shot to Luke. "What are you saying?"

Luke shrugged. "I caved."

The tented booth was filling with patrons buying jewelry and jams, pies and what was left of the brownies.

Trent saw Danny as he watched his friend, Timmy, leaning against his father's leg, eating a brownie. Luke was talking to Sarah and Mrs. Beabots, absentmindedly running his hand over Timmy's thick hair, then down to the boy's shoulder. Timmy barely made any sign that he felt his father's endearing touch; he was used to love and comforting caresses.

Danny's expression showed sadness sifted over jealousy. And yearning.

Trent knew that feeling. He felt it now, knowing that he'd never have a son of his own to hold and love.

"Danny," Trent said, breaking the boy's concentration.

Danny's gaze slowly peeled away from Timmy and traveled to Trent. "Yes, sir?"

"Nearly all of Mrs. Beabots's treats are sold. But I see one brownie that's left. I'll buy it for you."

"You will?"

"Remember? I promised you one?"

"Uh-huh, but I have to ask my mom first. Okay?" Danny asked excitedly.

Danny rushed over to Cate, who was talking to Sarah. She leaned down to listen to Danny.

Cate whirled, the soft fabric of her blouse floating around her like a cloud. The sun struck her face as her thoughts nearly pierced the brown-colored contacts. Distrust.

Trent didn't have to look at her to feel her wariness. What were his intentions toward her son? Why was he being kind? What was in it for him? They were the same thoughts that filled the heads of the crime victims he endeavored to protect—even the minds of the perps.

Sarah asked Cate a question. Yet Danny persisted. Cate relented. Trent saw her nod, and Danny made a gleeful sound.

He raced to Trent. "She said yes."

"Great." Trent walked to where Drake stood. He took out a twenty-dollar bill and put it in the jar marked Donations. "I'll take that last brownie for Danny."

"Sure, Trent," Drake said, putting a napkin around the brownie.

"Let's go over here." Trent pointed under a tree to a group of folding chairs he'd set up earlier. Trent sat and patted the chair next to him. "Sit next to me."

Danny looked toward his mother for approval. She caught his eye and winked. "She said it's okay." Danny smiled and scooted into the chair. He took a bite of his brownie and, with a mouth full of chocolate, said, "I want to be a policeman when I grow up. Do you think that's a good idea?"

Trent was stunned. He hadn't expected this at all. "I, er, think it's a very good idea. Why do you want to be a cop?"

"Because policemen take care of people. They protect moms and kids." Danny looked at Trent with so much admiration and respect in his eyes, Trent didn't know whether to melt or puff up his chest.

Trent was used to kids saying they wanted to wear a gun, or they had visions that police work was like living in the middle of a video game. Danny didn't. He got it. Understood the reason Trent lived and breathed law enforcement. He wanted the world to be a better, safer place for people. Kids, especially. Danny was six years old, yet he looked at life like an adult.

"I think I'd be a really great detective like you."

"Oh, you do, do you?" Trent was intrigued.

"I do. Detectives are smart. I'm smart. I can read chapter books, and I'm memorizing multipliers."

"That's impressive," Trent replied truthfully. "I was kinda slow in school at first. I had a bit of dyslexia. But I learned to deal with it. Once I went into the army, I didn't let anything hold me back. Sorta like you."

"You were in the army?"

"Special Forces. Green Beret."

"Wow!" Danny's face filled with wonder. He put down the brownie. Even sugar couldn't compete with the glaze of hero worship. "That's even cooler."

"I suppose."

Danny beamed at Trent. "I could be a Special Forces guy. I'm really good at concentration games. Ask my mom. I practice all the time. My mom says I have the power of observation."

"Is that right?"

"Sure. You can test me," Danny prodded. "Go ahead."

For a short moment, Trent had begun to react

emotionally toward Danny. The kid was as cute as a button, smart and more outgoing than his mother. Trent opened his mouth to say something, when Cate walked up.

"Done with your brownie?" She smiled at her son but glared at Trent out of the corner of her eye. She held out her hand to Danny. "Time for us to leave Detective Davis to his work. I told Liz we'd come to her booth to see their baby."

Danny jumped off the chair. "Oh, right!" He turned and leaned a hand on Trent's knee, cupped his left hand over his mouth and whispered, "Miss Liz lets me hold the baby because she trusts me."

"I'm sure you're very good at it," Trent replied, feeling the small blot of warmth from Danny's hand seep through his pants.

Cate's practiced smile curved her lips. "Thank you for the brownie for Danny. He's been looking forward to it. It was very nice of you to spend time with him."

"It was my pleasure." Trent was astonished at the sincerity he'd heard in his own voice.

He watched them walk away. It *had* been his pleasure. He'd felt things that he wasn't sure he'd ever experienced before. Trent had been living on the surface of the ocean of life for so long, he had no idea there was anything in his subterranean waters. Joy had flitted into his day. So had compassion, and the awareness that his life was no deeper than a creek bed.

CHAPTER SIX

CATE TOOK A large plastic grocery cart from the bay and plunked her oversize, fake Louis Vuitton purse in the kid's seat. She looked at Danny as he took a child's cart and started toward the door. "I may never get used to the fact that you're too big to sit in the grocery cart," Cate said.

"I couldn't wait to be big enough to have my own cart. Now I am," Danny said with a slight puff to his little chest. "Can I get the mini carrots instead of the big ones with leaves?"

"The little ones are more expensive," Cate replied, looking at the bags of premade salads, organic broccoli crowns, zucchini strips, cut and ready to eat. Someday, she'd make enough money to afford such luxuries. In the meantime, she washed, chopped, cut and julienned celery, carrots, zucchini and yellow peppers at night after Danny went to bed. She insisted on organic fruits and vegetables and as few processed foods as possible. She was relentless when it came to the well-being and safety of her child.

Protect Danny.

Those words had been her mantra since long before he was born. They still were. Selecting a package of organic strawberries, she looked at Danny who surveyed pie pumpkins.

"Does Mrs. Beabots really make pumpkin pie out of these?" Danny asked.

"I'm sure she does. I've always used canned pumpkin, but I can try using a real one this year. I could make pumpkin bread, too. You should get one."

"Okay," he said, and carefully put the little pumpkin in his basket.

"What were you talking to Detective Davis about?"

Danny wheeled his cart to a large stack of ears of corn. "Things."

Cate dropped her head back and looked at the ceiling. This was going to be one of "those" kinds of talks with Danny. Pulling taffy was easier than getting information out of him when he thought he was keeping secrets. Danny liked secrets.

So did she.

"What kind of things?"

He held up an ear of corn. "Can we have corn on the cob?"

"Sure. Get four. And remind me to buy butter."

Danny bagged four ears of corn while Cate chose a head of lettuce and some organic spinach. "Do you like him?"

"Who?"

"Detective Davis." She ground out the words. She had a hundred questions she wanted to ask. All of them leading to the one important one. *What did you tell him about us? Things that would incriminate me? Things no one, especially a cop, should know?*

Logic told Cate she was being ridiculous. Danny didn't harbor half her fears and for good reason. She'd never told him the truth about her past. Which was precisely why she wanted to keep the status quo. She didn't need Trent Davis poking around in her life. The current one or the old one.

"I like him pretty much," Danny replied. "He's really big. And strong. Did you see his arms, Mom? I always thought Timmy's dad was the toughest-looking dad in our school. But Detective Trent, I mean Davis, he's got really big muscles." Danny spun around to face his mother. "Do you think I could grow that big?"

"Sweetie, I'm sure Detective Davis is very careful about what he eats, and he exercises to stay strong. So, yes. You could do that, too—someday when you're older."

"Good."

"What kind of questions was he asking you?" she ventured, feeling a bit frustrated.

"He didn't ask me anything."

"Nothing at all?"

"Nope."

"You two talked for such a long time I thought he was asking you, well, about us."

"No. But, Mom." Danny lifted serious blue eyes to her. "I told him a secret."

Cate swallowed hard. There was no telling what Danny thought was and was not a secret. This past year he'd become inquisitive and not easily satisfied with her explanations of why they had no other family. No grandparents, no relations. Why there was only the two of them. "What secret is that, sweetheart?" She braced.

"I told him something that I haven't even told you. I—I think I want to be a policeman. Just like Detective Trent."

Cate felt warmth flood her icy veins. It was okay. Danny was being a little boy. That was all. Nothing to be afraid of. She touched her hand to his cheek and realized she was trembling.

Brad.

This was his fault. He was the reason she'd been on edge for days. For years she'd lived in the cocoon of her lie. But all that she'd built, contrived and manipulated was about to come tumbling down if she didn't stop him.

Her first objective was to keep Danny safe. Keep him locked in the dream she'd invented. She needed to act normal. "What did he say to that? Was he flattered?"

Danny raised his shoulders and dropped them. "I dunno. He told me he was in the army. Special Forces, Mom. A real Green Beret. He's like a—a hero."

Cate knew how much Danny admired Luke Bosworth. Timmy's dad was the closest thing Danny had to a father figure even though Danny had seen Luke only on rare occasions. Now that Danny was in kindergarten, he saw more of Luke than before. All around, this was a good thing. Interestingly, in all the times that Danny had praised Luke, she'd never heard the kind of adoration she now heard from him about Trent Davis.

"He said he had some problems in school with reading. He told me he was impressed about me liking chapter books, Mom. He was impressed with me."

She crouched to his level and put her hands on his shoulders. "Danny, you are a very impressive boy. Everyone likes you. The kids in your class look up to you. Your teacher says you are probably the smartest boy in the class. Detective Trent should be impressed with you. Everybody is."

"But, Mom. The difference is that he told me so."

Cate couldn't argue that one. How many days went by that she didn't tell Danny that he was great. She told him that she loved him a half a dozen times a day or more. But to comment on his skills? His behavior? His accomplishments? She was guilty of lagging in that department.

She needed to pay more attention to this special person who, by sheer luck the universe, had been given to her as her son.

"You know, Danny, you're right. That was very nice of him to say that."

"I like him a lot, Mom."

"I can see that."

He reached into his jeans pocket. "He gave me his card so I can call him anytime I want." He showed her the card.

She glanced at it and smiled. He put the card in his pocket.

"Do you like him, Mom? He's protecting us. Right?"

She smiled. "He is. And that's not all that easy, is it? It's one thing to take care of your own family, but to watch over someone else's family, that's different."

Danny put his hand on Cate's arm and pulled at a thread on her blouse sleeve. "He doesn't have a family. There's just him."

"He told you that?"

"Yeah. I think he's lonely."

"How can you tell?" she asked.

"Because he looks at me like he wishes I was his kid," Danny said, balling the thread between his finger and thumb then flicking it away.

Cate was dumbstruck. Who was this forty-year-old adult in a child's body? Was he really that astute? Or was this Danny looking at Trent, wishing Trent was his father?

Either way, it was apparent to Cate that a bond was forming between her son and Detective Davis.

"Well," she said, touching Danny's nose with her forefinger and smiling at him. "I know one thing. If he does think that, he's smarter than

I'd imagined. I can't think of anyone I'd rather have as a child than you."

Danny put his arms around Cate's neck. "I love you, Mom."

"I love you, too, Danny. So much."

Danny pulled away and grinned. "Can we get ice cream?"

"Oh, you stinker." She laughed. "I suppose you'll want cookies to go with it."

"Uh-huh. Maybe some hot fudge?"

"I'll tell you what. We'll go to the Louise House for ice cream over the weekend. And I'll buy the ingredients for cookies. If we're going to have treats, I want to know what's in them."

He kissed her cheek and she rose.

"Okay, Mom. And don't forget the pumpkin bread."

CATE PULLED UP to her garage, hit the button and waited for the door to open. After parking the car, she and Danny unloaded the groceries into the kitchen. She went back, hit her remote to lock the car, then locked the garage and double-bolted the kitchen door behind her.

"Don't forget to turn on the motion light, Mom," Danny said.

"I always have the motion light on," she replied.

"I'll get it." Danny went to the switch, raised onto his toes and flicked the switch. "We need lots of lights."

Cate bent to put the broccoli in the refrigerator, straightened and as she did, she looked out the window.

There was no mistaking a man's figure in their yard. She ducked next to the cabinets. "Danny! Grab my purse off the island."

"What's going on?" he asked, staring at her with curiosity but no panic in his eyes.

"I need my cell phone. Do you still have Trent's—I mean Detective Davis's card? I want it." Then she motioned for him to sit beside her.

"Yeah." Danny shoved her purse across the floor and then crawled over to her. He pulled the business card from his pocket.

Cate punched in the number. Trent picked up on the first ring.

"Davis," he said.

He'd only said his name, but the sound of his strong, deep voice soothed her rattled nerves. "It's Cate Sullivan. Detective Trent—I mean, Davis—"

"Where are you?" he asked bluntly.

"I'm…we're home."

"Inside?"

"Yes. But there's a man in our backyard. I think it's the intruder you told us about."

"Doors locked?"

"Yes."

"I'm on my way," he said and hung up.

CHAPTER SEVEN

TRENT SPED DOWN Indian Lake Avenue as if the devil himself were on his tail. Though his lights were flashing like strobes in a night club, he purposefully didn't use the siren. The lights would warn most motorists to move out of his way. Those who didn't, he'd blast past those. Indian Lake Avenue was a busy thoroughfare with weekend tourists coming from Illinois to photograph the fall leaves. Fortunately for Trent, cars quickly pulled to the shoulder and allowed him to pass. Once he turned off Indian Lake Avenue, he shut off the lights but kept his speed. He needed to catch Le Grande this time.

Trent drove two blocks past Cate's street, then doubled backed. He turned off his headlights, dropped his speed to a crawl and scoured the neighbors' yards, the sidewalks and street leading up to Cate's house. He was a block away when he saw a black Mercury peel away from the curb.

Trent rammed his foot on the gas, turned on

his lights and focused his searchlight on the license plate. He memorized the first three numbers, just as his radio shouted at him.

"Officer—10-101. What is your status?"

"I'm in pursuit of a late model, black Mercury sedan. Illinois license M3Y. Negative on the rest of the number."

Trent glanced in his rearview mirror to see Danny and Cate running down their front sidewalk. Danny was jumping, waving his arms as if to flag Trent down.

He cursed under his breath. He spoke into his radio. "Send backup. Mercury heading north out of town on Indian Lake Avenue. Presumably toward I-94."

"Copy that," the dispatcher replied. "Sending an APB. State troopers on alert. Will apprehend."

"Dispatch, 10-19. Will report from the scene."

"Copy that. Do you need backup at scene?"

"Negative."

The dispatcher signed off, "Ten-three."

Trent yanked his steering wheel around and performed a stellar, illegal U-turn and shot back to Cate's house. She and Danny were standing on the front porch steps, their arms wrapped around each other.

Trent bounded out of the car and strode toward them in four long-legged steps. "Are you two okay?"

"No," Cate replied and instantly burst into tears. She hid her face in her hands.

Danny went straight to him and flung his little arms around Trent's thigh. "We were scared. It was just like you warned us, Detective Trent."

Trent put his hand on Danny's head and pressed him into his leg. He rubbed his back affectionately. "Don't worry. I'm here." Danny heaved a sob and clung tighter.

Every protective bone in Trent's body ached for Cate. Of all the calls, all the assignments he'd been given over the years, this one reverberated inside him like church bells on a summer morning. It didn't take a genius to understand that his reaction was all about the woman. Not that she was defenseless, but that she'd been so strong for years. Like a stalwart angel against all odds, she'd chosen to obliterate her old life and don a new one.

He respected her and admired the kind of character it took to create a life for herself and her son that appeared normal to all outsiders when, in fact, the underpinnings were held by the sinewy fingers of evil. An evil not of her making.

Trent reached out to Cate and pulled her

hands away from her face. She was trembling even more than Danny, if that was possible. She opened her mouth to speak, but only a funny sound, like a little dog's bark, came out. Mascara ran down one cheek, and her face was red and blotchy. But her eyes were like searchlights in a storm, warning ships away from treacherous, rocky shores. More tears streamed down her face as she gently shook her head, as if she didn't mean what she said.

"No," she uttered thickly. "No. I shouldn't have brought you into this."

"Don't say that. It's not your fault. It's my job—" Already, he knew he'd moved beyond professionalism where Cate—and Danny— were concerned. If he could steal her away, then he'd be the savior.

"Your job," she said, then sniffed. "Yes."

Her eyes swam in a sea of tears, and though he could not see beyond the fake brown of their color, he felt the explosion of emotions in her. In that moment, he read the suffering she'd experienced at her ex-husband's hands. He couldn't imagine what it had been like for her back then. Pregnant. Afraid. On the run.

Trent had probed Luke for information about Cate and had been satisfied to hear that his own observations about her had been spot-on. Cate was the kind of person who did everything for herself and by herself. She didn't ask for favors. She didn't lean on anyone. Cate was more likely to help her friends than to ask for help.

What Trent knew was that everyone had their breaking point, and Cate had come to hers.

Trent wanted her to know she could depend on him. She knew him only as the cop doing his job. But he wanted to be a friend to her, just like Sarah, Luke and Mrs. Beabots. He wanted her to feel comfortable allowing him into her circle. Not because he thought he'd wheedle some information from her, but because, after being around her and Danny at the Sunflower Festival, he liked how he felt when they were together.

He realized with a jolt that he might need her more than she needed him.

He took her hand in his. "You're trembling."

"I'm scared."

Trent pulled her toward him. She relented like a flower in a spring breeze. "Come here," was all he said.

She fitted against his chest like she'd been born to inhabit that very spot. He slid his arm around her shoulders and pressed her head into his chest, just as he had done with Danny. He made comforting noises that were half words and mutterings that he remembered his mother using when he was small and terrified of monsters in his closet.

For Cate and Danny, their monster was very real.

Standing in the dark with woman and boy clinging to him for comfort, safety and protection filled Trent with a sense of belonging he'd never experienced in his life.

And he didn't want it to end.

But it had to. He was Trent Davis, former Green Beret who'd seen too many things, done things—top secret things—he could never share with another living human being. Yet, they were part of him. Part of what told him that as much as he wished this moment would go on forever, he had to push Cate away. He was damaged, and he never wanted to hurt her.

Trent smoothed his hand across Cate's shoulders, noticing that as he did, her trembling eased and her sobs had abated.

Oddly, as much as Trent knew he should release Cate, she seemed in no hurry to move away.

She turned her head on his shoulder and looked at him. "My hugging you probably isn't in your department manual, is it?"

"It's on page 27. Section E."

"You're joking."

"No. It specifically states there is to be no fraternization."

Her eyes probed his as a gentle smile uplifted her pink lips. Kissable lips. He was losing his focus, and he didn't give a hoot.

"Is that what this is?" she asked teasingly.

"Absolutely not," he lied. It was so much more.

"Darn," she replied, and lowered her head.

Trent kept his arm firm around her, and allowed his hand to slide comfortingly up her arm. She smelled like a spring garden that he could spend a lifetime roaming.

Cate was a conundrum that baffled and beguiled him, and he didn't care. At the Sunflower Festival she'd been professional, rehearsed in her manner toward him, yet she'd scrutinized him as if he were under a microscope. Even so, she'd allowed Danny to spend time with him. Yet, like quicksilver, she'd changed her attitude and couldn't wait to get away from him.

It was just as well because, in the end, Trent wouldn't and couldn't ever allow himself to get involved with a woman.

Cate was his informant. The victim. His case. That was all.

He was on thin ice, but as long as Cate was

on it with him, he'd take the risk. After all, it was possible they would share only this moment. It wouldn't happen again. Would it?

"Are you okay to go inside?" Trent finally asked.

Cate nodded but didn't move away from him. She lingered as if she needed him. Was he just the cop to her, or was she feeling the same attraction he was?

He felt a clutch at his heart and a snap in his head as if a connection had just been made. Was it his epiphany? Or had Cate come to abide in his head and his heart?

She placed her hand on top of his right hand, which was resting on her son's head. "We should. It's getting chilly and Danny only has a sweater."

Danny leaned his head back and looked at Trent. "I'm okay."

Trent smiled at him. "You were a brave guy tonight, Danny. I don't know when I've met anyone with so much courage. Except for your mom."

She mouthed *thank you*.

They might have done the right thing, but they were both a bit shell-shocked, and he believed it was up to him to allay their fears.

Thinking quickly of ways to lighten the mood, he rubbed Danny's back.

"Your mom's right. You're chilled. Maybe a cup of cocoa would warm you up."

Cate sniffed, and when he looked, he could see more tears. He didn't blame her. He'd be out of his mind if his kid had been threatened in any way.

"I'm sorry, Danny. No cocoa. I didn't buy any mix."

Trent guffawed. "You don't make it from scratch?"

"Uh, no." She stepped out of his embrace and wiped her face, seeing the mascara on her fingertips. "I'm a mess. Let's go inside. I need to wash my face."

Trent took a step, but Danny wouldn't let go of his leg. "Come here, kiddo." Trent reached down, grabbed Danny's arms and flung him onto his shoulders. "I think you deserve a ride."

"Whoa! Wow. I'm really far up here!" Danny exclaimed. "Mom! Look how high I am."

Cate gave a light, quick laugh.

Trent thought her laugh was melodious, and he wished he could hear it more often. But no, these moments, with Danny chuckling and commenting on how the world looked from "so high up," would end the minute Trent began questioning them.

Tonight was truth time.

Trent ducked as he walked through the front door with Danny on his shoulders. Once inside, he put the boy down.

Trent started through the living room, this time taking more notice than the last. A white twill-covered sofa and aqua twill-covered club chairs flanked a white wood fireplace with a mantel. There was a glass coffee table filled with shells and corals. Boat paintings and posters on the walls. Fresh flowers. Rows of novels on the white-painted bookshelves. The dining room had a white-washed wood table and French ladder-back chairs with light green cushions. The walls were lake-water blue with light green painted trim. The whole place felt calm and tranquil. And just as he'd observed before, it was all very clean.

The kitchen was also a happy room with lots of white paint, a wood floor and blue-and-aqua cushions on the stools around the island.

Trent followed Cate as she went straight to the kitchen sink, lowered the blinds and twisted them shut. She turned on the water and splashed her face.

Danny scurried behind them and climbed on a stool.

Trent watched as Cate scrubbed her face with a near vengeance. She took out a towel from the drawer next to the sink and buried her face in it. Again she scrubbed hard. He was surprised she hadn't eliminated an entire layer of skin.

"Ah," she said. "Better."

"Are you okay? Really?"

"I'm okay," she replied unconvincingly. "Danny, you really were great."

"Why was that man at our house, Mom?"

"I don't…know." She turned pleading eyes to Trent. "Maybe you can help us out here?"

Trent looked at Danny. "In police calls like this, Danny, we believe the perpetrator has targeted the house. He might think you have something valuable. I believe he was prepared to break in, but you came home too soon. You called the police, and criminals don't like that. My guess is that we've probably scared him away for good."

"Really?" Danny asked.

"Really," Trent lied. From the email and report from Richard Schmitz at CPD, they knew the minions of Brad Kramer aka Le Grande were in Indian Lake. It made sense that Le Grande himself would show up at some point.

Danny folded his hands on the granite counter. "I'm hungry," he announced.

Cate narrowed her eyes and put her hand on her hip. "Just like that? I thought you were afraid."

"Not anymore. Now I need some hot cocoa. To warm me up. Like Detective Trent said."

Trent lifted an eyebrow, realizing he'd been suckered. He looked at Cate. "I didn't mean to cause a problem...if..."

She waved her hand at him. "Forget it. You'll find kids often have a short attention span."

"I see that." Trent smirked and rubbed Danny's hair.

Danny smiled up at him. "You can make it, right? The cocoa?"

"Absolutely. I can make it while your mom puts the groceries away. I'd help, but I don't know where things go."

Cate immediately went to the grocery bags. "I forgot all about these in the, er—" She looked at Trent for direction.

"I know," he said.

"So, Detective Trent. How do you make hot cocoa? With chocolate syrup, right?"

Before Trent could answer, Cate interrupted. "We don't have any. Sorry."

Trent shook his head. "Syrup is cheating. I

make it with cocoa, sugar and milk. Do you have cocoa?"

Cate's eyes narrowed. "Like baking cocoa?"

"Uh-huh." Trent smiled. "And I see you have milk." He nodded toward the gallon on the counter.

Danny pulled on Trent's sleeve. "We have lots of cocoa. It's in the pantry. Right over there." Danny pointed to a long narrow cabinet. "Sugar is there, too."

Trent started toward the pantry. He looked at Cate. "It is okay for me to make the cocoa for Danny?"

She looked at Danny's expectant face. "I think we should all have some."

"Done."

"There's a saucepan in the cabinet under the stove. What else do you need?"

"A whisk or slotted spoon?"

"Whisk is in the drawer in the island to your left." She went about putting fresh vegetables in the refrigerator.

Trent found the sugar and cocoa. He measured a half cup of sugar and a third of a cup of cocoa into the saucepan. With the whisk he stirred the two together until there were no lumps in the cocoa. Danny nearly crawled over the island to watch every move Trent made.

Slowly, Trent added the milk. He turned on the heat and continued stirring.

"You know, Cate, if you add tapioca or corn starch to this and not so much milk, it makes pudding," Trent said, not taking his eyes from the cocoa.

"Really? And who taught you to cook?"

"My mother. But actually I only know the fun stuff. Cocoa. Fudge. Pudding."

"I'm surprised," she said, putting the plastic grocery sacks in a recycle can next to the back door. "Given that flat belly of yours, I didn't think you'd indulge in anything sweet."

She'd noticed his physique. Hmm. That was interesting. "Two hundred sit-ups a day. I can have fudge from time to time."

"Two hundred!" Danny exclaimed as his eyes flew to his mother. "Should I start doing those now?"

"Danny, you're six. You can wait till you're sixteen."

Danny exhaled. "Oh, good. Ten years."

"Hey—" Trent smiled, taking the pan from the stove "—you are good at math."

Danny smirked and winked at Trent. "I told you I was good."

Trent looked at Cate. "Mugs?"

She went to the cabinet and took out three

blue-and-white china mugs. "I don't have any marshmallows."

"We don't need them," Trent replied, and poured three mugs full of the steaming brew.

"Danny," Cate said. "Sit properly on that stool before you fall off."

"Yes, ma'am," Danny answered, reaching for his mug. He blew on the surface and took a sip. He took another sip, closed his eyes and licked his lips. "Yep. This is the best I've ever had. Mom, we have to make our cocoa like this from now on."

Cate took a sip and raised an eyebrow. "This is delicious. Really good."

"Thanks." Trent wondered if he was blushing. He'd couldn't remember blushing before, but suddenly his cheeks felt hot. And the heat wasn't from the cocoa.

Danny downed his cocoa and used his tongue to lick the inside rim of the mug.

Cate barely touched hers. She looked at Trent from beneath lowered eyelids. "I should put Danny to bed. Then we can talk."

Trent only nodded.

Cate came around to the stool and lifted Danny off. "Say good night to Detective Davis, Danny."

Danny broke away from her and rushed up

to Trent, putting his arms up for a hug. Trent leaned down and hugged the little boy. "Good night, Danny."

"Night."

Danny skipped to his mother, and they disappeared down the hall. Trent heard water running and then the sound of Danny brushing his teeth. Cate giving instruction. Danny answering her. A door closed. Then a door opened.

He heard what he thought was the two of them reciting a prayer. It was the one about a guardian angel he remembered from his childhood.

Trent finished off his cocoa, then rinsed his and Danny's mugs. He found the soap and washed and dried them. He'd just put the mugs away when Cate came back.

"Do you want to sit in the living room to talk?" she asked.

"Whatever is comfortable for you," he replied.

He reached in his jacket pocket and took out a notepad. Several of the officers took notes on their cell phones, but Trent was wary of the phone crashing and losing his information. Paper notes became part of his personal backup files he kept on every investigation.

Cate sat on the sofa and pulled an aqua throw

around her shoulders. She looked vulnerable and ethereal all at once. A glimmering blue angel.

That's when he noticed it. She'd taken out the brown contacts. Her eyes were blue. Aqua blue. Like a sea nymph.

He stared at her.

She smiled softly. "You noticed that my eyes are blue like Danny's."

"I did."

"I told him I wear them to make me look professional. For a long time, they were part of my disguise, I guess. At home, they aren't necessary."

"And not so much anymore?"

"I think I should tell you that I know the man who was out there tonight. His name is Brad Kramer."

Trent scribbled in his notebook. He didn't want to stop or misdirect her. She'd come a long way to get to this point. He just hoped she told him everything.

She toyed with the fringe on the throw. "I haven't seen him for over six years. That's when I ran away from him." She squirmed on the sofa. "It's not a pretty story, but you seem to like Danny and he practically reveres you. Unfortunately, you're involved in this mess. I mean, I know you're the investigating detective, but I sense there's more to it."

She lifted her head, and her aqua eyes shot him with so much sincerity and intensity, she could have brought him to his knees. How could she know he was becoming invested in her? In Danny? Were his feelings that obvious?

"It's true," he admitted. "I want... I want you both to be safe." Instantly, he felt guilty. She'd been picking up on the emotions that were flying around inside him like bats in a cage. Violent emotions that, if unleashed, were so powerful, they could overwhelm him. He was torn between a gentle caring for her and her son, and the need to rip Le Grande to shreds for frightening them. The struggle to remain objective and aloof was agony. What he wanted was to have Cate in his arms. Just once more.

"I know you do, and that's so sweet," she said. "In all the years I've lived in Indian Lake, only three people know the truth about me. You'll be the fourth."

"Mrs. Beabots. Right?"

"No." Cate chuckled. "Though it wouldn't surprise me that wily old woman had me pegged from day one. She's uncanny."

"She is that."

Cate took a deep breath. "My father died

when I was fourteen. My mother worked to support us, but we were close. There was no other family. Just me and my mom. When I was seventeen my mother died in a car accident. Suddenly, my world was upside down. I was grief stricken, but I didn't know how to address the pain. I acted out. My girlfriends and I went to a public pool and flirted with the boys we met. I set my sights on the lifeguard—Brad Kramer. He was older and seemed very romantic. He also bought me my first beer. We could talk all night long. His parents were dead, too. Our sense of loss, abandonment and loneliness bonded us. I thought I'd found my soul mate. I rode on the back of his motorcycle through downstate Illinois. I felt free with the wind in my hair.

"I skipped school because Brad demanded it. I had promised my mother I would finish school, but he didn't understand. Brad was always angry. He'd been in and out of foster homes since he was twelve. Flushed out of the system, he said. He was nearly four years older than I was, and I thought he was wise. Always telling me to live life by the minute. Live in the present. Forget the past. Forget tomorrow.

"We had some bad fights. I didn't like his friends. I wanted a job and a nice house. He…"

"He was abusive?"

"Yes," she replied lowly, and put her hand to her cheek. "It's so embarrassing."

"Don't—please. You have nothing to be embarrassed about. Men like that are monsters."

Her eyes pierced his with intense gratitude. Trent nearly felt light-headed.

"He was, you know. Exactly that." She looked at her hands, seeming to gather her thoughts. "It took me a long time to realize that those motorcycle trips were to sell drugs downstate. I didn't want to believe it. I also wouldn't admit that he was using them, as well. What I thought was harmless recklessness was cocaine. Marijuana. Heroin. You name it.

"We were married only two weeks when he came home completely wasted. He could barely stand. When I confronted him about what he was on, he hit me. Not once but several times. I locked myself in the bathroom to escape him. He passed out in the hall.

"The next morning he brought two dozen roses and promised it would never happen again. But it did. A couple more times. The last time, I went out the back door. All I had were my clothes and running shoes and my wallet with a whole forty-two dollars. No cell phone. I ran. And ran.

"I know I ran over fifteen miles before I slowed and took a breath."

"Adrenaline can do that," Trent said quietly. "You were running for your life."

"I was. I found my way to Highway 20. I thought if I could hitch a ride and get far, far away from Brad, I'd be free."

"But you stopped in Indian Lake. You didn't keep going."

Her smile was wistful. Soft. Beautiful. "A nice lady picked me up. She was driving from Chicago to Detroit to see her grandchildren. To this day I can't remember what I told her, but I think she knew I was running away from someone." Cate touched her lip. "I might have had a bruise or two. I'm not sure."

"So you stopped here?"

"Uh-huh. For gas. We came into town because she said the price for gas was a lot cheaper here. We went to the marina mini-mart.

"The guy at the counter was so courteous to me and, though he asked me a lot of questions, I didn't feel he was prying. I kept going up and down the aisles, my stomach growling, but I didn't dare spend a single cent.

"He handed me a soda and a package of cookies and told me they were on the house. He asked my name and I gave him my new one, Cate Sullivan. Anyway, I asked him his name—Lester MacDougal. He told me that he'd seen the kind of look I had on my face because he'd run away from home, too. He said a woman in town had helped him a great deal. The soda and cookies weren't much, but they were his way of paying back her memory. He said her name was Ann Marie Jensen."

Trent stopped writing. "Sarah Jensen Bosworth's mother."

"Correct. Well, his story nearly made me cry. I told him I needed help. He explained he didn't usually work at the mini-mart. He was a landscaper and he was filling in to help Captain Redbeard. Then Lester went to the car with me and we told the woman who'd brought me that I would be staying. At first she wasn't so sure about leaving me on my own, but by that time, Captain Redbeard—Red—had come back. I explained my situation to Red and he gave me a job working the register."

"So, that's who knows about you? Captain Red and Lester MacDougal?"

"And Julie, Red's wife." She nodded. "There's more to it than that."

"Oh?"

"After about a month there, Julie complimented me on my natural sales talent. She was relentless about trying to find something that would better suit me. The pay was okay, and Red and Julie gave me a room to live in at their house. But I knew I couldn't stay there forever.

"Then I discovered I was pregnant." Cate's voice lowered an octave and was laden with guilt. "At the same time, Julie had heard that one of her friend's daughters had enrolled in real-estate classes. Red and Julie advanced me the tuition."

She shrugged. "Turns out I am a born salesperson. For me, it was so easy. I've been selling real estate ever since." She raised her arms and gestured around. "It took me a couple fixer-uppers to get to this house, but I love it. It's me."

"It sure is," he said, his gaze tracking around the room.

"After I sold the house to the new fire jumper, Rand Nelson, I saw Brad following me in his car."

"You're sure?"

"Positive. I'd swear it in court." She paused, then lifted her chin defiantly. "That's why it not only frightens me, but also angers me that Brad has found us. How dare he destroy the world I've built for us? How dare he?"

Trent leaned back. "And all this time, he's never contacted you?"

"No. There's been nothing. I'm really afraid, Detective Davis—"

"You can drop the formality. Trent would be just fine."

"Thanks. There's only one reason Brad would be here."

Did she know more than she let on? Maybe she'd figured out how big Brad's operation was and that he was branching out to Indian Lake… and points north and east from here. "What's that?"

"He's found out about Danny. He's seen us together. It wouldn't take much to put two and two together and realize Danny's his son."

"Danny doesn't look much like Ra—Brad. Except for the hair. He looks like you. Especially the eyes," he said pointedly.

Her expression held a tinge of challenge and defiance. "You figured it out, didn't you? About the brown contacts?"

"I did."

"I thought you did. The way you kept looking at me at Sunflower Festival, I knew the time had come to discard them."

Trent leaned forward and put his notebook

in his jacket pocket. "So, you want to tell me about the hair?"

She chuckled. "Oh, you saw that, too? I meant to do my touch-up this morning but time got away from me. Helping Mrs. Beabots and all."

"Natural blonde?" he asked.

"Yes. It's been so long since I've seen my real hair color, I have no idea what it is. Probably gray."

"Uh, not yet." He smiled.

"I meant from fright."

"Yeah. I see that." He slid out of the club chair and onto the sofa next to her. "And if Cate Sullivan is your alias, what's your real name?" He already knew, but he wanted her to tell him. If she told him the truth, then he knew he could believe everything she'd told him.

"Susan Castle Kramer."

Trent lifted his hands to pull her to him, but he checked the move. This was a police investigation. "You didn't drop his last name when you divorced him?"

Her eyes narrowed. "Did I say I divorced him?"

Trent could feel her shields shooting up. "No. I did," he returned confidently. "It was in the report I received from the Chicago Police."

"Chicago Police?"

"It seems acquiring an alias runs in the family. His name isn't Brad Kramer anymore. He goes by Raoul Le Grande now, and he runs one of the largest drug syndicates in the Midwest."

CHAPTER EIGHT

SHOCK ETCHED A gorge of uncertainty, distrust and betrayal through Cate's midsection. Blows like this always threw Cate into panic, which rendered her brain a malfunctioning glob of serotonin, irregular synapses and electrocuted defense mechanisms.

It had taken every smidge of courage she could gather to tell Trent the truth and, in one breath, he'd reverted to his cop persona. She didn't like that quicksilver switch, as though he were two different people.

That's how Brad had been. Dr. Jekyll and Mr. Hyde. Angel and demon. She didn't know Trent all that well, though her instinct had been to trust him. And she had, at least for a few moments. At the same time she knew he was bound to his duty as a cop to disclose that she was a suspicious person.

What would Trent do now? Did he think she was working with Brad? That she was part of Brad's gang? How far would Trent go to make his case? Could he hold her for questioning? Could he demand that Danny be sent to Child Protective Services?

Stop it, Cate!

She had to calm down and think rationally, which was becoming increasingly difficult.

"You need to leave," she said, biting back her anger as she shot to her feet. She flung the aqua throw behind her on the sofa.

"What? Why?" He rose slowly.

"I was a fool to tell you all this," she said, blaming herself. *Stupid move.* "My son doesn't even know the truth. But now you do. I suppose you'll hold that against me."

Trent put his hand on her forearm. "I'm not going to hurt you, Cate. I swear to God."

"But you could! You know everything." She'd tipped her hand and messed everything up. She was angry with herself. For more than six long years she hadn't trusted another person with her entire story. Even Red and Julie didn't know about Brad's drug dealing. They knew only about the abuse.

No, Trent Davis was the only one she'd chosen to bare her soul to. She'd chosen poorly. She could only blame herself.

Her emotions boiled over and ran down her cheeks in the form of tears. Visions of Danny being ripped from her terrified her. "It's your job to disclose everything." Her head was about to explode. She had to keep it together.

She'd do it again. Run. She could escape. She'd take Danny, and they'd head to another town. This time far, far away. South Carolina. No, to another country. She could do that, couldn't she? She'd need a passport. Didn't have one.

She felt her knees giving way. Sinking. She was dying. Without Danny, she would die.

Trent took her by the shoulders. She knew he was talking to her because she could see his lips moving, but she didn't hear a word. Then he left.

Good. Trent was gone.

The police didn't always help someone like her. She remembered a night when Brad was drunk and high. He'd slapped her around and hit her hard in the ribs. She'd escaped to the bathroom and called the police on her cell phone.

The dispatcher had made a point of asking if the perpetrator was her husband. When Cate had replied in the affirmative, she'd heard the snarl and disdain in his voice as he said, "Domestic dispute."

During the fifteen minutes it took for the

cops to arrive, Brad had shot up again and was sitting on the sofa in a quiet stupor. He was polite to the officers and acted as if nothing had happened.

When the officers asked if she wanted to press charges, she'd declined. She'd been a coward.

If she'd put Brad away then, her entire life might have been different. Maybe she'd never have come to Indian Lake.

Still, she remembered the policemen talking as they'd left her. "I hate these domestic dispute calls. There's never any charges," one of the officers had said.

"Yeah, we'd be better off ignoring them."

The sound of Trent's footsteps—sturdy and purposeful—broke through her memories.

"Here," he said, sitting beside her again. "Drink this." His voice was kind, not condescending. He wasn't like those cops from the past at all.

He reached behind her and picked up the throw and covered her shoulders. "You're trembling and as cold as ice."

Why was he being so nice? Was it his job? Or his nature? She'd never met a man like Trent before. She drank the water and handed the glass to him. When he took it, his fingers touched hers. He set the glass on the coffee table.

Despite the promises she'd made to herself never to allow a man in her life, her heart strummed a nearly imperceptible cadence that this time, this man was different. A peace settled over her, calming her nerves and hitting the brakes on her adrenaline-activated brain.

"That better?" he asked soothingly.

It was.

She felt his arm slide around her shoulders, then he pulled her close. Again. For the second time in one night.

It made no sense that being near him made her feel safe, but it did. What was he saying? She felt as if she were underwater or that he was talking to her from a faraway place.

"I want to help you, Cate. I mean that. In any way I can." He continued to rub her shoulders, warming her. She hadn't realized how impossibly cold she'd gotten. When she delivered Danny, she'd bled out. Her heart had stopped. They said she was going to die.

Was she going to die now?

Her head nestled in the crook between Trent's chin and collarbone. He smelled like lemons and vanilla and something very masculine. Perhaps it was his persona of reassurance. She couldn't be sure because he was the man she wasn't supposed to trust.

No, that was Brad.

Her heart ached to trust Trent, but her heart had betrayed her once before. The nightmare of Brad still haunted her.

Since the day she'd escaped Brad, she'd been her own savior. But now, there was Trent. She knew he felt empathy for her. Even if he was used to comforting his case victims, she believed she read something more in his eyes, something profoundly sincere that told her that he cared.

She knew that only time would tell if she was right.

He and Brad were polar opposites. The bad and the good. The ugly and the beautiful.

Trent was beautiful, she mused. Handsome. His strong jaw rested on her head and kept her wedged next to him. She could feel his heartbeat. Strong. Steady. Dependable.

Cate had never thought about a man except in negative terms. Even Brad she had thought to be a cure for her grief. Not a person. Not someone to share things with. Trent was different in so many ways, her mind was flooded.

"You're warmer. Are you feeling better?"

She nodded slowly. She didn't want to leave

this space, this place where, for a moment, she'd felt safe. "I'm okay."

He removed his arm and immediately she felt the loss. Was that possible?

Putting his forefinger under her chin he lifted her face. "Please believe me, Cate. I'm not going to expose you to your friends. This is none of their business. Frankly, the fewer people who know about my investigation, the better. I want to catch Le Grande and put him and his syndicate down. More importantly, I will do everything to keep you safe."

"And Danny? How can you keep us both safe and not tell him?" She put her hand on his shoulder. "Trent. He's not your responsibility. He's mine. I've lied to him all his life. I told him that his father died in a motorcycle accident. But now that he's getting older, that's harder to maintain. Just little things. He keeps asking if he's going to be big like his father. He asks if his feet are the same. His hair. His—"

"Danny is the spitting image of you, Cate. Not Le Grande."

"Except for the hair. Danny thinks I have black hair like him."

"So, who said you need to change it back?"

She pursed her lips to squelch a smile. "Funny, isn't it? Lately, even before Brad appeared, I thought about dropping my ruse. Bit by bit."

"Either way, you'd be beautiful," he said with a slight croak to his voice. He lowered his hand.

"You think I'm beautiful?"

"I do. I probably shouldn't have said so."

"I'm glad you did. It's been a long time since anyone said that to me. My mother did."

"You miss her." His voice was a soft whisper. "I can't imagine not having my mom in my life. She thinks she might move to Indian Lake."

"That would be nice for you," she said. "I'd give anything to talk to my mother again. She always gave good advice."

"So does my mother."

His thumb slipped along the edge of her thumb. How easy it would be to allow herself to drop her shields. Unfurl the iron wings she kept folded around her. She should step back. Keep her distance. She didn't know much at all about Trent. Yet, at the same time, she knew he was gentle, concerned and caring.

His rapport with Danny was easy and familiar as if they'd known each other forever. As if they were father and son. That had to count in his favor for something.

As the investigating officer, Trent probably wasn't allowed to touch or hold her. But there was no one around to file a report on him. Unless he feared she would turn him in.

She moved back and forced a smile. "I think you should tell me more about Brad."

"Le Grande," he corrected and edged away from her as well.

She felt the few inches of distance as if it were a mountain gorge. Was it possible to feel such emptiness when they were only getting to know each other?

"For years he's worked out of Chicago. Just recently we learned he'd started moving into Indian Lake. I spearheaded a sting operation for months. I was so certain I had him. And I did," he said forcefully. He grasped his knees and slid his hands up his thighs. "But he slipped away. We arrested the other members of his gang, but without Le Grande—"

"I think I understand. Drug dealers have ways of replenishing their forces faster than our military."

"That's the God's truth," Trent replied.

"So, do I understand you to say that you think he's in Indian Lake for the drugs? Not because of me and Danny?"

"Initially, he was here to set up a network. Our town is situated perfectly between five major state highways and has a web of country roads that all lead into Michigan. The drugs come from Mexico, Central America and Colombia. They make their way to Houston on boats usually. From there, they go straight to Chicago. They're cut, resold, then trafficked to the east and into Canada right through downtown Indian Lake."

"It seems preposterous. This lovely little town where everyone is so friendly."

"That's just it. Because the psychology of this town is trustworthy, the dealers slip in and out, and they're never noticed because Joe Citizen can't imagine that a major crime syndicate would be interested in this little town. To the Indian Lake citizenry, criminals should be in Vegas or LA. Not here."

"Exactly."

"Routing drug dealers here is a full-time job. Believe me. But if we can take down Le Grande and his gang, we'll have scored a major coup."

She studied his face for a long moment. There was no enthusiasm in his eyes. No hint of victory. Only wariness. Gone was the earlier caring glimmer.

"What do I do if he comes back?"

"I've been thinking about that."

She dropped her forehead to her palm. "This is all so insane. I never in a million years thought any of this could happen to us. I'm terrified to tell Danny anything about his father—"

"Don't. Let me think about things. Make a plan for you and Danny. In the meantime, I'll put my detectives on stakeout here. No more regular cop cars. Or just a few passes every hour or so. If Le Grande comes back, we will be close enough to nail him. That's for starters. I want you to put my number into your cell phone. You call me directly. I sleep with my cell next to my bed. You do the same. No more charging it in the kitchen."

"How did you know I do that?"

"I saw the cord in the kitchen."

"Observant." She smiled wanly, though she could feel her lips start to quiver with fear.

"What is it?"

"I have to tell you something about the first time I saw Brad here in Indian Lake." There, she'd said it. She took a deep breath.

Trent took out his notebook. "Go on."

"At Jack Carter's house he did something... He made a mocking motion with his finger, like he was shooting me with a gun. He used to do that—right before—"

"Before he hit you?"

She nodded.

"Then he was threatening you."

"Yes, he was," she replied morosely.

"What kind of car was he driving?"

"Black Mercury sedan. I didn't think to look for the license plate."

"It's the same car I saw tonight. The station is running a trace. Le Grande is smart. Probably already switched vehicles. I want to talk to my chief about this."

Cate fidgeted with her hands, rolling her fingers over each other. She felt like jumping out of her skin.

Trent put his hand on her shoulder and slid it to her elbow. "You gonna be able to sleep?"

She nodded. "Sure. Maybe. I don't know. I need to. I have a big appointment tomorrow."

Trent rose. "Well, good luck with that. Now, I'll keep my cell on. If you hear anything, see anything…you call me. I don't know how you'll warn Danny without frightening him too much, but he needs to be on guard."

"I'll sleep on it," she said. Telling Danny to look both ways before he crossed the street was one thing. Telling him that their lives were in danger was another.

Trent went to the front door. "Listen, I'm here. Okay? Any ideas you have and want to bounce off me, call. And if you think of any kind of idiosyncrasies about Le Grande, er,

Brad, write them down, text them to me. But don't let them go, no matter how silly or mundane they might seem. Okay?"

"Yeah. I understand." She folded her arms over her chest. "Goodbye."

What wicked twist of fate had put her here? Until she figured out what Brad wanted from her and how to deal with it, she knew she couldn't trust anybody. Not even a kindly cop.

"Well, good night," he said, then opened the door and walked quickly away, disappearing into the night.

Cate closed the door and locked it.

She felt as if she were the tiniest speck in the vast universe. Alone didn't begin to describe the emptiness.

CHAPTER NINE

DAWN CREPT SLOWLY over Indian Lake, burnishing the water and the remaining leaves with amber, crimson and lavender rays. Trent eased his unmarked car into the visitor parking lot at the marina and watched as Cate, wearing a black wet suit and a fluorescent yellow bathing cap, joined Sarah Bosworth, Maddie and Liz Barzonni, and Isabelle Hawks.

The morning chill hung over the lake like a ghost, no doubt lending credence to Halloween tales, he thought as he parked near a spruce tree. Keeping close to Cate was his job, he told himself. The black Mercury had been found abandoned just over the state line by the Michigan State Police. Trent had been on his way to investigate, but decided to take this detour when he remembered that Luke had told him Cate rowed with Sarah on Saturday mornings.

He turned off the engine.

He hung his forearms over the steering wheel

and leaned his chin on his hands, peering at the boathouse—at Cate.

Cate. Susan. No, Cate. Pure. And a woman of courage. The name suits her.

He watched as she hugged each of her girlfriends and they carried the sculling boat to the water. Their laughter about the frigid water skittered across the distance to the wooded area where he moved to a lonely picnic table.

He called in his position to the dispatcher. "I've made a short stop. Then I'll check on the Merc."

"Copy that," Ned replied.

The women expertly steered the boat into the lake, sluicing through the glassy surface as swift as a razor, barely causing a wake with their precision rowing.

Awestruck, he watched as they performed synchronized movements. He heard Sarah's voice cut through the morning mist, giving instructions.

When they broke through a low cloud of fog and into the sun's light, he saw that Cate's face was intent on her task, devoid of the joviality he saw on Maddie's face and even the strain that Liz displayed. Perhaps Liz was thinking of her baby son and not her rowing.

As they rounded the end of the lake and shot

toward him, he could see Cate's narrowed eyes, the deep furrows in her brow. Her lips were pursed so tightly, they'd almost disappeared. Cate rowed as if she were being judged on every movement, every dip and turn of the oar.

Trent found he was more intrigued by her than ever.

They turned again and bolted into the sun.

Trent stood just behind the evergreens where he could see Cate, and he knew his presence would not intrude—at least not yet.

The women rowed back and eased to the shore. In unison, they lifted their oars straight up at the command of their leader, Sarah.

The bow swept into shallow water and stilled.

The women got out, and moving as a single unit, they hoisted the boat over their heads and carried it to the boathouse.

Trent waited patiently while they said their goodbyes and grabbed their belongings. Each woman went to her car, waving and chatting. Calling out future sculling dates to each other. None of them saw him.

Walking toward her car, Cate whipped the fluorescent cap from her head, shook out her short hair and caught sight of him. An apprehensive smile crept onto her face.

"Hi," he said, though he didn't move. "You were magnificent."

"How did you know I'd be here?"

"Checking on you is my job. Remember?"

"Uh, right." She frowned and continued to stare at him.

He shrugged. "Luke told me about the sculling. Sarah said you were rowing with them today."

"Oh," she replied, looking down at the sand and then up at him. "I forgot you know them pretty well."

"I do." He paused. "Listen, I'll be honest. Yes, I was on my way to check on something—police business. I apologize if I'm intruding. But I was curious."

"About what?" She took a small step toward him. Could anyone be this beautiful? No makeup, her hair rumpled from the cap.

Trent felt as if he'd walked into a dream.

"The rowing. You were beautiful. I mean, er, it was beautiful to watch you…all…out there."

She chuckled lightly—a tinkling sound carried on the wind.

"We practice whenever we can."

"Apparently. It's gotta be freezing out there."

"I hardly notice. I'm in another world on the lake."

"And what is that world?" he asked, moving even closer. He had to be nearer. He was getting the feeling that was the only way to be with Cate. Close.

"Freedom. Utter, boundless freedom."

"You deserve that, Cate," he said sincerely.

Her eyes delved into his. "You really mean that, don't you?"

"I do. I'd like to make sure that happens for you."

"Well then, Detective Davis—" she smiled and rocked back on her heels as if ready to walk away "—I'll hold you to that," she said with more wariness in her voice than he would have liked.

"Good."

It was all Trent could do to resist touching her. He was on duty, and she was like a shot of hot bourbon to an addict. Enticing. Forbidden. "I'd better go."

"Yeah," she said. "Don't let me hold you up."

He lifted his hand to touch hers. Kiss her palm. But that was crossing the line. Breaking the rules. Again.

He dropped his hand. He didn't want to frighten her. She had enough in her life to deal with. He didn't need to add to it. "Call me if you need me," he said.

She nodded. "I have your number in my cell phone."

"Promise. If anything—"

"I promise, Trent," she replied, then went toward her car.

Trent watched her, unable to move from the spot. He had to see…

Just as she opened the car door, she stopped, looked at him and waved.

"Yes," he whispered to himself. It wasn't much, her looking. But it was a sign that maybe, just maybe, he'd made some kind of a favorable impression.

He knew he shouldn't be feeling this attraction to her. He had serious baggage, and after being with her, holding her, he realized she was not only a good person, but kind and sweet, as well. She deserved the best life could offer— not a guy who was half-whacked with PTSD.

Sure, he'd vowed to himself never to get involved with a woman. And he hadn't. For years. But that was before—Cate.

He waited until she drove away. He believed that when she'd looked back at him, she was looking at Trent and not simply Detective Davis.

Trent had always been a man of few illusions, but for today, he wanted to hold on to this one.

CHAPTER TEN

IT WAS AFTER ten when Trent emailed Richard Schmitz at the CPD inquiring about Raoul Le Grande. He leaned back in his desk chair and looked around the station. Nearly everyone had gone home. He was always the last guy to leave. And why not? He had no "home" to go home to. He was where he should be. That's what he told himself—constantly.

He could hear Ned Quigley, the dispatcher, cracking jokes with the patrolmen who were cruising the town. Sixteen minutes ago he'd gotten a report that all was quiet on Cate and Danny's street. He was amazed at how much that information settled his nerves. Not that he was anxious. Nah. No reason to be. She was one victim on the department surveillance list. She was in need of protection, and she was getting it.

"Officer down!" Ned yelled across the room.

Trent bolted out of his chair, grabbing his

jacket as he raced past the paper-littered desks. "Who? Where?"

"Washington Avenue. It's that new kid, Johnson. He wasn't responding to my calls, so I asked Henderson to drive his route and see what he could find. He found Johnson unconscious. Davis," Quigley said with a sputter, "he's at that warehouse where your Le Grande sting—" Ned respectfully didn't elaborate.

Trent muttered a curse and rammed his arms through his jacket sleeves. "How long ago?"

"I just hung up with Henderson."

"Call him. Tell him I'm on my way. Did he call for an ambulance?"

"On its way." Ned waved him off.

Trent raced out of the building. It was less than a quarter mile to the abandoned building where Johnson was. At this time of night, few people were on the streets. Even the majority of the bars shut down around nine thirty. There was only one bar on Main Street that stayed open until curfew at 2:00 a.m. When the shifts at the manufacturing plants changed at midnight, a few patrons would go there before heading home, but even they didn't stay longer than an hour. Indian Lake was a quiet town. Exactly the kind of demographic to make a drug kingpin drool.

Trent sped around the corner and headed down Washington. Instantly, he saw Officer Henderson's patrol car lights flashing red and blue against the crumbling brick walls. Trent could hear the ambulance siren in the distance.

Trent shot out of the car, slamming the door behind him. "Was he shot?"

"No." Henderson shook his head. "They hit him over the head with something."

Johnson was lying on the ground next to Henderson, conscious but dazed. "Sir? What happened?"

"Lie still," Trent said as he crouched to inspect Officer Johnson's head. "That's a real goose egg, all right." He chuckled, hoping to dispel his own tension. "You were lucky. If you were attacked by the Le Grande gang, they could just as easily have shot you and not thought a thing about it."

"Yes, sir." Johnson closed his eyes briefly. "I was trying to see the license plate. I should have radioed in…"

"Yes," Trent replied. "You always call the station before getting out of that vehicle. Basic rule."

"I know that, sir. I screwed up."

Trent remembered being this young and naive. That was a thousand lifetimes ago. In the military. Trent almost smiled. Almost. "You're going to have one heck of a headache." Trent peered at him. "And did you get the plate number?"

"Yes, sir. I memorized it. OMY435. It was an Illinois plate. New model Ford Transit van. Black."

"That's a common vehicle. Paneled sides. Commercial looking. No one would suspect it of being anything other than a delivery truck or a construction van."

"I thought the same thing, sir. Except that a brand-new van like that wasn't local. Construction guys here have rusted-out pickups."

"So you went to investigate."

"Yes, sir."

"Good man." Trent patted his shoulder.

The ambulance screamed down the street and pulled to a stop in the parking lot. Two EMTs flew out of their rig and hustled to Trent.

He stood. "Take care of him, guys. He's one of my best."

Trent looked at Johnson, who smiled broadly at him. "Get some rest. We'll talk tomorrow."

"Sir. Yes, sir," Johnson said.

Trent walked to his car, got in and radioed the dispatcher. "Run a trace on a black Ford Transit van. Illinois license." Trent gave the number. "I'll stay here until Johnson is taken to the hospital. I want to look around. I'll keep Henderson with me. Can you get his regular patrol covered?"

"Ten-four."

ONE HOUR LATER, Trent was no closer to any clues than he had been before. The one thing he assumed was that Le Grande must believe there were still drugs in the building. The cops had confiscated everything they'd seen. Surely, Le Grande knew that. Or was it something else? The cops had used their drug-sniffing dog, Max, to find drugs. Heroin specifically. Max was not a marijuana-sniffing dog. Nor a bomb-detecting canine. Each of those talents was specific to a single dog. A heroin dog would miss marijuana.

"And there's no such thing as a money-sniffing animal," Trent mumbled to himself as he and Henderson explored the elevator shaft. The elevator, no doubt installed in 1903 when the building was erected, ran from the first floor to the basement only. A staircase on the other side of the building went to the second and third floors. The elevator mechanism was broken. A set of twelve folding metal steps had been placed on the elevator floor so that a person could climb from the first floor down to the elevator floor. However, the platform had apparently broken in transit, which left it hovering two and half feet above the concrete basement floor.

"They should condemn this place," Henderson grumbled as he jumped off the rickety wooden platform, high-powered flashlights in both hands.

Trent swept his light around at the open pipes running across the ceiling, the brick walls whose mortar was only a memory. It smelled musty, but wasn't wet. The electricity had been turned off, and Trent assumed the water had been, as well. Stacks of old furniture—chests, mirrors, armchairs and tables—huddled at one end, looking like forgotten refugees. A rocking chair sat by itself in the middle of the room as if someone had recently used it.

Maybe they had.

Trent walked toward the furniture, shining his light on a particular chest of drawers.

"Sir?" Henderson asked, following behind.

Trent pointed at the chest. "Shine both your lights on those drawers. Notice anything?"

"Looks like an antique to me, sir. Colonial drawer pulls. Maple wood. Not my taste," he joked.

Trent shook his head. "Your light beams are reflected off the brass. There's no tarnish," Trent said, walking over to pull on the drawer. "Which would signify that it's been polished by someone opening the drawer many times. Presumably to hide something."

Trent yanked on the drawer as Henderson walked up and stood next to him.

"Holy crap!" Henderson exclaimed. "What is that?"

"Thousands of dollars, I'd say," Trent replied, looking at the stacks of cash. "Wrapped and tagged, neat as you please." Trent smiled to himself. "No wonder Le Grande sent his minions back here. My guess is that Johnson interrupted them. They got spooked and ran before getting what they came for."

"So, Johnson's a hero."

"Uh-huh." Trent shoved the drawer in. "After he gets a reprimand."

Henderson kept his eyes on the drawer. "Yes, sir."

"I have to call this in. I was certain Forensics came down to the basement after the bust. I need to read that report. If they did, then that means that the money was put here after that, and Le Grande is still using Indian Lake as his hub. Le Grande's gang stashed the money here thinking it was safe now that the investigation is over. These guys in the black Ford van tonight could have been the buyers or some of Le Grande's pickup men."

Trent pulled out his cell phone and tried to call the station. "No signal." He looked around the basement. "This place is built like a tomb." He walked toward the elevator shaft. "Probably lead lined."

"Yes, sir," Henderson replied.

"I meant that as a joke," Trent said, climbing onto the elevator platform.

"I got it," Henderson replied. "A reference to superheroes and comic books."

"Exactly. And I'm hoping that Le Grande is stupid enough to think he's a superhero."

"Why is that, sir?"

Trent climbed the metal steps. "Because superheroes aren't real. And in the end, they have to have someone else write their story. I intend to be that somebody. And what an ending I'll write for Le Grande."

STAKEOUTS WERE THE bane of every investigator's existence, and yet, given patience and time, they almost always produced results. Trent unwrapped a tuna sandwich he'd bought at dinnertime from the Indian Lake Deli and hadn't had a chance to eat. He took a bite—whole grain bread and guacamole spread. No question about it, Olivia Melton and her mother, Julia, made the best tuna in town.

Trent had parked his unmarked car nearly a block away from the abandoned building where Johnson had been assaulted earlier that night. It was past four in the morning, but Trent's adrenaline had been flowing since he'd found the drug money.

Forensics had come and gone. He'd finished his report in record time, and now he was spending his off-duty hours doing what he did best. Catching bad guys.

Chief Williams had told Trent that after the sting, the team had scoured the building, including the basement. No money had been found.

From that information, Trent's gut said the guys in the Ford van were most likely the buyers, and if so, they'd be back to get their money. None of them would risk having the cops find it.

But find it, he had.

Fifty thousand dollars was a lot of cash. The department had it counted three times before processing, reporting and locking it up. That was big money for Indian Lake. But was it big for Le Grande? Trent knew dealers who would murder for only five grand. Fifty was a lot more motivation.

Trent washed down the last few bites of his sandwich with water from his sports bottle. Picking up his binoculars, he zoomed in on the alley behind the building. No activity.

He put down the binoculars just as his cell phone pinged with an incoming text. Because thoughts of Cate punctuated his mind regularly, he realized that he hoped she would call him. Not because she was in danger, but because she wanted to talk to him.

It was a selfish wish. He had no right to expect anything from her. No right to foist his very flawed life upon her.

But if he were different, healthy and the circumstances were normal... It was easy to imagine being with her.

He looked at the screen. It was his mother reminding him about Sunday dinner. He'd have to drive into Chicago. She still worked as a nurse at Rush-Copley Hospital, although was set to retire in two years. She'd come to Indian Lake in June for the boating Grand Prix and had fallen in love with the place. Suddenly, she was talking about moving to Indian Lake to be closer to him. Trent had asked her if there was a problem with her health. She assured him that she was fine. Maybe that was what retirees did. Pull up roots. Start over. Have an adventure. His mother had worked all her life. After his father died eight years ago, when Trent was still in Afghanistan, she'd put up a good front. She kept busy, but he could tell her life would never be the same. She always said they'd had a real romance.

Trent leaned his head on the neck rest. He closed his eyes, suddenly feeling the weight of the day. His mind drifted. He saw Cate's face in his mind. He conjured a romantic scene of the two of them walking hand in hand along Cove Beach. He could almost feel the sand under his feet.

Taste the grains…

Instantly, he was in Afghanistan. *Back there.*

There were four men in his team. Since they were being thrown out of a helicopter, they traveled light. Lightweight guns. Backpacks with only the essentials for this mission. Special Forces knew their purpose was to outsmart the enemy, not engage them. They packed smaller guns and less ammunition than their colleagues. They planned well and always left an escape route if things went south.

Trent and Parker Adams had been on every mission together. They practically read each other's minds. Their CO expected them to lead the two younger SF members.

The fact that the army's helicopters were all in need of massive repairs after years of service was accepted. Part of daily life.

The mission had been to extract an American businessman who was being held captive in Kandahar by al-Qaeda terrorists. The building had been located. A Special Forces sniper had been placed on the roof of a building across the street. Timing was set for ten minutes after midnight. They were to rappel to the alley behind the building. Go in through the back door, which was unlocked by their informant. They were to walk down two hallways to a rear room where their package was located. The guards ate at midnight in the front rooms before the new crew came on duty. The army's informant had sent exact specifications with measurements of the hallway and rooms.

Nothing about an extraction was ever simple, but Trent had believed this one was the most thorough reconnaissance he'd seen.

Trent carried his M4A1 carbine and took point. Silently, they entered the building. He heard the guards' laughter coming from the front rooms. Trent remained at the door to the prisoner's room while his three men went inside.

In seconds, Parker came out with the middle-aged man. The two other men in the team followed as Trent walked backward down the hall, his M4A1 aimed at the front of the building.

Just as they raced out the door and down the alley to meet their helicopter, Trent received word that the Apache was having engine trouble. The pilot gave Trent new coordinates.

Trent slapped Parker on the shoulder and signaled that everyone was to follow him. Crouching, they shuffled quickly down the alley to a street. They crossed and headed west.

This street was broader with bombed-out buildings on both sides of them.

Trent heard the chopper; he pointed upward.

The chopper hovered. Parker remained next to a building, watching the alley for signs of approaching enemy.

Trent ordered the two men to get the hostage hooked up to the guide wire.

He watched as the first three were pulled off the ground like angels ascending. Trent turned and signaled to Parker to follow.

Parker raced toward him. And stepped on the IED. He was only a few feet away from Trent. The blast sent Trent flying, and he landed on his backside, covered in his best friend's blood.

There were body parts everywhere, smoke. Blood. Death.

Trent reached for Parker and opened his mouth to call to him. He heard his radio. The pilot ordered him to board. The guide wire dangled from the chopper.

Trent scrambled to his feet. Training took over. He did as he was told.

He didn't remember boarding the chopper or what was said to him. He could only stare at the blood-soaked ground.

Trent woke from the dream and realized he'd been screaming Parker's name.

His hands had a death grip around the steering wheel. He was covered in sweat. He pulled himself up and looked down. Somehow he'd bent the gearshift so badly, the car was inoperable.

Something else that will come out of my paycheck.

He had no idea how he'd explain this one.

What he did know was that his memories were as vivid and as painful as the night Parker died. A wave of anger and sadness washed over Trent as if it would take him away in its undertow.

Half the battles in the Middle East hadn't been as all-consuming as these psychological wars he still waged. There had to be some way to fill the emptiness inside him.

His only hope was that some psychologist would figure out how to rewire his brain and make the past disappear.

Trent wiped the sweat from his forehead. His hand was trembling. He took deep breaths and blew them out as he'd been taught by therapists and psychologists. He felt his body ease. He was returning to normal.

He grabbed his cell phone and got out of the car, locked it. The walk to the station would do him good. He needed to clear his mind.

If only that was possible.

Standing under the streetlight on the corner of Washington and Maple Boulevard, he punched in his passcode. He saw he had a voice mail from Cate. It had come in while he'd been asleep.

His first thought was that something had happened. Had Le Grande come to call on her again? Or was Danny in danger?

"Hi. I wanted to thank you for…well…for being there. For Danny and me, I mean. I was wondering if you'd like to come to dinner sometime. Gimme a call."

She had stumbled on her words. Oddly, she'd

called late at night. Maybe she couldn't sleep. Apparently, she was thinking about him.

Trent felt a warm glow catch fire inside him. He remembered much too quickly how good it felt to hold Cate. She hadn't resisted his need to care for her. That was important to him. He liked feeling needed.

He continued walking toward the police station. He walked past Danny's school—St. Mark's. Trent wondered if Danny was sleeping well tonight. Or was he tormented by night terrors about the stalker in their backyard?

It wasn't right that a little kid like Danny should live in fear. Or sweet Cate. There were a lot of things about this world that weren't right. But Trent couldn't fix the world.

Cate and Danny?

He might be able to fix their world.

CHAPTER ELEVEN

EVERYONE WAS TALKING at once. Cate couldn't follow a single conversation. At high noon and without a cloud in the sky, the sun warmed her back through the gold maple leaves at the deli's street-side café table. Sophie, Katia McCreary—a newlywed who worked with Jack, Sophie's fiancé—and Sarah were discussing floral arrangements for Sophie's upcoming wedding. Mrs. Beabots, who sat next to Cate, was huddled with Gina, Julia and Olivia looking at invitation samples for Olivia's wedding to Rafe in February.

Cate's mind wasn't on weddings, it was on Trent. She sipped her raspberry tea.

I must have been out of my mind to call him last night. And I asked him to dinner!

Of course she was crazy. Who wouldn't be with a stalker ex-husband who was also a criminal wanted by the police—in two states. Last night Cate had tossed, turned, paced and nearly pulled out her suitcases to pack. Knowing Trent was a phone call away had stopped her from running.

She didn't know what it was about him, but simply hearing his voice had put her at ease. When she'd started to leave the message, she'd glanced at the clock and realized it was in the middle of the night. She'd been so confused and upset, she hadn't paid any attention to the time. Once the call had gone through, it would log the hour automatically. She'd heard the beep, and then she bumbled her way through. The dinner invitation just came out.

The truth was, she did want to see him, and that fact was nearly as upsetting as another visit from Brad.

For so long Cate had kept her heart unplugged. No energy, no force had fed it until Trent had put his arms around her and soothed her. Once in the circle of his arms, she couldn't get him out of her head. But that was what she had to do. Wasn't it?

"Cate, what do you think?" Sophie touched her arm.

"What?" Cate looked into Sophie's brown eyes. "I'm sorry."

"Are you okay, sweetie?" Mrs. Beabots asked. "Something is bothering you. I can tell."

Cate put on her real-estate agent smile and

forced her eyes to be merry. She was a sales-person after all. "I'm fine. I've got a big deal I'm working on, and I was thinking about how to handle it. That's all."

"Really?" Katia's green eyes grew wide with curiosity. Katia was without a doubt the most beautiful woman Cate had ever seen. Her glorious auburn hair spilled down the back of her cashmere sweater. "Is it somebody's house we know? Are you the listing or buyer's agent?" Katia drew a long sip of tea through her straw.

Cate couldn't help noticing Katia's beautiful new wedding rings. The diamonds glittered in the sunlight. Austin McCreary was the wealthiest man in town, and he didn't spare a dime on his new bride. From what Cate understood, they'd been in love since Katia was sixteen and had been separated by circumstances—family disapproval, since Katia was the housekeeper's daughter—for over ten years before being reunited.

Cate seldom took note of any of her friends' apparel or jewelry. Her life was one of buying only what was necessary and every extra dollar went toward saving for a better house. A safer house. Until now.

Suddenly, no place was safe for her. Even now, Brad could be across the street watching her. Sooner or later he would make a move. That she knew.

She also knew him well enough to know that he liked playing games. Cat and mouse was a favorite. His abusive nature preened and thrilled over watching her squirm. He was planning something. She was sure of it.

"Katia, you know I wouldn't disclose private information like that."

"Aw, c'mon. Give us a clue." Katia leaned forward. "The Appletons' house next to ours just went on the market. Is it that one?"

Cate smiled. "No, Katia. And I can't tell you how much I wish I'd gotten that listing."

Katia let out a deep sigh. "I know. I gave her your card as soon as Austin heard about them moving to California. If it makes you feel any better, he said that house will sit on the market for a long time. It needs a lot of repairs and updating, and they weren't willing to do it. They just wanted to leave."

I know that feeling.

Cate nodded. "He's probably right. The only way to move it quickly is to drop the price."

Mrs. Beabots speared a forkful of salad. "I think they'll come back," she said blithely, and gave Cate a knowing wink.

"You know something," Cate said.

"I might."

Every woman at the table turned her eyes to Mrs. Beabots. "Tell us."

"Yes. Spill," Sarah urged.

"Gretchen Appleton told me at the grocery store. She said they'll stay in California if they get the price they want for this house. Things out there are very expensive. But the weather is nice. If Austin is right about the repairs, the house may not sell, and they'll come back. Personally, I think they're bored. I told her to book a cruise or two every winter and stay in Indian Lake."

"Good advice," Katia said.

Mrs. Beabots looked at Cate. "If you could sell the Appleton house to someone who was handy, say, like Luke, you'd make a good commission, wouldn't you?"

"I sure would," Cate agreed, and picked up her sandwich. "I could use it."

Why did it always seem like everything in her life came down to money? If she had more of it, she could easily pack up and move away. She and Danny could disappear. Live well in Florida or Arizona for that matter. Money gave her vanishing power.

If. If. If.

Her head pounded with another dozen thoughts and complications that sprang up.

As she looked around the table, she wondered what they all would think if they knew the truth about her. Would they still support her? Be willing to refer her like Katia had?

"Sophie, dear," Mrs. Beabots said. "Did you ask Sarah about using Luke's truck?"

Sarah turned to Sophie. "What about Luke's truck?"

"I'm moving out of Mrs. Beabots's apartment day after tomorrow. I wondered if I could borrow his truck."

"I'm sure it's fine, but I'll ask him after lunch. We can help you get your things packed if you want."

The conversation buzzed around Cate, but she wasn't following any of it. Then she heard her name. She was being addressed again. She smiled, but she didn't know who was talking to her. Her mind was a maze, and she was getting lost. Maybe she'd finally gone over the edge.

Mrs. Beabots put her hand on Cate's shoulder and whispered, "Cate, dear. You're not yourself at all. Would you like to come over after lunch and talk?"

"I'm okay." She pressed her fingertips to her temple. "A headache coming on, I think."

"Oh, that's not good." Mrs. Beabots dropped her hand. "But you know my door is always open."

Cate leaned over and kissed her cheek. "I do. Thank you."

Mrs. Beabots picked up her glass of lemonade. "I think we should toast the two brides-to-be."

"Cheers!" they all said, and clinked glasses.

They finished their lunch, and as Sarah and Katia helped Olivia clear the table and take the dishes inside, Sophie hugged everyone goodbye and jogged to the hospital for an afternoon surgery.

Mrs. Beabots buttoned her blazer and looked at Cate. "I'm very happy for Sophie and Jack, you know. But it seems like I barely get used to having one of the girls in the house and suddenly they're getting married and moving away. The house will be empty again. At my age, you'd think I'd be used to these bittersweet times, but I'm not." She looked at Cate with sad blue eyes.

Cate put her arms around Mrs. Beabots. "Don't you worry. I'll find a tenant for you."

"Would you do that?"

"Sure. No fees, either."

Mrs. Beabots brightened instantly. "What a

lovely idea. I'd forgotten you handle rentals as well." She picked up her vintage Louis Vuitton purse. The brass lock and key dangled from the edge of the leather handles. "You take care, Cate. And bring Danny around soon."

"I will. I promise," Cate said.

Sarah, Gina and Katia came out of the deli and said their goodbyes. "I'm getting a turkey sandwich for Danny," Cate said.

Sarah hugged Cate. "Julia made her brownies. I bet Danny would like one of those, too. I have to run. See you soon."

"Bye." Cate waved to them.

She swallowed a lump in her throat. These women were her friends. Real friends. They helped each other; supported each other through trials and crises. And celebrated joys together. The capacity of their ever-expanding hearts was astounding to Cate.

All those years ago, they'd taken her in and hadn't asked questions. They respected Captain Red and Julie, and when they vouched for Cate, that was all that was necessary. The rest had been up to Cate.

Something told her that if she ran, she'd never find this kind of home again.

Yet, she had to find a way to keep Danny safe from Brad.

Cate was out of ideas. The only person in her life who knew the truth was Trent. He was her only hope.

CHAPTER TWELVE

"Stakeout? You? I hate stakeouts," Richard said to Trent on the phone.

"So do I," Trent replied, looking at the repair bill he'd be paying when he picked up his car.

"Listen, Trent. I've got a report on my desk that says Le Grande was spotted coming out of the John Hancock Building yesterday morning. I have another report that his car, a 2015 Cadillac CTS known to be his personal vehicle, was parked at a garage at Randolf Street for two hours last night.

"We've also got a license plate on this Ford van. Turns out the van is hot."

"No surprise there." Trent tossed his pen on the desk.

"The guy is as slippery as an eel. My team went into the Hancock and arrested a couple of his dealers. For the most part, these idiots have superglued their lips. But we nabbed one punk this morning. He's in the interrogation room now. No one has stepped up to bail him out, either."

"An independent?"

"That's my guess. He's trying to get into the gang. But he did say one thing that was very interesting."

"What's that?" Trent asked, taking his long legs off his desk. Richard never said *interesting* to anything unless it was big.

"He said that Le Grande had told him that if he crossed Le Grande, he personally would go after his family and kill every last one of them."

"He said that?"

"It's in the report. That's why we're keeping him in custody."

"That paints a different picture," Trent mused uneasily. "Drug dealing is one thing, but murder? That's another."

"I've said all along that Le Grande is a real scumbag. We believe he sees himself as a real mafioso type of leader. He's got connections to smuggle half a million bucks' worth of heroin into the region. You can bet he's going to make sure he sells every bit of it. Your raid has to have made him very, very angry."

"And when murderous men get desperate…"

"They get even," Richard finished. "If I were you, buddy, I'd watch my back. If Le Grande is in the city today, that doesn't mean he's not headed your way tonight. Know what I mean?"

"I do," Trent replied, his mouth going dry.

"Like I said. Watch your backside."

"Will do. Thanks." Trent hung up.

He looked at his watch. Nearly one thirty. His car should be finished by three. In the meantime, he was starving. He took his cell phone from his jacket pocket and listened to Cate's voice mail once again.

He liked listening to her voice. He'd gotten her cell number from one of the many flyers she'd posted about town. He sent her a text message.

I need to see you. When would be convenient?

That was professional and hopefully wouldn't cause her stress. Once he told her this new information about Le Grande, she'd be more than stressed—she'd be alarmed.

He rose and went to Ned Quigley. "I'm going out for a sandwich. I'll be on my cell."

"Sure, Trent." Ned gave him a quirky grin. "Gonna pick up your car, too?" Ned burst into laughter.

"Funny," Trent replied, shoved his hands in his pants pockets and left.

CATE HAD LEFT her friends and gone into the deli to get Danny the sandwich she'd promised him. She went up to the counter. Olivia and Julia were busy filling orders. Most of the lunch crowd had left, but there were still a few stragglers.

"Olivia, could you wrap up a brownie for Danny?"

"Sure, Cate," Olivia replied.

"And I'll have a tuna on whole grain," a familiar male voice said from behind Cate.

She spun around. "Trent."

"Hi." He smiled.

Cate felt her heart trip. Maybe from too much caffeine. No. That couldn't be right. Olivia's raspberry tea was decaf. It was the nearness of Trent that made her smile.

Olivia came up to the counter. "You want the usual guacamole spread, Trent?"

"Yes, please," he said. "Chips and fruit on the side today."

"Do you eat here often?" Cate asked, making small talk.

He shook his head. "I get it to go. Always working. But it's such a nice day I figured I'd walk from the station. Before we know it, winter will be here."

"Yes. Winter," Cate replied as she realized

that ordinarily she'd be thinking about the up-coming cold weather, which meant a slowdown in business. But not this year. All she thought about was this danger zone she occupied. There was no escape. No respite.

"I could make an exception today. On the to-go thing, I mean," he said. "What I mean is, would you have lunch with me?"

"Oh. I'm getting something for Danny. I just finished lunch with my girlfriends."

"Ah. I saw Mrs. Beabots on my way in. Must not have been fun. She looked sad, which is unusual for her."

"She is sad. Sophie is moving out day after tomorrow. Mrs. Beabots will be alone again."

"Really?"

Olivia came to the counter, took Cate's money and handed Trent his order. He paid, then walked out with Cate.

"Cate, I want to thank you for the call last night. I sent you a text—"

"About that—"

"Look, Cate," he said. "I need to talk to you about, uh, your situation."

"What about it?" Every tiny nerve ending sparked. She held her breath.

"Listen," he said, taking her elbow. "My car is being worked on. Is yours nearby?"

"Yes. Just down the block. Why?"

"I want to talk to you where we won't be overheard." He glanced up as two patrons walked out of the deli. "Do you mind?"

"Uh, no." She reached in her purse for her keys. "C'mon."

THEY DROVE TO Cove Beach, parked the car and then walked to a bench and sat. There was only a slight breeze, creating ripples across the blue water. Indian Lake was ringed with oak, maple, sweet gum and walnut trees dressed in their blazing autumn finery.

"I love this lake," she mused.

Trent watched her face soften. She was obviously a loving parent, and her relationship with Danny was priority number one. She was an excellent real-estate agent. Most importantly, he admired her courage in telling him the truth about her past.

He sensed a need in her to love and be loved that had etched a place in his heart already. He wondered if she would ever release the dark ties that kept her bound to Brad Kramer. It wasn't the fact that they shared a child, Trent thought. He believed it was fear of choosing love again that kept fortress walls around her heart.

He knew those walls. He'd built some around his own heart.

"I come out here and run sometimes," he said. "Of course in the winter, I work out at the YMCA with Luke, and Scott Abbott."

"Danny loves Scott's bookstore—it's the pop-up books."

"Me, I love Scott's coffee," he said, staring across the lake at the Lodges.

"I don't run," she said, then cleared her throat. "For exercise, I mean."

"I know what you meant." He quirked a half smile as a breeze blew a lock of her hair across her eyes. He brushed it away. "So, when you're not sculling, I bet you do yoga."

"Uh-huh. In the winter." She watched his lowering hand. "Was that in my file?"

"No, but you move so gracefully. It was that or ballet." He felt like a teenager on a first date, and this was supposed to be all about Le Grande. Trent didn't feel like going there yet.

"My parents didn't have the money for ballet lessons."

"Mine, either," he said straight-faced.

She laughed and covered her mouth with her hand. "Was it an option? I mean, you're rather big for ballet…"

He liked that she kept the joke running. It

showed a sense of humor, even when life was dark and frightening. "I never learned rowing, either."

"It's not hard, just takes coordination and practice," she assured him.

"I'd be a klutz," he joked.

"I doubt that," she replied firmly. "You remind me of a ship's captain. Taking charge of the vessel, the crew, the storm and bringing everyone to safety."

She looked at him with absolute conviction. This was the confidence he'd hoped to win from her.

It's so beautiful." Cate's eyes roamed the lake. "I wish I could do this every day. Just sit here. Gaze. Find peace."

"I know what you mean," he replied. He needed her to believe in him. Because he wanted to be the guy who gave her and her son real safety. But the truth was that he wasn't that guy. He wasn't her captain or her savior.

He was the messenger of impending danger.

"Cate," he said, easing his voice back to his professional tone. "Today isn't that day."

Her back stiffened as she turned to look at him. "I can see that. What now?"

"There was an incident last night. I can't go

into all the details, but Le Grande's gang was involved."

She nodded solemnly. "There was no mistaking him that day at Jack Carter's condo."

"I talked to CPD and was told Le Grande was in Chicago. He has an alibi—for part of the day. But what I wanted to talk to you about is the fact that the Chicago cops believe he's capable of a lot worse than just dealing drugs."

Her hands were trembling. He wanted to hold them. It took all his strength to keep his distance.

"Cate, we have information that Le Grande will stop at nothing to get what he wants. Just as you indicated."

"And he wants me."

"Yes. You're an object to him, just like his drugs and money."

She held up her shaking palm while placing the other hand over her mouth. Her eyes filled with tears. "When we were married, he told me often that he owned me. I wasn't a person to him, but a possession."

"Le Grande isn't Brad anymore, Cate. He's a different animal all together. CPD believes he sees himself as a cartel leader—a kingpin. He's all about his drug business and making money now."

"I see." She paused, gazed out to the lake. "Trent. I have to ask. Do you think he would kill me?"

"We have no intel to suggest that he's crossed that line," Trent said.

Her eyes darted from right to left, surveying the beach around them. "Can you help me get out of town? Somewhere where he can't find me? Ever again?" Her voice cracked, and he could hear the eruption of terror.

Trent leaned closer, feeling empathy for her, but she almost cowered from him. Almost. Then he put his hand on hers.

"Cate. That's the sacrifice I want you to make."

"Sacrifice?" She braced.

He felt her hands turn icy.

"I need your help. I want to bring Le Grande and his gang down. Now and for good. To do that, I need you to—"

"Stay. You want me to stay. Help you reel him in," she said bluntly. She lifted her chin. "Is that right?"

He hesitated. He had no idea how much more courage she had in her arsenal. It must have taken so much to run from Brad then to sustain her disguise. But Trent needed her. "Yes," he said finally. "I need you to draw him out."

"I told you, Trent, I know Brad better than anyone."

"I'm counting on that, and if what you believe is true, that he's still emotionally invested in you, then so much the better."

"You are his Achilles' heel. You and Danny."

He paused and studied her face. "Cate, we have a man on the inside. He's deep undercover, and he's how we know so much about what Le Grande is thinking. Yes, Le Grande sought you out. But listen to me. Criminals make mistakes, and when he trips up, I'll move in."

"You sound so sure. So confident."

"Because I am, Cate. This is what I do. Protect people. You and Danny." He squeezed her hand.

Cate swallowed hard. "So, what do we do?"

"My counterpart in Chicago is Richard Schmitz. We have a plan to trap Le Grande."

"A plan?" Her voice skipped over her words. "You've collaborated with the Chicago Police. Sorry. It's just all so insane, you know? To think that the father of your child is a drug lord. I'm having a hard time getting used to the idea."

"I understand. Le Grande is in the process of forming a partnership with a drug lord out of Detroit. They want to create a syndicate that would supply drugs to most of the midwestern United States. Their plans are grandiose, but they have to start somewhere."

"And that's in Indian Lake?"

"Yes. We've fabricated a story about a large buyer who wants to meet here. We're trying to set a drop date, but it's not easy. Le Grande wants to call the shots. Everything is a secret with this guy. He doesn't tell any of his minions his strategy until the day of the deal."

"He was always like that. Even with me. For a long time I thought I was stupid or not observant. Then later, I realized that was how Brad worked. It's part of his cunning nature."

"You're so right," he said. "We need an edge to smoke him out. That's why we need your presence.

"We believe Le Grande will show his face here more than he would in Chicago because of you. He might try to see you at church or the grocery. Danny's school." How frightening this must sound to her. "Highly trained officers will watch you and Danny every second. They'll have the best surveillance equipment. At the same time I want to take precautions to keep you as close to me, er, the police as possible."

"That's a lot to ask."

"It is," he agreed.

"This is happening so fast."

"Cate." He put his hand on her shoulder. "I know you're afraid, but listen to me. Just now when we were at the deli, you said that Sophie was moving out of Mrs. Beabots's house."

"Yes. Day after tomorrow."

"If I call Jack Carter and make some arrangements, I'd like to see if we can move her out tonight and move you in at the same time."

"Tonight? You're kidding?" She peered at him. "You're not kidding."

"No. I'm serious. Mrs. Beabots's house is directly across from the rear of the police station parking lot. I see her house every time I get in my car. With Danny's school nearby, we can keep a very close eye on you. I can go to the school and pick up Danny and take him to the station with me. When you finish work, you come to the station, get him and take him to Mrs. Beabots's house."

Cate wrung her hands in her lap. "I just don't know. I mean, Trent…can this work?"

"I believe it can. This afternoon, after I talk to Jack, I'll get my men to move all of Sophie's things out after dark tonight."

"It's just that tonight is so soon. My house— you don't understand. I've worked hard, saved and scrimped for every dollar. For Danny and me to have a safe place to live."

He let her continue. She was in shock. The words had to sink in and then logic would reign. She was a smart woman. He trusted in that.

"But even my home isn't safe anymore."

"It isn't right now. Cate, I want to send a crew to your house with you to pack up what you and Danny need for the time being. Under no circumstances are you to go back there alone today. Do you understand?"

She nodded. He saw a tear fall onto her cheek. His hand was against her skin before he could stop it. With his thumb he wiped away the tear. "I know this is hard. But I swear I won't let any harm come to you or Danny."

"I believe you."

"That's all I wanted to hear." He leaned over and kissed her cheek where another tear had fallen.

"Thank you." He could feel her sigh of relief. Felt the pulse of her heartbeat beneath her skin as he slid his lips to her temple. Her hair smelled like lavender and lilacs. Like a spring day.

Trent could rationalize all he wanted about his PTSD, but his emotions begged to be heard. It had been a long time since he shared any part of himself with a woman. Not since Afghanistan, and even then, his relationship with a female officer had come more from the war-torn atmosphere than it did from their hearts. Once he was stateside, Trent had believed he could go forever without meeting someone.

Until Cate.

"What about Danny?" she asked. "He gets out of school in an hour."

"What do you usually do?"

"He walks with Annie and Timmy to their house. Miss Milse meets the kids just outside the school yard. Then I pick him up after work. If I'm home early enough, I'll meet him after school."

"What's the plan for today?"

"He goes to Sarah's."

"Stick with the routine. We don't have time to talk to Danny about the move until later. A lot of wheels have to be put in motion."

CATE WISHED SHE could think of even one way to talk to Danny about his father. First things first, she'd have to tell her little boy that she'd lied to him. The worst blow was that Brad wasn't a good man. Danny was such a sensitive boy, she could already imagine the questions he'd come up with. Above all, she knew she had to reassure Danny that Brad had made wrong choices in his life. That Danny wouldn't have inherited his nature.

Cate felt as if harpies from hell had perched on her shoulders. They pecked at her head. Tormenting her with her one underlying fear: that she was a bad mother to Danny.

"Hey." Trent put his hands on her shoulders. "Stop that."

"What?"

"Anguish is scribbled all over your face. It's going to be all right. I'm here."

Lowering her eyes from his, she muttered, "It's not about that."

He whispered in her ear, "I know exactly what you're thinking. Explaining Le Grande to Danny. That's going to be rough, but he's a smart kid. I have faith in him. And in you."

"You...do?" Her head jerked up to see sincerity in his eyes. She felt warm where she'd been cold. And not quite so alone anymore.

"I do," he said gently, and grazed her cheek with his lips.

It was the softest fluttering. Not a kiss, really. But she'd reacted as if he'd flung his arms around her and pressed his lips to hers in the most heart-stopping, knee-buckling, earthquaking kiss ever. Time stopped. The world ended. Then began again. But everything was different, powerful. Had Trent made that happen with the touch of his lips? Was she so desperate for closeness that she would take it—even from the cop who knew far too much about her lie?

He pressed his palm to her cheek. "I'll have an unmarked car watch Danny from the time he leaves school until he's at Sarah's. That gives us time to make the arrangements for the move."

He was giving her logistics. But she could only focus on his hand against her skin. How was it possible to feel so much comfort right now when she should be listening? Thinking about how to wade through this massive undertaking he'd arranged.

There were so many details. So many ways it could blow up. Would it be the end? Or would they succeed? Cate had taken so many risks in her life she was terrified of taking Danny to the county fair each year. Bumper cars and roller coasters were for people who lived normal lives. Not for Cate Sullivan.

"Cate. What do you think?" Trent asked. "Have we covered all our bases?"

What was he talking about? He'd taken his hand away. Why? Didn't he know that he'd given her strength?

Of course not. How could he know? Cate Sullivan didn't tell people the truth. She lived undercover.

"Trent, you forgot one thing," Cate said.

"What's that?"

"We haven't asked Mrs. Beabots."

He looked at his watch, stood and held out his hand to her. His hand. What did he want? To touch her again? Did the kiss mean anything to him, or was it a mistake? Maybe he hadn't meant to skim her cheek like that. Yes. That had to be it. He was acting too normal. Too much like a cop.

"Do you want to drive? Or should I?" he asked.

She handed him the keys. She told him the truth. "I'm still a little shaky."

"Good thinking."

CHAPTER THIRTEEN

MRS. BEABOTS BROUGHT out a sterling silver caddy piled with pastries, scones and miniature muffins. She'd put an English cozy over the Haviland china teapot. She started to pour the tea into three cups. "Goodness. You two look as if you're about to jump out of your skins," she said, handing a cup to Cate and filling a second for Trent.

Her blue eyes tracked from Cate to Trent and back.

"Frankly, I'm more than worried," Cate said, trying desperately to tamp down her fears.

Trent took a sip. "That's…really good tea. What is it?"

"Mint, dear. I grow it in my garden. But not the bourbon. I get that down at Indian Lake Fine Liquor Store," she said with a mischievous smile. "You don't fool me. Something dangerous is afoot, and you think I can help."

Cate clanked her cup against the saucer. "How do you know?"

"I'm old. I'm supposed to know these things."

"That's not true. I know lots of clueless octogenarians," Trent said.

"Fine. Chalk it up to experience."

"How would you—"

Mrs. Beabots waved Cate off. "Trent. Out with it. What can I do?"

"I need you to rent your apartment upstairs to Cate and Danny."

Mrs. Beabots stared wide-eyed at Cate. "But your home is so darling."

Cate nodded, tasting acid from her stomach. For days she'd thought about running away, and now she was doing just that, even if she wasn't going far. Irony spread a large cloak over her life right now. "It's not about my house. I'll go back there. Hopefully. And soon. This is... temporary."

"My, you are in trouble, aren't you?" Mrs. Beabots looked at Trent. "With the law?"

Trent put his teacup on the end table and said, "Cate is being stalked by a dangerous, possibly murderous man. I want to protect her and Danny as best I can. Since your house is across from the station, I can keep an eye on them."

"That is serious," Mrs. Beabots said. "Then why not put her in one of those protection programs you all have out in Nevada or Iowa or somewhere."

"Because we need to catch this guy. His power is growing by the day. If we can—" He flexed his hands.

"Snare him," Mrs. Beabots supplied. She looked at Cate. "And Cate is the bait."

"Yes," Cate said. "We're hoping it doesn't get nasty, but you have to know there is a possibility."

"I see."

Mrs. Beabots was silent for a moment, and Cate was suddenly worried that perhaps her friend wouldn't want her to stay. Maybe Brad and his criminal buddies would be too dangerous for her.

Cate stood. "You know, this is too much to ask. Trent, we should never have come here. To involve Mrs. Beabots in my problems is—"

Mrs. Beabots took Cate's hand and pulled her back into her chair. "Nonsense, dear. You act as though I've never known danger. Nothing could be further from the truth. Believe me." She turned to Trent. "But you aren't here to investigate me, you're here to help Cate and Danny."

"That's right. I just got off the phone with Jack. He and I have made plans to move Sophie to his house tonight about six thirty. He tells me Sophie doesn't have all that much to move."

"She doesn't, poor thing. Always working. Never shops." Mrs. Beabots shook her head. "Sad. Anyway, Trent, tell me everything. I need to know what we are up against. You said murder. He wants to kill Cate?"

Cate put her hand on Trent's sleeve. "I should tell her. It's my mess."

"Cate, it's not. You're caught in a web," he said, covering her hand with his and giving her a reassuring smile. "But you're right. You should tell her."

Cate took a deep breath and a long sip of the bourbon-laced mint tea. "Trent has been trying to apprehend a big drug dealer for months. A few weeks ago, his team came very close, but the ring leader got away. That man was…is my ex-husband, Brad Kramer."

Mrs. Beabots folded her hands in her lap. "I thought your husband was dead. Apparently, he was just dead to you. Is that right?"

"Yes," Cate answered, feeling surprisingly lighter with each disclosure, as if she was finally doing the right thing. Unweaving her lies had often frightened her more than the idea that she might see Brad again. Having Mrs. Beabots on her side was monumentally important to her.

She realized the elderly woman was the mother and grandmother figure in her life. Her heart expanded with the love she felt. She wondered if Mrs. Beabots could see it.

"Go on, dear."

Cate told Mrs. Beabots everything she knew about her ex-husband. Her abusive marriage. Her flight to Indian Lake. Captain Redbeard and Julie taking her under her wing.

"And they never introduced me to you until you were in real-estate school. I think it was during the Christmas Candlelight Tour of Homes," Mrs. Beabots interjected.

"It was. Danny was just an infant. It seems a lifetime ago," Cate murmured.

Trent chimed in with statistics that had come from the Chicago police. "His gang is over two dozen strong and growing. The CPD is working with us."

"And, Trent, you believe that this Le Grande character will come after Cate?"

"I hope to intercept him. That's my plan. He knows where Cate lives. I'm not sure if he's had enough time to find out where Danny goes to school. He should be busy trying to cover his tracks now. I'd hoped that his battles would be on Chicago turf, but in the event that he's still as controlling as Cate remembers, there's a chance that he would come here again. One thing is clear—she can't go back to her house right now. We want to smoke him out, yes, absolutely, but only when we have Cate under tight surveillance."

He continued. "I've got two policewomen assigned to pack up clothes, toys and essentials that Cate will need for a couple days."

"I understand completely." Mrs. Beabots nodded.

"Would you allow my team to install surveillance cameras around the perimeter of your property? I've requisitioned them. What the department doesn't pay for, I will."

"I can't ask the police department to do that, young man," Mrs. Beabots countered. "I'll pay for it myself. I've thought for years it would be a good idea to have cameras. I'm not getting any younger. It's been a long time since I took a self-defense course." She raised her chin. "Have them get some of those timer lights, too. I'd like a few of those. Safety is quite a bit different today than it was in my day," Mrs. Beabots said.

"Oh?" Cate asked. "What did you use then?"

"A Colt .45 1911 myself. Raymond preferred a Ruger." She picked up her tea and took a long drink.

CATE HAD TO take Sarah into her confidence since she had to arrange for Danny to stay overnight with her, Luke and the kids while she and Trent helped Sophie move out and move Cate's things in to Mrs. Beabots's apartment.

"You know I'll do anything to help you and Danny, Cate," Sarah said. "You don't have to tell me everything. We trust you. You know that."

"I do. But there's so much about me—my life—I've kept secret, and now my ex-husband is stalking us. You see, he's a drug dealer, and it's because of him that these gangs have been moving into Indian Lake. Now the local police and the Chicago force are trying to catch him. Can you believe it? My ex turns out to be public enemy number one." Cate raked her fingers through her hair. "You have to know that it could be dangerous. And I don't want anything to happen to the kids. So, after today, Trent will get Danny after school and take him to the police station if I'm at work. I'm so thankful it's just across the street. Trent has promised that I'll always have a surveillance car nearby. If Brad tries anything—even comes close— they'll be there."

Sarah threw her arms around Cate and kissed

her cheek. "Oh, honey. I had no idea this was going on. I can't believe you're still sane!"

"Am I? I'm not sure." Cate made a stab at humor.

Suddenly, Cate realized how her deceptions were truly like a spiderweb, snaring her friends into possible danger.

Through it all, Trent was strong and commanding. She'd thought men like him were characters in books. They weren't real.

"Trent is a good guy," Sarah said. "Luke thinks the world of him. Since they were both in the military, they have a lot in common."

"That's right. I forgot that. You're lucky to have Luke.""

"You're a good friend to me. Don't you worry about anything. We're all here for you. If you need Miss Milse to babysit for Danny whether my kids are home or not, just let me know."

"Thanks, Sarah," Cate said as two pickup trucks arrived. Luke pulled into Mrs. Beabots's driveway instead of his own. Behind him was Jack in a rented truck. Luke waved at Sarah.

"Hey, hon. I'll be helping Jack and Trent. Can you bring me a ham sandwich?"

Cate looked at Sarah disbelievingly. "He's helping? How does he know?"

"Trent, probably. You know Luke, Trent and

Scott Abbott go to the firing range a couple Saturdays a month to keep up their skills."

"No," Cate replied, looking over at Mrs. Beabots's house as Trent drove up in his unmarked car. "I didn't know."

"Come help me with the sandwiches and coffee I made for the guys. If they're going to get this switch done tonight, we need to feed them."

Trent got out of his car. He waved to Cate. She waved back. Sophie and Mrs. Beabots came out the front door. Sophie raced down the steps and into Jack's arms. After a joyful kiss, they rushed up the steps together.

Trent walked to where Cate and Sarah were standing.

"Everything okay?" He looked from Cate to Sarah.

"Yeah, it's fine," Cate replied, unable or unwilling to take her eyes from his. "What do you want mc to do?"

"Go inside where no one can see you," he said. He twisted around and scanned Maple Boulevard. "I love this street. I don't want anyone to disturb it. Ever."

"Neither do I," Cate replied.

"Then go help Sophie pack. I want to get this part over as quickly as possible."

"All right." Cate turned and hugged Sarah.

"Thanks for everything, Sarah. I'll be over in the morning to get Danny."

"Call me if you need me," Sarah said. "Night, Trent."

"Good night, Sarah," he said, taking Cate's arm.

They walked in silence across the yard. Silence didn't bother Cate ordinarily, but now it thundered in her ears. "Are you mad at me?"

"No." He blew out a sigh. "Just tense, I guess. I saw you standing there, and all I could think was what a perfect target you made."

"I'm sorry. This is new to me in many ways. In some ways it's not."

"I'll bet."

They walked up the drive to the back steps, which led to the private entrance for the second-story apartment. Trent stopped Cate at the bottom of the steps. "I want to tell you that I think you're very brave for doing this. You could have bolted like you did before."

"I thought about it."

"I'm sure you did," he said, touching her cheek. "Why didn't you?"

"Because this is my home. I've put down roots, and I don't want to see anything happen here if I can prevent it. Maybe we wouldn't be in this position if I'd turned Brad in years ago.

This time I'm standing up to him. If you and the police need me to rout him out, then I'm willing to do it as long as Danny is never in danger."

"I swear I'll do everything—"

She put her fingers over his soft, full lips. Ones she wanted to kiss. "Don't promise. Nobody knows what's going to happen. Brad is a cancer in this world. He needs to be surgically removed. I know that now."

Trent kissed her palm. "Like I said, you're a very brave woman."

"I'm not that brave," she whispered. "Because right now I'm terrified to be standing in the dark with you."

"I thought so," he replied, and kissed her. It was a kiss like none other. Compelling, thrilling and comforting all at once. She felt heady, as though she'd had a glass of champagne. He drew her close to that iron-hard chest of his that told her she needn't worry ever again. Trent could take care of her. But it was the feel of his tender lips against hers that caused shivers to race down her spine.

She put her arms around his neck and pulled him closer. If she could stay here, kissing Trent, she didn't have to think about nightmares and a murderous ex-husband. At this moment, she lived another lie—that she was worthy of having a real love with a man like Trent.

CHAPTER FOURTEEN

CATE WAS ASTOUNDED at how many of her belongings the police had managed to move to her new apartment in a single night. Trent put together both her and Danny's beds while Cate fitted them with sheets and pillows.

There were two policewomen helping. Jordan Ames, whom Cate knew from her work with the symphony committee, was an amazingly talented violinist in the orchestra. Cate knew that Jordan had hoped to play in Chicago or New York, but her mother was ill and Jordan was her mother's only support.

Cate had met Nadia Sokolowski six years ago when she was still living with Captain Redbeard and Julie. Cate knew little about her except that she was close to thirty years old and had been born and raised in Indian Lake. She had no ambitions to live anywhere else. Nadia's dream was to make detective like Trent.

Nadia walked up with a huge box of inexpensive pots and glass pans. "I can put these in the cabinets for you."

"Gosh, you've both done so much already and it's after midnight. I'll do it tomorrow sometime."

"It's no bother," Nadia replied. "You'll need these to make breakfast. I packed up nearly everything in your pantry, and Jordan has a cooler with everything from your refrigerator."

Cate was tired, but they all had to be exhausted. Trent had told her that their shift ended at midnight, but they were willing to stay on. "You guys have been great," Cate said. "Seriously, you can call it a night."

Just then Jordan walked down the hall pulling a plastic cooler on rollers. "Thanks, Cate. I'll put these things in the fridge for you, then I'll take off."

Jordan was a very pretty woman with short blond hair and sparkling green eyes. Cate wondered where she got her energy. "Thank you, Jordan. Honestly, I don't know how you both did so much so fast."

"I'm getting used to assignments like this," Nadia groaned. "Instead of real work."

"I heard that," Trent said, coming from the living area where he'd placed a box of books and the same aqua throw that Cate kept on her sofa. The sofa wasn't here…yet. But the throw was. Interesting, she thought, that he'd ordered it packed for her.

Cate watched as he gave orders to Jordan and Nadia. Jordan checked her watch and shifted her weight on her feet. Nadia stood stock-still, receiving his orders with intense scrutiny as if she were going into battle. Cate expected Nadia to salute him as she left, but she didn't.

"I'll be going, as well," Trent said, glancing around at the disarray. "I can help you tomorrow after work."

"It's not necessary," she said, yawning. "Sorry."

"We're both tired. And yes, I will see what I can do about getting some of the larger pieces of furniture here for you, but it will have to be after dark." He raised his eyebrow. "Okay?"

"Yes. I understand." She looked at him—the tower of strength. "Tomorrow."

His blue eyes delved into hers. Her heart was a jumble of terror about Brad, concern for Danny and anticipation about Trent's role in her life. Was he just here to protect her? Did he consider her only as the bait to nab his perp? Or did he feel something else for her?

"Good night, Cate."

"I'm sorry," she said.

"For?"

"Kissing you."

"I thought I kissed you," he said, moving closer, his face very close to hers.

Placing his fingers under her chin, he lifted her face to his. It was late. Moonlight streamed in through half-bare October trees outside. He looked like a hero from a Gothic novel, dark, handsome and purposeful.

That's when she noticed it. The look in his eyes was withdrawn.

She knew she wasn't going to like what he was about to say.

"I'm the one who should apologize, Cate. I was out of line. I'm a police officer and you're my—"

She held up her hand. "I know. I'm just your case. Once you have Brad, this…association will be over. Part of a record that you file."

"Yes. I'm sorry," he said flatly.

Cate wished she could erase emotions from her speech as easily as he did. She wondered if he'd learned that in the military. Or the police academy. Maybe she should take lessons. "Ten-four, or whatever it is you cops say."

"Good night, Cate," he said again. "Good luck in the morning talking to Danny. I know that's gonna be hard."

She forced her lips into a smile. She was practicing being stalwart. "Thanks."

Trent dashed down the hall to the stairs and was out the back door in record time. She heard the door slam. In anger? Or finality?

Cate dragged herself to the bedroom where her bed was made up. "Thank goodness."

She flopped on the bed and looked at the ceiling. She hadn't noticed the ceiling fan before. She closed her eyes and was surprised to feel a tear slip out.

It was just as she'd thought. She'd pushed Trent too far, and he wasn't interested. At least he was honest with her—and all that mumbo-jumbo the shrinks said was good when trying to build a relationship. She didn't care. Right now, she could do with a strong dose of illusion to get through these next days.

Maybe that's what Trent thought he was doing. She wasn't falling for the real Trent. She hardly knew him.

Just once, she'd like to experience a sweet romance. Dates, flowers, Ferris wheels and picking a song to be theirs, but that wasn't Cate's life. Her life could be cut short tomorrow or the next day by a vengeful ex-husband.

She put her forearm over her eyes.

Great. More tears.

She knew it would be a long time before they stopped. Funny, she'd thought she was too tired to cry.

And then she fell instantly asleep.

"MOM! WHAT ARE YOU doing here?" Danny asked as he sat in Sarah's sunny kitchen next to Annie and Timmy, who were eating hot oatmeal and baked cinnamon apples laced with cream. Beau sat on his haunches at Timmy's chair, waiting for the boy to slip him a bite.

Sarah held up a spoon. "Cate, you want some? It's my mother's recipe."

Cate smiled. "No wonder they love it. All your mother's dishes are delicious," Cate said, glancing at the coffeemaker. "I will take a cup of that coffee instead."

"Coming up!" Sarah took a mug from the cupboard. "So, what are you doing here so early?"

"I thought I'd drive the kids to school," Cate replied.

Danny frowned. "We were gonna walk today."

"Well, I like that," Cate teased with a wide smile. "I didn't see you all night, and now I want to spend a couple extra minutes with you and you'd rather be with Timmy. I get that. I'm sure he's a lot more fun."

"Mom!" Danny said. "We put up Timmy's tent in his room last night and pretended we were camping in Yosemite Forest."

"Really?" Cate replied with wide eyes as Sarah passed the mug.

Sarah chuckled. "Timmy's class is learning geography by campsites. His teacher is a camping and hunting buff, so he has slide shows of his camping trips."

"Yeah, Mom!" Danny said with oatmeal dribbling out of his mouth. "Timmy knows a lot about camping and fishing, and his dad said he would take me sometimes, too." Danny turned to Timmy. "Didn't he?"

"Yep," Timmy said, shoveling a huge piece of baked apple into his mouth.

Danny beamed. "His dad is the best."

Cate felt something sharp stick in her chest. This was the day she would tell Danny about his real father. About Trent's plan. About the danger. About his new schedule for after-school pickup. None of it could wait. Cate had telephoned Danny's teacher this morning and explained that Danny wouldn't be in school for the first hour, perhaps even two. Cate knew that she'd have to take the teacher and the principal into her confidence. Danny's safety was paramount.

Trent had suggested that she give the school officials Brad's description in case he showed up at the school. Cate intended to do just that. But not until after she talked with Danny.

The kids finished their breakfast and cleared their dishes.

"I took the liberty of making a lunch for Danny," Sarah said. "He told me last night he likes turkey and mayo. I hope that's okay."

Lunch? Cate had forgotten an ordinary part of their everyday routine—making lunch. Already Brad was making too many changes in their lives. She didn't like it. At all.

Cate sighed. "Thank you, Sarah. I completely forgot."

"Understandable." Sarah put her hand on Cate's shoulder, then whispered, "Just let me know what else I can do. And good luck this morning."

"Thanks," Cate replied quietly. "I'll need it.

"So," she said brightly, turning to her son. "You kids ready to go?"

Timmy was petting Beau. "I'm never ready to leave."

"Tomorrow is Saturday, and you can play with Beau for two days straight. Maybe we'll take a ride in the country. Look for some apple cider. I might even make doughnuts," Sarah said.

The kids jumped up and down and shouted, "Yay!"

"Come on, you guys," Cate said, ushering Danny out the back door. "Thanks for everything, Sarah. I'll call you later."

Sarah winked at Cate. "I'm always here."

Cate went back and hugged her. "Thank God for you, Sarah. I don't know what I'd do."

CATE DROVE THE kids to school. Annie, who was nine, rode in the passenger's seat, preening because she was old enough not to have to sit in a kid's seat anymore. Danny and Timmy sat in the back.

"I can't wait to be big," Danny muttered to Timmy, who rolled his eyes.

"Too soon for me," Cate said as she parked the car. "You two go on inside. I want to talk to Danny for a minute."

Annie and Timmy jumped out, closing car doors behind them.

"I can get out myself," Danny said, unhooking the shoulder straps.

"Hang on, Danny. You aren't going in to the school just yet."

"Why not?"

"I have to talk to you about something. I told your teacher you'd be a little late today."

"You did?" Danny's smile was born of pleasure. Then he looked at his mother's reflection in the rearview mirror. "What's wrong, Mom?"

"I'm going to park in the police station parking lot. It's only a block away, and Trent said it was okay."

When Cate had parked the car again, she got out and helped Danny out of his seat. Then they both sat in the front seats of the car.

"Danny, I have something to tell you that in a way, I'm not very proud of, but I hope you'll understand."

"Mom—"

She put her hands on his cheeks and looked into his aqua eyes, her eyes, thinking that it couldn't be possible to love a child any more than she loved Danny. From before his birth, she only wanted one thing…for him to be safe. And now, they were both in more danger than she could ever have imagined. And it was her fault.

Her fault she hadn't faced up to Brad back then. But how could she have done that when he came at her with his fists and enough venom to annihilate anything and anyone in his path?

"Sometimes adults do things that aren't right,

but they're necessary. We mean well and we're hoping for the best, but in some cases that doesn't happen. Am I making any sense?"

The look in Danny's eyes was blank. "No, Mom."

"Okay. I was trying to be diplomatic, but that's not working. The truth is Danny, that your father isn't dead," she said in a rush.

There. She'd said it. Amazing that it came out at all. She'd had it locked away for so long.

"He's not?" Danny asked, then fell silent as he processed what this meant. "But you said he died."

"He didn't. I—"

"Then I can meet him. I can have a real father like Timmy. He can take me camping, and he can teach me to fish. I can get a real fishing pole and lures like Timmy and his dad—"

"No, Danny. Your father isn't like Luke." Danny's mind had landed in a magical place that didn't really exist.

"He's not? How do you know? Did you talk to him?"

"No, I haven't seen him since before you were born."

"Then Trent found him, right?"

"No, sweetie. It's not like that."

Danny's eyes darted around the car like they

always did when his mind was going faster than a motorboat. "Do I look like him? Is he a big guy? Will I be big like him?"

Cate felt a rush of tears, but she fought each and every one back. This wasn't the time for her to be emotional. She needed to go slow.

"Actually, sweetheart, you look like me. Except your hair is like your father's."

"Uh-uh. It's black like yours."

"Danny, my real hair color is blond. I've been dyeing it black for a long time. It's been so long I barely remember what I really look like."

"You dye it?" Danny inspected Cate's head with probing eyes. "Did you want it to look like my dad's?"

The sigh Cate expelled was filled with angst and worry. "Sweetie, it was part of my disguise. I've been running away from your father for years. He wasn't very nice to me."

"How? How was he not nice, Mom?"

"I shouldn't tell you everything—"

"Why not?" he asked with a defensive jerk to his chin. "Because I'm just a kid? Because I'm not big?"

She dropped her jaw. Awestruck at his astute perceptions. He was exactly right. "Yes. Because you're a child. But it's also wrong of me not to explain everything. Danny, your father was violent. He hit me, and one night I was afraid he would kill me. So I ran away. And that's how I came to live here." She smiled at him, hoping to soften the blow.

Danny didn't smile back. He was silent for a long moment. "Since he was so mean and bad, then I have bad blood in me. That means I'll grow up to be like him."

Cate grabbed his face and touched her nose to his. "No, it doesn't. Don't ever think that. Your father made choices, and those choices were bad. He wanted to be mean and hurtful." She drew back. "And he still does."

"He does?"

"Yes, Danny. You see, he took drugs and after I left, he kept on taking drugs. Then he made more bad decisions. Illegal decisions. He sold drugs and now he's graduated to being a drug lord, and the police want to put him in jail."

"Mom." Danny started picking at a piece of lint. "The teachers tell us that drugs are bad for us. I didn't know they made people mean."

"Yes, Danny, they do. And hateful and crazy. Those people will do anything to get more drugs. They'll lie. Steal. Murder. I want you to promise me that you will never, ever take any drugs."

"I won't."

"And if any big kids come to you and offer you drugs, you tell me or Sarah or Luke right away."

"I promise," he said solemnly. "But, Mom, it would be better if I told Trent."

"Why's that?"

"Because he's a cop. And he can arrest the bad guys and keep them away from little kids."

"That's very true, Danny. I'm glad you see that." She looked at her son, who was doing an extraordinary job of absorbing so much information.

"Danny, I want to ask you a question."

"Okay."

"Do you feel safe when you're around Detective Davis? Trent, I mean."

"I bet he's the best cop ever. I want to be just like him someday."

"Wow. I didn't know you thought that much of him." She ruffled his hair. "That's a good thing, because he's promised to protect you and me from your father."

Danny straightened in his seat. "He thinks something bad is going to happen?"

"I'm afraid it's possible. You see, the man that we saw on our back porch was your father."

"Mom!" Danny's eyes widened. "Why is he here?"

"Trent tells me that he has a new name now and is the leader of a very dangerous drug gang. Trent and the Chicago police want to arrest him and all his gang members and put them in jail. They've come to Indian Lake to sell their drugs."

"How can Trent stop them?"

"He needs our help, Danny. Yours and mine."

Instantly, Danny's chest puffed up and he squared his shoulders. "Trent needs me to help him?"

"He does." The way that Danny was looking at her, she knew no action hero had ever had a more determined, fierce look in his eye. She was proud of her son. For the first time, she was seeing the man in the boy.

"Trent has a plan, Danny, and we have to follow his rules to the letter. This is not a time for games. Trent fears that your father may try to kidnap you or me. Or both of us. You have to be careful. Do you understand?"

"Yes, Mother. I do," he said, sounding too adult.

Cate explained to Danny about their move to the apartment in Mrs. Beabots's house, the new schedule for going to and from school, and that anytime he wanted to go anywhere, even to walk Beau around the block with Timmy, Sarah, Luke or Cate had to accompany him.

"Promise you'll do all these things?" Cate asked.

Danny threw his arms around her neck. "Yes. I will. I don't want any bad men to take me away from you. Ever."

"I don't, either, Danny."

He sat back and was silent.

"Have I frightened you too much, sweetie?" Cate asked.

"No. It's not that."

"Then what is it?" She held his hand. "Tell me."

"I was just thinking that I don't really know what it's like to have a dad, but I've been hoping—lately, I mean—that it's good, like when I'm with Trent."

Cate pulled Danny into her arms and kissed the top of his head. "I think it would be just like that."

CHAPTER FIFTEEN

A POLICE ESCORT to a wedding had never been on Cate's bucket list. In fact, the entire idea was almost enough for her to decline going to Jack and Sophie's wedding. Almost.

Mrs. Beabots mentioned at least half a dozen times that she needed Cate or Trent—or both—to drive her there and back. Cate happily agreed. It was the least she could do for her friend who was putting herself at some risk to rent the fabulous apartment to Cate and Danny. Cate had to admit, though, she didn't think any perpetrator would dare take on Mrs. Beabots. From what Cate had witnessed, nothing intimidated the woman. Her nerves were so steady, Cate was certain the octogenarian was capable of leading armies.

Perfect. I'm in the war of my life. I need a general like her. And an archangel like Trent.

Whether it was Mrs. Beabots's influence or her air of imperviousness, Cate didn't know, but since moving into the big Victorian house and spending more time with Mrs. Beabots, Cate actually felt bold, if not brazen.

At moments, she imagined being courageous enough to spit in Brad's eye if he showed up. She'd lived in fear for too long.

As small a stand as it was, Cate wanted to go back to her natural blonde self and discard her brown contacts completely.

The session at the hairdresser was a strategic maneuver. She had to clear it with Trent.

"I'll be there four hours," Cate had told Trent on the phone.

"What kind of barber is that?"

"I'm having my color done," was all she'd said. She didn't want him to know what she was doing because this was about her. About being Susan and Cate at the same time. She couldn't believe any man would understand.

"Cate, we had a report earlier that Le Grande was spotted at the toll road booth. They've got our APB flyers with his photograph. I'm on my way to check it out. I'll have one of my best men watching you."

"He can come inside and sit with me if he wants." Despite her best efforts, she couldn't keep the quaver from her voice.

"As long as I know where you are, and that

we have you in plain sight, I'm okay with that. How about you?"

"I wish Brad was behind bars."

"So do I. Look, since you'll be a while, I'll tell my man to pack a lunch."

As IT TURNED OUT, the session took four and half hours to get her expertly highlighted and low-lighted.

What she had to ask herself, as she got in her car and checked her reflection in the visor mirror, was whose skin was she more comfortable in? The old Susan? Or the new Cate? Before she had a moment to dwell on her thoughts, her cell phone pinged with a text message.

"Danny." She smiled as she always did whenever she thought of her son.

Danny had been instructed by Trent and Cate to have his teacher text her when he was ready to leave school. If she was in the vicinity, she would pick him up. Otherwise, Trent would meet him at the school yard and take him to the police station.

Today, Cate had finished both work and her hair just in time. She texted him.

Stay inside the school. I'm on my way. Five minutes.

She pulled away from the curb, reflexively glancing in the rearview mirror. Earlier, Trent had texted her that Brad had indeed been seen at the toll road, but he was on his way out of town. This time he was in a Cadillac SUV. The black Mercury had been abandoned. However, this was a white Malibu she knew to be an unmarked Indian Lake police car.

Four minutes later, she pulled up to the school. She texted Danny to come out.

"Hi, Mom!" Danny waved as he raced toward the car, then slammed to a halt as he looked at her. He nearly toppled over. He rushed toward the driver's door. His hands splayed on the window. "Mom. What did you do to your hair?"

She lowered the window and he backed up, inspecting her with very critical eyes.

"Do you like it? It's for the wedding tonight."

Danny gaped. "It's—different. But you still look pretty."

"That's good." She smiled. "Notice anything else?"

"You're not wearing your brown lenses! Our eyes match now!" he gasped.

"They do," she agreed. "I'm not going to wear them anymore. I thought they'd make me look older and that people would trust me more. Kinda dumb, huh?" She jerked her shoulder.

"I've been noticing that adults do a lot of dumb things," he said, sighing.

"They do," she replied. "Get in. We have to get ready."

Danny climbed in the backseat and buckled himself in. "I gained another pound, Mom."

Cate couldn't stop the guffaw. Here they were in the most tension-filled time of their lives, and all Danny cared about was getting out of his child's seat.

"And so that would—"

"Put me over the top, Mom," he said forcefully.

"Okay. You got me. I cave. When we get to Mrs. Beabots's house, we'll take the child seat out, but you still have to have a booster seat."

"Yes!" He raised his hands over his head. "I thought the day would never come."

Cate laughed. It felt good. "You are so dramatic."

"I know. I was thinking I should try out for the school Christmas pageant. Timmy said he thought I could get a part."

"How would he know?"

"He's been a shepherd three years running. He wants to be a wise man because he's getting old."

Cate's eyes flew to the rearview mirror. Danny

was looking out the window, serious eyes trained on nothing in particular. She wished to heaven he would stop growing up so fast.

"Do you think I'll fit in my suit?" Danny asked. "After all, I *am* taller than I was when we bought it last summer."

"If the pants are too short, you can wear those new black ones we got. Those will look good with the navy jacket. And you haven't gotten so big that it won't fit," she assured him.

"Good."

"So, what's the sudden concern with how you look?"

Danny's face spun from the window and glared at her in the rearview mirror. "Mom. Are you kidding? This is important!"

"How's that?"

He looked at her like she was an alien. "Mom," he said in that indulgent tone that made her feel completely uncool. "It's my first wedding. I think Mr. Carter is so super. He came to our school and talked about not taking drugs. And Miss Sophie. She was with him. She's a very important nurse. Dr. Barzonni told me so. Besides, my friends are going to be there, and they'll be all dressed up, too."

"You've been to many of your friends' birthday parties and my friends' dinner parties with me, and you said you didn't like being dressed up."

"That was before."

"Before what?"

"You know. I'm big now. So, it's different."

What could be different now?

Other than the fact that he'd spent a great deal of time at Sarah's house with Annie and Timmy.

Annie.

Just this morning Danny had asked if he could take an extra cookie to school for Annie. When she'd asked if he wanted one for Timmy as well, Danny acted as if Timmy, his best friend, was an afterthought. Last Saturday night, when the kids had all watched *Finding Nemo* at Sarah's house, Cate had thought Danny had lingered at the door talking to Annie a bit longer than normal.

Duh. Bingo. Cate exhaled through her nose. She'd been so concentrated on her own problems that she hadn't seen what was going on right in front of her very eyes.

Danny had a crush on Annie.

"You know, sweetheart. You're right. We have to make sure your clothes look good." She checked the clock on the dashboard. "Once we get home, we'll try everything. Shoes. Shirt. The works. If it's not right, we'll go get you something new."

"Mom? Are you sure? Can we afford it?"

Cate clutched the steering wheel. Ten thousand ifs ran through her brain. All of them boiling down to the real and frightening fact that if Brad had his way, she and Danny wouldn't have a tomorrow. Money was the least of their worries. "Remember that guy I told you about? The firefighter? Rand Nelson? Well, I closed on his house this morning. So, yes. We can afford it."

Danny exhaled loudly, closed his eyes and leaned his head against the headrest like a man who'd just come through a very tough battle. He opened his eyes. "You're the best mom in the world."

She was far from the best mom. She was about as bad as they came. What if the police protection wasn't enough and something happened to her? Who would care for Danny? Was she doing the right thing? She wanted to help keep the town safe. She did believe there were times when a person had to stand up to evil. But at what cost?

Fear had infiltrated Danny's world. She

couldn't ignore the fact that her little guy had been forced to alter his schedule to accommodate her commitment. She'd had to tell him the awful truth about his father.

Nope. She was far from a good mom.

BEAMS FROM A harvest moon filtered through the maple and oak trees surrounding the brick patio at the Mattuchi farmhouse. A drape of gauzy material formed a canopy over six violinists, a guitarist and a cello player who filled the night air with rhapsodic strains of "The Shadow of Your Smile." A portable wooden dance floor extended past the patio behind the farmhouse. Wooden barrels, clay pots and square wooden planters were overflowing with potato vine, blue cornflowers and red geraniums.

A half dozen round tables, seating ten people each, were covered in bright floral prints in yellows, reds, blues and pinks. Each was accented with enormous vases filled with the sunflowers from Sophie's grandmother's garden.

Dripping from the trees were long strings of clear lights.

Trent had arrived early in the evening while all the guests were at the church. He'd had two of his undercover men watching Cate and Danny as they drove to the church with Mrs. Beabots and Sarah's family. Trent received nearly minute-by-minute reports and updates from his men via text or radio as they ran surveillance around the church, the route to the Mattuchi farm and all of the surrounding area. Trent had posted a man at the neighboring Crenshaw Vineyard. If he'd had the resources, Trent would have requisitioned a helicopter to patrol from the air. As far as he was concerned, no measures were too extreme.

The cars arrived in a ribbon of headlights streaming along the country road toward the farmhouse.

Trent had arranged for a rental car for Cate, which she was to exchange every week. In the event that Le Grande himself or one of his minions tailed her, the change would throw them off the track. He wanted Cate hidden and under his care until the time came when they were ready to spring their trap. Until then, he wished she were invisible.

Le Grande was cunning, devious and possessed the kind of criminal mind that twisted down paths of reasoning that defied logic. It was Trent's job to push his own brain to the edge of reason in order to outwit him.

As much as Trent wanted to believe he was a match for Le Grande, all it took was one tiny miscalculation, one missed clue and Cate would pay the price. And that was utterly unacceptable.

The massive buffet table groaned under the weight of butternut squash ravioli, eggplant parmesan, spaghetti and meatballs, penne and shrimp, and a mountain of Italian bread. The cake was five layers of traditional Italian wedding cake studded with small clusters of sunflowers. It sat on a round table skirted with yards of lace under which tiny crystal lights had been lit. It glittered as Trent passed behind it, his eyes scanning the shrubs and the shadows around the dance area.

There was no telling how far Le Grande would go to take what he believed was his.

Trent knew the drug lord had to want revenge for the bust and the subsequent confiscation of his half million in heroin and fifty grand in cash. Little things like that were not taken lightly in his world. Things like that got a cop killed.

"Hi, Trent!" a child's voice shouted from the distance. Danny.

Trent touched his earpiece. "They're here,"

he was informed by the undercover man he'd assigned to follow Cate.

Trent smiled as he looked to the pathway that led from the front of the farmhouse to the backyard. He saw Sarah and Luke coming toward him with their kids. Trent had spent an hour that morning working the barbells with Luke at the Y. They saluted each other.

"Hey, Trent," Luke called, thrusting his thumb over his shoulder. "Cate's right behind Liz and Gabe."

Sarah winked at him. "I like her new look. She was pretty as a brunette but blond really suits her. All these years I never guessed she was wearing brown contacts. She's like a new person. It's really fun."

He looked over Sarah's shoulder, trying to see Cate, but couldn't make her out in the crowd. "Thanks," he said. "See you later."

Trent spied Liz, walking with her arm hooked through her husband's. In his other hand Gabe held a baby carrier.

"Gabe," Trent said to the eldest of the Barzonni clan of four brothers, who looked like mirror images of each other.

Gina, the stunningly beautiful mother of Gabe, Rafe, Mica and Nate, walked with Sam Crenshaw, Liz's father.

Trent cocked his head. Was there something going on between them that he'd missed?

"*Buonasera*, Trent," Gina said sweetly as she passed. Then she immediately looked at Sam, who winked at Trent.

"Evening, son," Sam said in his gruff voice.

Nate followed his mother with his arm around his wife, Maddie.

"Dr. Nate," Trent said.

Nate stopped and shook Trent's hand. "Perfect night for a wedding, huh?"

"I'd say so."

Nate looked at Maddie. "And some moonlit dancing."

"Now you're talking," Maddie said as they walked away.

Lastly, he saw Austin McCreary and his new bride, Katia, walking toward him.

Austin shook Trent's hand. "Nice night for a wedding. No storm clouds."

Trent had to laugh. "The fact your wedding took place in the middle of the worst thunderstorm in Indian Lake history is already legendary."

"Not as much as his proposal during a tornado," Katia said, beaming as she put her head on Austin's shoulder.

"You got that right," Trent said. "Good to see you both."

Finally, at the very end of the group, he saw Cate. He felt his heart trip. She wore an aqua dress with a matching long gauzy coat that fluttered around her legs, causing him to question whether she walked on the earth or above it. Her hair was blond, and even with just the moon for light, it shone softly. This transformation was mesmerizing because it suited her. It was authentic, honest. No more disguise, and that made her look vulnerable to him.

At the moment he'd thought how beautiful she was, she raised her head and looked at him with aqua eyes.

He held his breath and wondered why and how she had such an impact on him.

Cate had taken Mrs. Beabots's arm and was leading her down the walkway, chatting quietly. Though Cate smiled and chuckled at Mrs. Beabots, she never took her eyes from him.

Trent forced himself to breathe. She was beautiful, yes. But in her eyes he read a thousand emotions and thoughts—all of them stealing into his being like moths around a flame. He was bewitched, and he didn't know how to react.

Danny wove in and out of the group, moving

forward until he met up with his friends, Annie and Timmy. Then Danny waved. "Trent! I was hoping you'd be here!"

Danny rushed away from Annie and up to Trent. He wrapped his arms around Trent's thighs. "Hi!"

Trent ruffled Danny's thick hair. "How're you doin', kiddo?"

"Great! Mom already said I could have two pieces of wedding cake when they cut it. Do they do the cake first?" Danny asked with so much anticipation, Trent couldn't stifle his laugh.

"I think it's last."

"Darn," Danny groused, shoved his hands in his pockets and walked toward Luke and his kids.

Trent raised his eyes and Cate filled them.

"Hi," she said.

That was all. Just a hi and he was toast. Burnt to a crisp on the spot. His tongue swelled in his dry mouth, and his words caught somewhere deep in his throat. "Hi," he managed to croak.

Mrs. Beabots unwound her arm from Cate's and said, "Here, Trent. Take care of Cate. I want to talk to the bride and groom."

Before he knew it, his hand was wrapped

around Cate's soft fingers. "You look lovely tonight."

A slow smile, like dawn rising, filled her face, and her eyes glistened like moonbeams on a summer lake. "Thanks."

What was happening to him? He was on the job. On duty. Working. But he didn't feel that way. He had the odd sensation that the most prudent action for him was to grab Cate and Danny, race to his car and start driving…to Brazil. Or Marrakech. Some fantasy place.

What was he thinking? Not thinking, that's what he was doing.

"Isn't this amazing?" Cate asked. "I love that waterfall of lights over there."

"Just don't go beyond the curtain," Trent warned, suddenly back on the job, feeling the tingling in his nerves that he always felt when anticipating a sniper, an IED, a suicide bomber dressed as an innocuous old woman or worse, a child strapped with timers, detonators, C-4 and Semtex. He closed his eyes and willed the vision away.

"Why not?" she asked, withdrawing her hand from his and crossing her arms.

Trent recognized the move. Protective. Anxious. And wary.

He knew instantly that she felt his caution

and apprehension. This rural area was the perfect setting for a kidnapping. Le Grande's men could slip in through shrubs and grapevines, snatch Danny or Cate while the guests were distracted. A professional could do it in seconds. They would disappear in the middle of the night. He'd never see her again.

Trent shook his head. "I shouldn't have allowed this."

"This?" Cate asked. "What? Me and Danny attending my friend's wedding?" She jammed her face close to his. "You listen to me. This is my life. My son's life. I understand you want to get your man, but there are some places where I draw the line. If Brad shows up here, I swear, I'll kill him myself. It's only been a couple days of this—terror—and I hate it already. I won't let him control any more of my life than he already has." She stepped back and took a deep breath, rubbing her arms.

Trent was aghast. No charge of his had ever blasted him like that. Ordinarily, he would have given it back to her.

She had a point. A valid one.

All terrorists stole lives. They did it to intimidate. Threaten.

That was precisely what Brad had done to her. So had he. In a legal, professional kind of way. Still, it had nearly the same result. Was he trying to control her? And why? Because of his reaction to her? What had happened to his training? His by-the-book mentality that had been drummed into his head from army boot camp through Afghanistan? Where was all that?

Turned to dust the minute she'd incinerated him with those eyes. He should demand she put the brown contacts in. He didn't know if she'd be safer, but he might be.

She smiled. He felt his stomach flip.

She folded her arms across her chest, the aqua gossamer coat floating in the breeze. "I should go," she said anxiously.

He didn't blame her. She had a lot to risk by being with him. He should tell her about his PTSD and why he was a bad choice for any woman. He should tell her about the treatments he'd undergone during his time in the military.

But it always came back to unexpected, rogue wave triggers that took him back there. Set him off and frightened others.

He didn't want any of that to affect Cate. She was too precious to him.

"Yeah, you should probably see to Danny." He said the excuse aloud for her.

"Listen, Trent, I should be honest with you."

She pierced him with a look so earnest and strong he held his breath.

"Please."

"I should never have kissed you. Or let you hold me that night at my house. I don't want you to think I'm...well, a maiden in distress. I can take care of myself. One of the things I've realized is that I'm a magnet for guys who... are inappropriate for me."

"That's diplomatic." He frowned.

"I can't stand losing control. You have to know that, and right now I can't let you take over my life—"

"I wasn't trying to do that."

"Sure you were. Our situation gives you a control over me and Danny that isn't healthy... in the long run, I mean."

He nodded but let her continue.

"Listen, I admit I've been attracted to bad boys. Adrenaline junkies like Brad. Like cops can be—sometimes. I think it's best I take a step back."

Best for whom? She was right and he hated it.

He was without a doubt the absolute wrong guy for her, but as she stood bathed in moonlight, the orchestra playing an old Johnny Mathis ballad, he caved.

"Before you take off, can I have just one dance?"

He held out his hand.

Unsmilingly, she said, "Absolutely not."

She turned and walked away.

And Trent was alone. Again.

CHAPTER SIXTEEN

THE BAND TOOK a break, and Trent watched the dancers applaud. Cate stood not far from him, watching as well.

Jack rang a steel wind chime that sent peals of sound echoing across the farmland. He and Sophie together announced that the dinner was being served. Four women, dressed in white shirts and black pants, immediately went into action pouring wine at the tables as the guests lined up for the buffet.

Trent felt a tug on his jacket and looked down. "Danny." He noticed that Annie was standing next to the boy—with a very wide smile on her face. Her hands were clasped behind her back, and her full skirt swished as she rocked from side to side. At first, Trent couldn't get a take on what the two were up to, then he realized Annie wasn't looking at him at all. She only had eyes for Danny.

"Have you seen my mom?" Danny asked.

"She's right over there." Trent pointed and

noticed Cate walking toward him. She was looking at Danny, too.

"There you are, Danny," she said.

"Mom. You didn't see us?"

"I did," Cate answered, putting her hand on Danny's shoulder. "You two look like professional dancers."

"Annie, tell her," Danny urged with a slight jab of his elbow.

Annie's smile grew to a grin. "I think Danny and I should enter the city dance competition. He's really good. He said you taught him, Mrs. Sullivan."

"I did," Cate said, beaming at her son. "He's been dancing with me since he could walk. I didn't know there was a competition. How did I miss that?"

"It's new," Annie said. "My mom thought it up to raise money for the school. She's always doing that, you know. She's pretty good at it."

"Yes, I know," Cate replied.

Trent heard a voice in his earpiece as one of his team members addressed him. "Detective. North slope. Eleven o'clock. We have intruders."

"Copy that," Trent replied smoothly.

He addressed Cate formally. "Why don't you

all get some dinner? Sit next to Luke as we planned."

Cate stiffened. "What is it?"

He knew his face was calm. He'd practiced this look for years. "It'll be fine. I'll be back. But stay close to Luke."

Trent leaned down to Danny. "Do as your mother says until I get back."

"Yes, sir."

Trent moved out of the glittering lights and into the shadows in a nanosecond.

Trent signaled to Sal Paluzzi to circle up the left side of the hill and flank the perps, while he and Bob Paxton took the right. They were all dressed in dark suits, dark shirts and ties. The other two wore work shoes. Trent's shoes were dress wing tips, as he'd hoped to blend in with the rest of the guests. Now, he wished he had soles that gripped the ground.

Crouching low through a line of grapevines, Trent knew he was well-covered. A cloud moved away from the moon, and then he saw them. There were three men. All dressed in dark jeans and black hoodies.

They blended with the evergreens. Trent could tell from their nonchalant body language that they didn't know they'd been spotted.

Bob Paxton pulled his Beretta from his

shoulder holster, then dropped to one knee, allowing Trent to take the lead. Trent moved in with panther-like stealth. He signaled to Sal Paluzzi to move forward and come from behind the trio. Trent took his gun from his shoulder holster. If these were Le Grande's men, it was highly possible there would be gunfire. Trent didn't plan on dying tonight.

At times like this, Trent felt as if time stood still. He heard every insect buzz and rustle of each leaf. He heard birds half a mile away and the voices of the wedding guests below. Another cloud scudded across the moon, casting shadows across the terrain. He heard his heartbeat in his ears, and the blood in his veins felt like rushing spring rivers.

The air seemed charged with electricity. Adrenaline did that to him.

He often wondered if, at these moments of action, danger and possible death, he became more instinctual—nearly animal. More mechanical than man.

Suddenly, the tallest of the perps halted the others and they stopped chatting. He looked around, realizing he was being hunted. He turned, and his eyes zeroed in on Trent.

"Police!" Trent bellowed. "Freeze. Stay where you are!"

All three perps stood stone still. Then they yelped almost in unison.

That was when Trent lowered his gun. Their voices hadn't even broken yet. "What are you kids doing out here?"

Trent walked up to them in a few strides. Sal was behind them. Bob sauntered up, chuckling to himself.

"Sir? We heard there was a weddin' out here," the tallest one said, his voice croaking, as he pulled his hoodie down to reveal a full head of recently barbered blond hair.

These weren't street kids. Probably neighbor boys. Curious. Having fun. Hoping to swipe a bottle of wine or beer at the end of the night.

"How old are you, son?" Trent asked.

"Fourteen," the boy answered proudly.

"And your parents live…?" Trent continued his interrogation with detached, professional cool.

"I'm a half a mile over. The next farm up the country road. Johnson. You aren't going to tell my pa, are you? He'd kill me. He's really good friends with the Mattuchis."

"Hmm. And so your parents are at the wedding." Trent pointed down the hill.

"Yeah. Yes, sir."

"And these two are…"

"My cousins from in town. They came out to spend the night. Their parents went to Chicago for the weekend. We didn't know they'd have police out here. I mean, at a wedding? What for?"

Trent didn't like how smart the kid was. He was the kind who would rush to school and blab to all his buddies. Word that Trent's team had been at the wedding would spread all over town by Sunday afternoon. He had to think fast.

"Since your parents own a farm, then you know that trespassing is against the law. The Mattuchis have reported incidents of intruders lately." Trent grabbed the kid by the collar and lifted him up, nearly out of his sneakers. "Would that be you?" he growled.

"No, sir. No way!"

The kid shook as if he were a puppet on a string.

"Swear?"

"I swear."

Trent looked at the other two boys. Sal moved over to the boy to the left and hovered. He breathed hard against the kid's back. Bob grabbed the arm of the other one and squeezed.

"What about these two? You kids into drugs? Trying to steal tools and rakes to pawn for some heroin?"

"No, sir! I ain't even had a beer yet! Tonight was supposed to be my first," the youngest, who Trent guessed to be twelve or thirteen, squeaked nervously.

Bob coughed. "We should take them in and book them. Call their parents home from Chicago."

"Please don't do that, Officer," the tall one said. "Please. Honest. We're not criminals. We were just looking for some fun."

Trent released the kid and he stumbled forward. "Regulations say I have to take you in. The Mattuchis reported possible burglars, you three are here. Add it up. What do you get, kid?"

"It's not us!" they chorused.

Sal backed away. "You won't agree, Detective, but I believe them. These guys are just young and stupid. Besides, the farmhouse has camera surveillance. If they come back, we'll have them dead to rights."

Trent paused for effect. Sal was smooth. "Here's the deal." Trent turned to the tall one again. "You kids go home. If we find out you've said a word of this incident to anyone—your parents, your friends, kids at school when you're mouthing off trying to be hotshots—

we'll come back and throw the full weight of the law against you."

The tall one stared at Trent. "For real? You won't tell my pa?"

"No."

"Awesome."

Instantly, Trent stuck his face next to the kid's. "You get this, mister, and get it good. There are consequences for every behavior. You have a consequence. You may not realize it now, or a year from now. But sometime in the future, if you don't straighten up, you will have hell to pay. You got me?"

"Sir." The kid gulped and dropped his smile. "Yes, sir."

"Now leave," Trent commanded.

The three kids took off running across the top of the slope toward what he believed was the Johnson farm. For good measure, Trent would check out their story. If the Johnsons did own the next farm, most likely they were telling the truth.

If not…he'd deal with that, too.

TRENT RETURNED TO the party while Sal and Bob remained in the shadows—watching.

Cate sat next to Luke with Danny on her right. Next to Danny were Annie and Timmy.

All three children were engaged in a lively conversation. Cate's dinner plate was still mounded with food. Luke and Sarah had finished theirs, as had Mrs. Beabots. A server came up from behind and took their plates. Another server poured champagne in their glasses.

Jack's brother, Barry, rose from his chair at the head table and gave the best man's toast. Everyone applauded, including Trent.

He circled the perimeter of the patio and stood far enough behind Cate to keep an eye on her. She hadn't seen him approach. But he noticed that rather than listening to the speeches, Cate looked around. She rubbed the back of her neck, then hugged herself. She shoved her arms down and put her hands in her lap. Then she lifted her hand and toyed with her fork.

She was nervous. Worried.

Was she worried for him?

The bride and groom cut their wedding cake, and the band started playing "Night and Day" while Jack and Sophie danced their first dance.

A photographer nearly bumped into Trent as he hustled across the expanse.

Trent saw Danny, Annie and Timmy huddle together, giggle and then race over to the cake table to be the first in line.

Luke reached his arm around his wife and

pulled her close. He kissed her temple and then her lips. Trent never thought he'd be envious of another man's life, but he was now. Luke was a military man. Married to the love of his life with two great kids. The guy had the world by the tail.

Trent could only dream about that kind of scenario.

Or could he?

Trent walked to the table and eased into the chair Danny had left. "Luke, why don't you dance with your beautiful wife? I'll watch over Cate from here."

"Good plan," Luke said eagerly, and held Sarah's chair for her.

Sam Crenshaw came over to the table and asked Mrs. Beabots to join him and Gina at their table. Then he promised her a dance, as well.

"You don't mind, do you, dear?" Mrs. Beabots said to Cate and Trent.

"Please, join your friends," Trent replied.

"Why aren't you two dancing?" Sam asked, and then urged them by pointing at the dancers. "It's too beautiful a night to waste it sitting on the sidelines." He winked at Trent.

"Uh…" Cate looked at Trent, but all he saw was trepidation.

"I'm game if you are," he said.

"Well, all right." She rose from her chair.

Trent walked behind her onto the dance floor. He took her hand and put his other one on her back. The music was romantic, and the night air felt like cool silk. And Cate felt perfect against him.

"Where did you go off to?" she asked.

"It was nothing. Some kids—joy riding without the car."

"Huh?"

"Three boys looking for mischief." He chuckled. "They reminded me of me when I was fourteen."

"Were you a hell-raiser?" She looked at him as if the answer were important to her.

"No. But I was always taking risks to help others. Once there was a flash flood when I'd been on the riverbank camping with some buddies. The rains north of us had been a deluge, but we didn't know it. We'd been too busy telling tall tales around the campfire. Drinking beer we'd taken from one of my friends' houses. I can't remember which one.

"The water appeared in seconds. Fortunately, I woke up first and ordered the others to hurry up the bank to the highest part of the hill. I was trying to rescue our tent and not doing a very

good job of it, when I heard a woman screaming. She was trapped in the water, flailing her
arms around. She yelled at me that she couldn't
swim. Without thinking, I dived in and got her
to shore."

"That was really brave," she said with a touch
of awe in her voice.

"Or stupid. But I've been doing that kind of
thing ever since. I wanted to save the world. I
still do."

"The world is a big place."

"And it needs saving."

Trent didn't think he'd ever seen a woman as
beautiful as Cate. Reflected lights from above
glittered in her hair as if she'd been struck by
fairy dust. It wasn't just her physical beauty, but
something from inside that shone through her
eyes. She was strong. Determined. Intelligent
and caring. She cared about her town enough to
risk her own life. Sure, he did the same thing,
but it was part of his job. He was different.
Most importantly, he was different around her.

He tugged her a bit closer, and she flinched.
"What's that?"

He realized she'd bumped his shoulder holster. Of course she would feel it being this close.

"Sorry. I'm packing."

She looked away anxiously. "Oh. I forgot."

And there it was. Tonight, she'd been pretending that she wasn't in danger. She'd taken a holiday from her situation.

He, on the other hand, was here as her bodyguard. Her protector. He was aware of every snap of a twig. Every light that flickered in the distance—wondering if someone with a flashlight or laser gun was out there waiting.

He held her with one arm while adjusting the holster with the other. Then he pressed her to him, her head nestled in the crook of his neck. "Is that better?"

"I'm sorry," she whispered. "I know you're here to...to take care of things. But while we are dancing, it all seems sweet, sort of like the senior prom I never got to go to."

"You never went to your prom?"

"No. I had Brad."

"Oh." His head jerked back as if he'd been shot. He knew her history, but it came at him differently hearing details like this.

The song blended into another Cole Porter tune that kept them holding each other. Trent didn't know where the notes ended or the next song began. All he knew was that he was holding Cate. It was his turn to get lost in the magic of the night.

He heard the guests as they left the dance

floor, got up from their tables and the metal chairs scraped the patio. The music kept playing and lulled him into a dream…

The explosion came from the distance.

And Trent was—*back there.*

An IED.

That's what it had to be. Or a land mine. Had one of his men left the safe area?

Another explosion. Then another. He heard shouting.

It was one of his men. Shot. Screaming. Bleeding. Dying.

Trent braced. He had to save them. All of them. It was up to him. It was always up to him.

He tasted Afghanistan dirt and sand. That awful fine-grain sand that cut like a razor. God. He hated that country. Hated the terrorists who stole lives as if it was their right. Fanatics were always part of human history, no matter the era or age, but Trent wanted to annihilate them and change the course of history.

"Trent!" Cate shouted. "Trent! Please. What are you doing? You're hurting me!"

"What?" He blinked. Once. Twice. It wasn't an IED. It was fireworks. Party fireworks for a wedding. That's all it was. He was in Indian Lake, not Afghanistan.

Cate broke away from him, pushing her

palms against his chest. He had her in strong-hold. Trying to keep her still. His hands were on her upper arms, holding her in a tight grip.

"Cate. I'm sorry. I—I…"

"What happened just then?" Her gaze bore into him. "You didn't hear me. You were…you were someplace else."

"I know."

"You do? Then what is it?"

It was the reason he could never let himself love any woman. *It* was the harpy that kept him cut off from people he wanted in his life. *It* was the monkey on his back.

And there was nothing he could do.

"Cate. I'm sorry. I shouldn't have done this."

"Done what? Hurt my arms?"

"Yes. No. Dance with you. I'm here as a po-lice officer. I shouldn't have let myself…go like that. I just can't."

"I don't understand," she said, stepping away from him.

That's good, he thought. *She should keep her distance. I can be a monster. One day my mind may snap and I may never come back, but I can't tell her that. Can't tell anyone that.*

That was Trent's greatest fear—that he would lose his mind and live forever in the war. A prison with no bars and no escape.

He looked at her. "The party is over. You need to get Danny and Mrs. Beabots and go home. I'll follow in my car. I'll watch your house all night."

She rubbed her sore arms. He hoped he hadn't bruised her, but he knew he probably had.

"Okay," she said, and walked away calling Danny's name.

Trent felt a cold breeze cross his face as she left. And he was alone—again.

CHAPTER SEVENTEEN

FOR THREE DAYS after the wedding, Cate had struggled with a sticky web of thoughts, assumptions and assessments about her feelings for Trent. One minute she was gooey with romantic visions, and the next she was ensnared, like a spider's prey, in a cocoon of distress.

Trent had unnerved her in the same way that Brad had right after they'd married. Back then, she'd thought she knew the man she loved, but she hadn't seen his dark side. It had snuck up from behind, stealthily, like a silent monster and grabbed her unaware. All these years, she'd promised herself she'd never fall into that trap again.

Trent wore honor and righteousness like a badge. Protection and kindness oozed from him, but as she'd let herself believe she might have feelings for him, possibly even be falling in love with him, his true self had been exposed.

Cate realized now that Trent wrestled with

demons. He was a good man. Yet there was something he was hiding. There had to be a reason he shied from relationships, but she felt his need to love.

If Trent wasn't ready to reveal his problems, then it wasn't her place to investigate. Perhaps he didn't trust her with his truths. Maybe he thought he'd jeopardize his case against Brad. Maybe he was beginning to have feelings for her in return. Maybe they both knew it best to keep their emotions dialed down.

Cate started making Danny's lunch for school.

Danny poured milk on his cereal and crunched happily while listening to the morning weather report on the television.

Boy, she'd really set herself up for that one, she chastised herself as she made his sandwich. She must have some kind of bad-boy homing device implanted in her psyche. If there was a troubled man within twenty miles of her, she managed to find him.

What was there about her that drew these men to her?

"Mom. Mom?" Danny said, getting out of his chair and standing at her elbow. "Why are you putting ketchup on my sandwich?"

Cate looked at the bread. Instead of mayo,

she'd smeared the bread with the ketchup she'd intended to add to the baked beans she was making in the slow cooker. "Oh. Sorry. I'll start over."

Danny frowned slightly. "I can do it."

"It's okay. I've got this," Cate assured him, forcing a smile.

Danny put his hand on her forearm. "Are you worried about me again?"

She looked into his upturned face. The summer freckles across his nose had faded now that the days were growing shorter and colder. Danny, Timmy and Annie had already turned to indoor play after school, but Cate couldn't blame all of it on the weather. They stayed indoors because they were afraid. All three kids knew about the police car down the block. As much as Cate, Sarah and Luke assured the kids that they were protected, the kids would feel the strain until it was over and Brad was in jail.

She felt it, too.

"I'm always worried about you. Things are just a bit more intense now, that's all."

"I'm not worried," Danny said confidently. "Trent will take care of everything."

"You think so?"

"Sure, Mom. Don't you?"

"I do." She nodded quickly and fought back her trepidation. She kissed his cheek.

"Yeah," Danny said, putting his arms around her neck. "I trust him."

"Good," Cate said, and stood once again. She put his sandwich together and shoved it into his insulated lunch bag along with his fruit and snacks.

"Okay. We're ready. I'll take you to school, and then I have an early-morning appointment for a walk-through on a house."

Danny put on his jacket and fumbled with the zipper. "Mom, I was thinking. We should invite Trent to dinner. You could make my favorite spaghetti. You haven't made that in a long time."

Cate had picked up her keys and purse, then froze. "Dinner? With Trent?"

"Sure. To thank him for helping us."

"You like him that much? I hardly ever invite a man to dinner with us."

Danny zipped his jacket and flipped the hood to cover his head. Then he grabbed his lunch bag. "Yeah. I noticed that."

Cate didn't know whether to laugh or keep a straight face. Danny was noticing all manner of things about their lifestyle that she'd never had the time or reason to explore.

Besides the fact that she needed to start paying attention to the details of her life, she also needed to staunch his blooming admiration for Trent.

Clearly, Trent was not the man for her. Keeping Danny away from him was impossible as long as the spotlight of the Indian Lake Police was shining on her and her son. Trent was a focal point in their life right now. But he wouldn't always be.

Trent and Brad apparently had some kind of genetic disposition for risk-taking. *Adrenaline junkies, both of them*, she thought. The only difference was that Trent chose the side of the law. Brad chose evil.

Light and dark. Good and evil. The battle was as old as humankind. It would never stop.

It wouldn't stop for her.

Unless she ended it.

"I don't think dinner with Trent would be a good idea."

"Why not?" Danny asked, crestfallen.

"Sweetheart," she said, putting her hand on his cheek, "Trent is just doing his job. He has to be nice to us because he's protecting us. Sometimes it seems like he's closer to us than other people, but the thing is, all the people in this town rely on him and the other policemen to take care of them. So, it's not that he doesn't like us. I'm sure he does. It's that we aren't special to him."

"Uh-uh." Danny shook his head so vigorously his hood fell back. "He is *so* my friend. I can tell." He tapped his forefinger to his heart, the way he always did to show her that he believed deeply in something or someone.

Danny's feelings had crossed into new territory for Cate. Not only had she felt drawn to Trent, but Danny had been experiencing emotions of his own. She knew she might be able to stash her feelings away in some mental file, but Danny was a child. Children didn't know how to turn feelings off and on.

But then, did she? Really?

Even more importantly, what if Danny was right? What if Trent truly was their friend? But nothing more. Nothing romantic. Children felt things more immediately than adults, and sometimes more intensely. At least Danny did. He wasn't the kind of self-centered child who was oblivious to others or the world around him. Danny was aware. Oftentimes, he was more aware than she was.

She was the only person who could put strings on a dinner invitation to Trent. For Danny, she would do it. For him she'd do anything.

"Okay." She smiled. "I'll send him a text today after my showing."

Danny scrambled over to the kitchen chair where she'd put her purse. He pulled out her phone. "Here. Call him. Tell him it's spaghetti!" Danny grinned widely.

"Fine." She took the phone and hit Trent's number. It rang three times and then went to voice mail.

"Hi, Trent. It's Cate. Danny is here with me, and he wants to know if you'd like to come to dinner. Spaghetti. His favorite. Call me when you get a chance. Thanks." She hung up.

Danny grabbed the phone and looked at the screen. "I forgot how early it is. Maybe he's in the shower." He stared at the phone.

"Yes, well, in the meantime, I have to get you to school, young man."

"Mom," Danny groaned, rolled his eyes and shoved his hood back into place. He trudged with slumped shoulders to the door.

CHAPTER EIGHTEEN

CLANK. CLINK. ZWOOP. Clink. Shunk. Trent successfully ejected the magazine from his Smith & Wesson M&P 45 semiautomatic pistol. He then racked the chamber to extract the remaining bullet. He disassembled the gun. Carefully he laid the bottom piece on the work cloth he'd smoothed out on his desk in his home office. He cleaned the gun methodically.

Holding the newly cleaned gun by the grip, he carefully put it back together. He tried the trigger. No resistance. No hitch to any of his movements with the slide or the trigger.

He shoved a full magazine of bullets into the gun. Racked it.

"Ready," he said to himself as he laid the gun on the battered desk.

The desk had been with him as long as he could remember. He'd learned his multiplication tables at it. He'd built model airplanes and plastic army tanks. He'd repaired his Star Wars toys and Transformers on this desk. It still bore a clump or two of glue from those days. Reminders that he'd had a childhood. That there had been a life for him before he'd gone to the Middle East.

Before *it* had all happened to him.

He looked out his apartment window. The trees were bare now. It was raining. Midnight and the town was dark. Silent. Much like his apartment. There was no music playing. No television station blaring the weather or the latest news.

Thanksgiving was approaching, and he supposed he should call his mother again. He tried to call her once a week—mostly so that she knew he was still alive.

He'd told her that he was working a case that wouldn't allow him to leave Indian Lake for the holidays. At least Thanksgiving. He'd have to wait to see about Christmas.

"What kind of case?" his mother had asked him.

"Never you mind. You know I don't discuss my cases with you." He'd chuckled, but half-heartedly.

"Dangerous case. That's what you're not telling me. That's why you can't come home for Thanksgiving. I hate not seeing you," she'd said with enough weight to her words that he knew her disappointment had gone deep.

"I'm sorry, Mom. It can't be helped. I can't promise anything, but if this case breaks—and I have good reason to think it will—I'll be home for a three-day, no make it a four-day weekend once it's over. I promise. I'll put up your tree. Take it down, whatever you want."

"A hug," she said in a way that threatened to rip his heart out. "You know, I could take early retirement and move to Indian Lake, and then I could see you all the time."

Trent bit his lower lip. The stinging truth was that he didn't want his mother within fifty miles of him. If she saw him more regularly, she'd know. She'd see he was still suffering from flashbacks.

Trent didn't want anything to interfere with his hopefully imminent apprehension of Le Grande and his nest of rattlesnakes. He wanted them all; every last one of them.

Trent had placated his mother with half promises of shopping in Chicago. Dinner at Gino's for a supersize pizza, knowing that she probably hadn't eaten well since he last saw her. She hung too much of her future on Trent.

Just like Cate.

Trent looked down at his gun.

All of his bulletproof body armor, tactical vests and lightweight ripstop fabric slacks hadn't protected his heart from falling for Cate.

Oh, he'd dodged her texts and managed to stay out of her line of sight when he checked on his men who tailed her. He'd declined her dinner invitation, even though he knew Danny would be deeply disappointed. He hated that. He liked that kid. Too much.

In some ways, if it was possible, he'd felt he couldn't be any more emotionally invested in Danny if he were his own son. If Cate was five seconds late picking Danny up from school, it terrified Trent. She didn't know that Trent never let her or Danny out of his line of sight every single afternoon. He watched them from between houses, behind cars, from the side of the church, wherever he thought she might not be looking.

But look she did.

He'd caught her always glancing around as she walked Danny from the doors of the school to her car. Each week, she'd traded rental cars, just as Trent advised. He was grateful she hadn't fought him on that issue. But every day he wondered if she was looking around for him—or Le Grande.

Was it fear that twisted her head and caused

her eyes to scan the playground? Or was she hoping to see him?

He had to leave her alone. Leave her behind. It was too dangerous.

Dangerous because if he slipped up—if he faltered in any way—his error could cost her life. Or Danny's.

If anything happened to Danny, Cate would always blame him. He'd never get close to her.

And he wanted to be close to her.

He swiped his face with his hand and was surprised to find cold sweat on his palm. Dang, he had it bad.

He pushed the chair away from the desk and went to the kitchen. He opened his small and very-used refrigerator and took out a beer. He popped the top and drank from the bottle. It was icy cold as it rushed down his throat. He hadn't felt all that parched a minute ago, but then he was getting used to Cate thoughts that too often wiped his senses clean.

He put down the beer. The only thing he really wanted to put his mouth against was Cate's lips. But it was past midnight.

Just then his phone pinged. He plunged across the room to the coffee table and grabbed it.

Trent read the text from Richard Schmitz.

You need to come to Chicago. I've cleared it with your chief.

Trent tapped his phone to call. If Richard had news about Le Grande, Trent wanted to hear it now. Not in the morning.

"Schmitz," Richard bellowed.

Trent could hear sirens, someone barking orders in the background. "What's going on?"

"Can you drive here? Now?"

"Now?" Trent looked at his watch. Then he dropped his arm. He went to the desk and picked up his gun. "It's Le Grande, isn't it?"

"Yeah. I'll text you the address where we are."

"We?"

"I've got Homicide here. And an eyewitness."

"I'll be there as fast as I can."

"Turn on your lights. This is official business," Richard said, and hung up.

Trent grabbed his tactical vest, keys, cash and a car charging cord for his cell phone.

Le Grande had killed someone.

CHAPTER NINETEEN

FIFTY-FIVE MINUTES LATER, Trent knelt and looked at the bloody face of the man Le Grande had murdered.

Flashing police car lights pierced the night as news teams filmed the scene. A young female newscaster was describing the scene to her camera operator. Her photogenic youth and beauty seemed surreal against the dilapidated projects behind her. Behind a strip of yellow plastic tape stood a handful of residents, their breath creating fog and the only warmth in the bitter November night.

The first-response teams had finished their jobs and hopped into their trucks. Sirens pealed through the air.

The pandemonium around Trent faded into the distance as he focused.

Richard stood behind him, talking to his forensic team members, both of whom were packing up their gear.

Though Trent's mind absorbed their conversation, cataloguing details and pertinent information, he was more interested in Richard's homicide team and the facts they'd gathered in the ninety-seven minutes since the nameless victim had been shot.

The medical examiner's forensic pathologist had issued cause of death as a homicide. He'd handed the onsite certificate to Richard so that he could continue his investigation.

Trent stood. "Who is he?"

"We have no idea. Personal effects turned up two knives, five bucks and a packet of cocaine."

"Was he illegal?" Trent frowned.

"According to our informant, he's Colombian and had only been here a week." Richard nodded as the medical examiner's team brought over a black plastic body bag.

Without pause or reverence, they shoved the body into the bag, loaded it on a gurney and rolled it into the van.

Trent glanced at the spray-painted outline of the sprawled body on the frost-killed grass. "And now he's dead." Odd that this guy's death affected him. Trent had never been squeamish. He had the kind of psyche that compartmentalized the job from reality. But this murder victim was a thread that connected him to Le

Grande, and that connection, in turn, brought Trent back to Cate.

He chewed the inside of his cheek, not breaking skin, like he always did when ruminating a case. "What about the eyewitness?"

Richard tipped his head and said, "I've got him in my car. Hank got him coffee and a sandwich. He's given us quite a statement."

Trent felt his neck hairs stand at attention. "How's that?"

"He was with Le Grande when he shot the guy."

"So, he's an accessory?"

Richard's mouth curled up on one side. "He wants witness protection. And for what he's telling us, we'll give it to him."

"And you're taking him downtown?"

"Not yet. You're here unofficially, but before the guys in Organized Crime Bureau get hold of him, I thought you might want to talk to him." Richard was nearly as tall as he was, and when he took a step closer and scoured Trent with his intense scrutiny, Trent held his breath.

"Continue."

"You and I are in this together. No one in the Bureau of Detectives knows about your scheme to lure Le Grande to Indian Lake. I could be reprimanded for not disclosing my part in it.

But, if it works, we'll get citations. Honestly, I think it's going to work."

Trent licked his dry lips and swallowed hard. Obviously, Richard was aware of the danger Trent had put Cate and Danny in, but until this moment, Trent hadn't known he'd also put Richard at risk.

"I wanted you to see this guy, but I can't actually let you talk to him. Let me do the talking. You just feed me the questions. If word of your involvement got back to my chief…"

"I got it." Trent put his hand on Richard's shoulder and gave him a reassuring squeeze. "I've got your back."

"Let's do this."

They walked to Richard's unmarked Camaro. Two uniformed officers stood close to the hood. They were young and no doubt fresh out of the academy, given the way their gazes kept sweeping the scene. They nodded to Richard, but barely looked at Trent. They didn't appear to register the fact that Richard was accompanied by a civilian. Trent carried his badge as he always did. He practically slept with the thing. Now, however, he wished he hadn't brought it because his presence could cause trouble for his friend.

Hopefully, Trent's plan would be executed

without glitches. He'd planned carefully. He'd stick to the plan.

Trent watched through the rear window of the car as Miguel answered Richard's questions.

Richard leaned down and looked at the thin, dark-haired man sitting in the back seat of his car. "You're Miguel, right?"

"Sí." Miguel looked at his hands, which nervously slid up and down his thighs, so much that Trent thought the guy would wipe the indigo from his jeans.

"I need to ask you a few more questions," Richard said.

"No. No more. I tell you everythin'," he mumbled.

"Oh, there will be lots of questions if you want witness protection."

"Wyoming. I want to go to Wyoming."

"You want a lot, Miguel." Richard's face was implacable. "But if you answer all my questions, I'll see what I can do."

"Okay." Miguel continued to rub his jeans.

"So you were the wheelman for Le Grande, is that right?" Richard asked.

"I drive. Only drive. Not kill."

"I get that. Okay. So, why do you think Le

Grande killed this guy? He's from Colombia, yes?"

"Yes. Medellín in the coffee region. He told me he hates coffee."

"Why's that?" Richard asked.

"No money. Money is in cocaine."

"Yeah. Go on."

Miguel inhaled deeply, and his words came out in Spanish at first. He stopped himself and started over. "Javier, that his name. He brought excellent cocaine. But when he sold on the streets, he take half the money for himself. He think Le Grande stupid. Javier think all Americans fat and stupid.

"Le Grande—he is *loco*. He screaming and hitting me because Javier steal the money. Le Grande say, 'I'll teach all you rats I'm the boss. I rule your life!'"

Miguel stopped, his voice hitched. Slapping his hand over his mouth, he closed his eyes. "He kill Javier to show us."

"Show you what?"

"That he the boss. He the king. He say, 'I am king in Chicago.' But I always think—" Miguel tapped his temple "—that he not."

Trent tapped on the roof of the car with his finger to get Richard's attention. Richard straightened and looked at him.

"Ask him if he knows about Indian Lake? The bust? The money?"

Richard nodded and leaned into the car once again. "So, Miguel. We know that Le Grande disappears from Chicago from time to time. Do you know where he goes?"

"*Sí.* Indiana. He has plans there, he say."

Trent was nearly out of his skin. He swiped his face and tried to remain patient.

"Tell me about these plans, Miguel," Richard said.

"He found a place where he can meet his partner."

"Partner?" Trent said aloud.

Richard remained cool. "Did he ever name this guy?"

"Triple X. From Detroit."

Trent curled his body around the roof and side of the car, wishing he could meld into the metal and hear every nuance, every breath, every tick of Miguel's eyelids lowering. Triple X was the biggest cartel in Detroit. For years, the Feds, the Detroit Police Department and CPD had tried to connect the Detroit gang to the drugs being run out of Chicago.

"Le Grande say he leaving Chicago and move to Indiana." Then Miguel laughed.

"What's so funny?" Richard asked.

"Le Grande say he has family in Indiana. He live with them now."

Trent leaned down and looked in the window. Miguel was shaking his head. Chuckling. Slapped his palm against his thigh. "*Loco*. He told my gang brothers long time ago he has *no* family. That why he make all of us in the gang never to see family again. Le Grande is the family." Miguel leaned his head back and laughed, tension and disbelief spilling out of him.

Richard stood and looked Trent squarely in the eye. "We need to talk. While my detectives take Miguel downtown and process him, let's get something to eat."

ROSE'S DINER WAS open all day and night, and everyone in South Chicago knew that their late-night cook served up extra gravy and larger portions, ostensibly to sober up the drunks before they drove home. Illegally. But then in South Chicago, few people cared. Except the cook.

Trent slid into the red plastic booth, and before hc'd picked up the menu from behind the jukebox selector, a gray-haired waitress with deep wrinkles around her eyes and red lipstick bleeding into the lines around her lips had plopped down two ceramic mugs and asked, "Coffee? Leaded or unleaded."

"Leaded," Trent replied.

"Same," Richard said. "I'll have steak and eggs. Gravy on the biscuits."

"I remember, honey," the waitress said, and winked at Richard.

Trent smiled. "Come here a lot, I see."

"What about you, handsome?" the waitress asked, taking out her pad and pen.

"Same. No gravy. But the cheese grits."

"Good choice. I'll be back with the coffee in a sec." She left.

Trent leaned back in the booth. "You need to shut up."

"I haven't said a word," Richard said with splayed hands. "What?"

"You want me to close it down."

Richard looked at his watch. "Ten minutes and I'm off duty. On duty, I have to say yes."

Trent rubbed the back of his neck. "Le Grande has upped the ante."

"Certainly has."

Plopping his arm on the table, Trent said, "I agree with you. I should flush this whole strategy of using Cate to lure him into the open. Le Grande is slippery as an eel. He plays a wicked game of chess."

"Your busted-up bust didn't help. But this... Trent, we're talking homicide now. And if what Miguel says is true—"

"I believe him."

"Me, too."

"That's why I'm not going to stop now." Trent curled his fingers in to a fist. "I'm nearly there. He's walking into my trap." Trent stared at his hand. All he saw was Cate's face. He heard Danny's voice, saying his name the way he did—suffused with hero worship.

"You can't do this, Trent. Think about it. Le Grande is now wanted for murder. If he crosses the state line, the Feds will be all over this. It will be out of our hands."

Trent drummed his fingers on the table. "What if he lied to Miguel to throw everyone off? What if he's moving to Detroit? Or Toronto?"

"Possible."

"But not likely. He'll show up in Indian Lake. He wants Cate. But what if you get your inside man to tell Le Grande that there's a new buyer for his drugs from Detroit? We set up another sting, using the fifty grand we recovered from Le Grande's warehouse. Then I use undercover cops to pose as the Detroit buyers. I could put a day and time on it."

"Trust me," Richard said, "Le Grande names his own days and times. That's how he stays invisible. Even to his own guys. My man in there says he gives them orders to make a buy at a certain time, then changes it. If I didn't know better, I'd say there's a cop on the take somewhere."

"You suspect your man?"

"No. Never."

"How can you know?"

"He's my son."

Trent's eyes widened. "I didn't know you had a kid."

Richard smiled. "I'm even married. I do have a life, you know."

Trent ground his jaw. That was more than he could say for himself. "That's great."

Richard finished his coffee. "I'm in this to win, but my worry now is that to our knowledge, this is Le Grande's first murder. Once he has tasted first blood, he'll be unstoppable. I want him off the street, and my son will be out of there."

Trent stared at his fork. "It's risky. But we need to force Le Grande to action. I say we do it."

Richard leaned closer. "The Feds find out

about a cockamamie gig like this, we're both busted back to patrol cops."

"Who's gonna tell 'em? Not me. If I lost this job, I don't know what I would do. Because if that happened, I'd lose Cate, too."

Richard's eyes flew open. "Lose Cate? What are you talking about?"

Trent felt like he was hemorrhaging emotions. Hot. Oozing. Draining. Losing Cate. The thought of never seeing her again. Holding her. Kissing her. It was too much to endure. He would just as soon be dead himself.

Le Grande had now committed murder— just to make a point. He'd done it blatantly. An in-your-face snub at the cops. CPD with their billion-plus-dollar budget didn't faze the guy. Le Grande was a sociopath with no sense of consequence or boundaries.

"Richard," Trent began, "I don't know how it happened, but this woman and her boy have come to mean something to me."

Richard dropped his forehead to his hand. "Don't say it."

"I love her. I know that now."

Richard looked up. "Then you gotta take yourself off the case."

"She doesn't know how I feel. In fact, she thinks I'm…well, indifferent. I need to keep it that way. At the same time, I know the only way I can protect her is to be even closer to her. I'll put myself on twenty-four-hour detail. I won't let her out of my sight."

"You're in too deep. Shut it down."

Trent stared back at Richard. Willful. Rigid.

"Once the Feds come in, you have to step away."

"When that happens, I will. I know the protocol, Richard. Trust me, I'm not going to be foolish. And I'm not going to lose my job over this. At the same time, I will get Le Grande."

Trent felt conviction rattle through his body. He'd never been so sure of anything in his life. Bringing down Le Grande would happen. He would risk his life for Cate. Die for her. He didn't know when or how he could tell her that.

Maybe never.

CHAPTER TWENTY

CATE HAD NEVER seen anything like it. Thanksgiving à la Mrs. Beabots was a production worthy of a Broadway opening. When Mrs. Beabots asked Cate to help her with shopping, flower arrangements and food preparation, Cate had gladly agreed. Little did she realize that Mrs. Beabots would need help for a full week.

"I've counted twenty-five guests," Mrs. Beabots said as Cate placed Royal Worcester casserole dishes on the island. Mrs. Beabots dragged a box filled with sacks of potatoes, carrots with long green tops, mesh bags of white pearl onions and enormous butternut squash out from under the island. "Thank goodness my table seats twenty-four." Mrs. Beabots beamed as she put the potatoes in the sink.

Cate gulped and looked at Danny, who stood on a step stool, an apron tied around his waist, as he polished silverware. He turned his head, his eyes wide. "All twenty-four? Eating in the same room? At the same time?"

"Why, yes, dear," Mrs. Beabots said. "I have leaves upon leaves to open it up. Luke is coming over tonight to help put the table together. I haven't had this many people since Raymond was alive. Oh, how he loved to entertain. We had such lavish parties. I decided this was the year I was going to do it again."

"What's so special about this year?" Danny asked.

Cate was curious, as well. "Yes. Why now?"

Mrs. Beabots fluffed the ruffled edge of her apron and winked at Cate. "I'm not getting any younger. That's the truth of it. One of these days, all you girls will be married off and gone, and I won't have anyone to share this with."

Cate saw sadness in Mrs. Beabots's face. Like the slap of reality that it was, Cate had taken Mrs. Beabots's presence for granted. They were more than just friends. For Cate, maybe for Danny, too, in the few weeks that she'd been living in this house, she felt as if Mrs. Beabots was family.

She put her arms around Mrs. Beabots. "I'm glad you chose this year. And I'm so glad we're here to help you."

Mrs. Beabots lifted her hand and wiped

away Cate's tears. "Me, too." Cate saw that Mrs. Beabots was about to cry.

She watched as Mrs. Beabots lifted her chin, shook off her gloom and turned to Danny. "You don't mind doing the silver, do you, Danny? If you do, Annie will polish it. She tells me she likes cleaning silver."

"She does?" Danny halted. "I mean, I like it, too. It's kinda fun to get the black stuff off. And I can see myself in the spoons."

"Good boy," Mrs. Beabots said. "Now, Cate, you know how to make cranberries, don't you?"

"Open the can?"

"Blasphemy!" Mrs. Beabots chuckled. "They're so easy and so good. Here's a three-quart saucepan. We'll make two batches. Everyone eats mine like crazy. The sugar is there in the canister on the center of the island." She pointed to a blue-and-white porcelain French canister that read Sucre.

Mrs. Beabots used a small potato peeler and skinned a large orange. Then she took out two nutmegs. "Here, Cate. Chop the rinds very fine and add them to the cranberries, sugar and water. Then grate nutmeg into them. Put them on the stove on medium-high heat and cook the berries until they pop."

"That's it?" Cate asked as she did as she was instructed. "This is amazing."

"After the berries cook, we let them sit and gel. Now, on to the creamed pearl onions in sherry sauce. We'll make the broccoli soufflés and put them in the second refrigerator in the pantry. I make my stuffing ahead…letting the sage sit a couple days enhances the flavor. Sarah and Luke are doing the two turkeys."

"*Two* turkeys!" Danny exclaimed.

Cate could practically see his mouth watering.

"Of course. And a ham. I have a lot of people to feed. That's why Sarah said she'd do the turkeys. I don't have enough oven space. Honestly, I've thought about having another oven put in. Over there where the baker's rack is."

"Wow. Two turkeys," Danny repeated. "So cool."

"Then we'll make the pies tomorrow."

"Pies?" Danny whirled. "You aren't buying them? Mom always does"

Cate had just placed the saucepan on the stove. "He's right, you know. I've never seen a Thanksgiving like this. I was raised differently, I suppose." Cate's Thanksgivings hadn't been all that different from any other day. Except for the parades on television. Her father slept all day on the sofa since it was his day off. Her mother bought a turkey, mashed potatoes and gravy, and a pumpkin pie at the grocery store already cooked. Cate's sole job was opening the can of cranberries and leading her parents in a Thanksgiving blessing that she learned when she'd stayed overnight at Mary Kelly's house, where they prayed all the time over food.

Mrs. Beabots's smile was knowing and gracious as she looked at Cate. "I'll bet if we compared notes, our backgrounds might be quite similar. I wasn't raised to cook or entertain, either. I learned it. That's what life is all about. Going down different roads. Exploring new ways. After all, it's the only life you have. Why not do it up!"

Cate felt her smile encompass her entire body. Yes. Why not do it up right? Hadn't she been doing that? Since the day she'd left Brad, she'd been doing the right thing. But was she still on that path? She'd agreed to help the Indian Lake Police capture him. But was it the right thing for her? For Danny? What if her decision was the wrong one?

Mrs. Beabots had lived so many more years. She had eagerly agreed to step up and help Trent. In fact, it had been Mrs. Beabots's willingness that pushed Cate forward. Even now,

Cate wondered if she would have done this alone, without encouragement.

Probably not. She would have run.

In the end, she wondered if she was courageous at all. Maybe she'd just joined the enthusiasm in the room that night she and Trent had come to Mrs. Beabots.

Cate's thoughts scattered. She jumped when Mrs. Beabots said her name.

"Cate, I didn't think you'd mind."

"Mind?"

"I asked Trent to join us for Thanksgiving dinner."

The dust motes dancing on the beams of sunlight that streamed through the window seemed to stop. The grandfather clock in the hallway ticked. Then tocked. Swung its pendulum. Time had not stood still. "Trent."

"Yes, dear. He has no family in town, and he's practically glued to the house these days. I see him in a different car day and night."

"You do? I didn't. I thought he'd disappeared."

"Oh, he changes vehicles every few hours."

"Really? How wily of you to notice," Cate said, her curiosity piqued.

"I notice a lot of things," Mrs. Beabots replied in a sweet singsong tone.

"I see that," Cate replied. "I thought his clipped answers to my texts were because he was undercover somewhere. You know, smoking out the bad guys."

"Oh—" Mrs. Beabots smiled as she picked up a ham-size butternut squash and raised a chef's knife "—I think he's doing precisely that."

TRENT TOOK A picture of the dazzling Thanksgiving table, resplendent with dozens of glowing tapers and votives in fall colors, and the center sprinkled with miniature gourds, fresh ivy and sunflowers in squat vases. He texted the photo to his mother, then shoved the phone in his jacket pocket. "What can I help with?" he asked Cate as she carried the cranberries to the table.

"Gabe is opening the wine. Will you make sure everyone has a glass? We're still making vegetables."

"Still?" He glanced over her shoulder toward the kitchen. "I thought I saw at least a half a dozen casseroles in there."

"Oh, you did," she assured him. "Now we're making fresh green peas. Grilled Brussels sprouts and steamed broccoli."

"Amazing."

"You have no idea," Cate replied as Danny rushed out of the kitchen. "What have you got there, Danny?"

"Turkey-shaped butter. Annie made them. Her mom showed her. They have a mold, she said." Danny handed them to Trent. "Here. I'll get more."

Trent smiled as he looked at the butter. Then at Cate. "He's excited."

"We've never had a Thanksgiving—or any holiday—quite like this," she said, taking the butter plates from him and placing them at each end of the table. "Living with Mrs. Beabots has been a revelation for him. He likes it here."

"He's with good friends." He moved closer, thinking that every argument he'd used to keep his distance from Cate had been faulty. "And what about you?"

"It's been—" she held her hands in front of her "—magic."

"What?" He couldn't have heard her correctly.

"It's like a fairy tale being here."

"But in the middle of a nightmare, as well."

"Aren't all fairy tales threatening? The dark villain? The white knight saving the princess?"

She was driving him mad standing this close. Each time she glanced at him with her aqua eyes, brimming with trust in him, hope in him, his breathing rattled in his chest. If he touched her, he'd be branded for life, and he'd never escape her.

He was in love with her. Completely. He was all in. She could crook her finger and he'd come running. Dance to her strings. Play her games. He didn't care. He would walk through eternity to find her.

Yet he was the one who just might have signed her death sentence. And if they all lived, the kindest thing for him to do was to walk away. She deserved a guy who was fresher. His PTSD hadn't abated over the years, though the military therapists said that it could.

He'd been so immersed in his work that he'd learned to live with his flashbacks and night terrors. He'd accepted his situation because there'd been no reason to try anything new.

There hadn't been Cate. Or Danny. There hadn't been a reason to heal himself.

He could hear everyone in the parlor clapping for Gabe and Liz as they poured their first bottles of last year's trial burgundy and pinot noir. Gabe was making a speech. Scott Abbott laughed. Liz cooed to her baby. He heard Nate tease Gabe. He heard Jack and Austin McCreary coming from the kitchen talking about tennis as they challenged Rafe to doubles. From inside the kitchen were the sounds of female voices—Mrs. Beabots, Sarah, Maddie, Olivia, Katia, Isabelle and Sophie—talking over each other. Children's laughter.

They all had a story. They all had their own fairy tale. Now Trent found himself in the middle of his own. But was he the white knight or the evil dragon keeper?

"I know why you haven't called me. Or texted much," Cate said, putting her hand on his wrist.

He wished she wouldn't do that. She'd feel his pulse, tripping like a jackhammer. "You do?"

"Mrs. Beabots told me that she sees you switching cars, moving your position out front all day and night."

"And I thought I was the detective," he said, trying to joke.

Cate's expression was unyielding. "Something has happened. Right? Otherwise, why would you make such a change up?"

"I can't say, Cate. You have to trust me on this." Trent knew from Richard and his intel that Le Grande had taken the bait about a big drug buy in Indian Lake. Richard's son had informed them that Le Grande was driving all over Illinois and Missouri meeting with Mexican drug dealers, buying cheap heroin, which he would cut and then sell to the Detroit gang.

Trent had gone to his chief and secured the fifty grand that had been kept locked in the evidence room at the station.

Trent had also asked the mayor for an additional fifty grand in marked bills to sweeten the deal. The mayor stated the city could not take the risk. However, she found a concerned citizen who agreed to supply fifty thousand in cash.

Trent didn't know who the wealthy concerned citizen was, but he suspected that person might be Austin or another of Mrs. Beabots's Thanksgiving guests, if it wasn't the hostess herself.

A tinkling bell rang loud enough to pierce the conversations. "Everyone to the table!" Mrs. Beabots announced. "Trent? Would you bring in one of the turkeys?"

Without thinking, he took Cate's hand from his, kissed her palm, squeezed it reassuringly and said, "Of course."

Mrs. Beabots signaled to Nate. "You're a surgeon. Will you bring the other turkey and carve it at the table for us? All of you have name cards. Find your seats."

Cate helped bring in the last of the steaming vegetables and dinner rolls.

Trent wasn't surprised that Mrs. Beabots had placed him next to Cate. Danny was to his right and Annie was next to Danny with Timmy on her right. There was a strain of the matchmaker about Mrs. Beabots that was both charming and, in his case, alarming. Ironically, being close to Cate was exactly where he should be.

Because Le Grande was amassing drugs for the setup buy, it was Trent's bet things were about to bust open. That being the case, Trent needed to alter his strategy.

He couldn't move in with Cate, though the idea was tempting. She'd never stand for it. Oh, she was being pleasant to him, sociable and hospitable, but he noticed the way she nervously tapped her forefinger on the knife handle. And was that a tiny tick in her lower eyelid? She looked lovely, but tired. Sleepless nights? Nightmares? Fear drained the best people. He'd experienced that in Afghanistan.

"Sam," Mrs. Beabots said. "Would you say grace for us?"

Everyone at the table held hands and bowed their heads. Trent reveled in the feel of Cate's skin against his. She might have been nervous, but the electricity that surged through her shattered him. He held her hand firmly. Confidently. She made no move to acknowledge a similar reaction on her part. She kept her head bowed.

He watched her out of the corner of his eye. The late-afternoon sun was dimming, and the flickering candles cast ethereal light on Cate's blond hair. The nearness of her, the intimacy of the moment took his breath away.

The prayer ended. Trent raised his head before Cate did, and when she opened her eyes, he saw they were misted. Rather than release her hand, he squeezed it. He whispered, "Everything is going to be all right."

Her smile was disbelieving.

Gabe was the first to stand and raise his wineglass. "To our lovely and most gracious hostess, Mrs. Beabots, who has performed the miracle of the year by bringing all of us together. To Mrs. Beabots!"

"Cheers!" they said in unison. "Happy Thanksgiving, everyone!"

Trent held his wineglass toward Cate and whispered, "To the bravest woman I've ever met."

She inhaled deeply, as if taking strength from the atmosphere in the room. Her shoulders straightened, and she lifted her chin as she pierced him with a hope-filled gaze. "Thank you, Sir Galahad."

It was Trent's turn to be nervous.

Trent slugged back his wine and reached for the crystal decanter that held the red wine. He poured a second glass. It was going to be a long holiday night.

CHAPTER TWENTY-ONE

CATE DIDN'T KNOW whether to scream or burst into tears. From the moment Trent arrived, she tried to be civil and not ruin this magical holiday feast. But the fact was he confounded her. The house was filled with good-looking men, but when Trent entered the kitchen, his presence overshadowed everyone and everything.

She knew Mrs. Beabots saw it. Probably Sarah, as well.

Had she been so tongue-tied that all she could say was "Hello"?

He'd been complimentary about the busyness in the kitchen. Had given Mrs. Beabots a kiss on the cheek. Showered Sarah with that radiant smile of his. And then he'd walked over to Cate as she made the gravy—her hands and apron sprinkled with flour and bits of chopped fresh sage still glued to her fingertips—leaned down and whispered in her ear, "Happy Thanksgiving."

The assault of his fresh-laundry scent nearly

made her forget how hurt she was. She'd closed her eyes, thinking she could block him out of her senses.

Foolish move, Cate.

There was no way around it. Trent was her narcotic of choice. She thought she wanted to be free of Trent because that was the way he wanted it—wasn't it?

Jack had come into the kitchen to fill the ice bucket. He shook hands with Trent and they left the kitchen together. But not before Trent had glanced over his shoulder and mouthed the word *later* to her.

She couldn't believe it. Where was the apology she'd been waiting for? An explanation for the distance she felt between them? Ever since Mrs. Beabots had told her she'd invited Trent and he'd accepted, Cate had anticipated talking to him. Getting some answers.

She lifted the whisk, fighting the urge to pitch it at the back of his skull. *Later?* They would do what? Talk? Then not talk for weeks? Or worse, she'd fall into his charming trap and kiss him again.

Cate didn't understand him at all. She didn't understand herself, either. Granted, she hadn't had many men in her life, only one, and her relationship with Brad hadn't taught her how to decipher Trent's actions.

Now here she was, sitting next to him at the dining table with all their friends to distract her, yet all she cared about was the magnetic attraction between them. When they were apart, it was as if he'd left the planet. To her mind, he went to extremes to avoid her.

And she'd had just about enough of it.

Then they'd had the toasts, and he'd said she was brave.

That had done it. She melted just like the turkey-shaped butter sitting too close to the votive candles. She put her napkin in her lap. She was a mess.

"I need to talk to you," Trent whispered as he leaned dangerously close.

His breath curled around her earlobe and set her heart on fire. "About what?" she asked quietly.

"Things. Everything," he said. "After dinner."

"After dinner everyone is invited to Gina's house for dessert and champagne. I'm driving Mrs. Beabots and her pumpkin pies."

Trent shook his head as he cut a piece of turkey. "No. I'll drive all of you, if you must go."

"Of course we're going. Danny is counting

on it." Why was it so difficult to concentrate on the conversation when she had a hundred other questions she wanted to ask him?

"Fine. But in my car. I rented a minivan. Cate, I have to talk to you. There are things I need to explain."

"Explain?"

Though his fork was halfway to his mouth, he put it down and slid his hand to her knee. "I'm sorry. So very sorry. I owe you an apology. An explanation. I owe you a lot."

Cate thought her lungs had collapsed. "What are you saying?"

His blue eyes expressed sincerity. Was she reading him correctly? She was angry with him. She was ready to take him to the mat, tussle, anything to assuage her ragged emotions. If she could end this pointless longing for him, she could move on. Or go back to being the Cate Sullivan she'd been before Trent. Before she'd agreed to help him.

But that was impossible because none of this was Trent's fault. It was Brad.

Austin chose that moment to ask Trent a question from across the table.

There was utter pleading in Trent's voice that she'd never heard from any man. She'd never studied the law, but she knew the verdict before she knew the extent of the crime. She'd forgive him. Anything.

"Mom, can you help me cut this turkey?" Danny asked.

"Sure, sweetie," she replied, and leaned over his plate. "I see you've eaten all the potatoes. Now try the Brussels sprouts."

"Aw, Mom," Danny groaned. "It's Thanksgiving."

"I know. Eat something green. Try the broccoli soufflé."

"I like that," he said, and speared a piece of turkey as Cate sat back.

Trent's arm was draped over the back of her chair. He was still talking to Austin, and now Rafe joined their conversation about car engines.

"My police car looks like a standard Crown Vic, but it's been reengineered. The engine is a Mercedes that will do 189 miles an hour. Zero to sixty in three point three seconds."

"I had no idea," Rafe said.

Austin took a sip of wine. "I have that very same Mercedes."

"Hardly," Trent said. "I got mine from a Chicago junkyard and did the work myself. Cops are only as good as our tools."

He looked directly at Cate.

A dozen images of fleeing across the country in Trent's ramped-up car skittered through Cate's mind. When his hand moved to her shoulder and then swiped across her back, she felt a waterfall of chills across her skin.

Austin and Rafe went back to talking about cars and tennis. Trent dug into his meal, but his gaze continued to scan the table.

For the first time, Cate realized that even now, on Thanksgiving, he never stopped investigating. Not that he suspected anyone here of wrongdoing. This was something else.

She settled into her meal as he had.

The clinking of a fork against a crystal glass got everyone's attention. Luke stood. "I propose that since Mrs. Beabots was kind enough to cook for us, we should all do the dishwashing."

"Absolutely!" Nate and Mica said in unison. Everyone raised their glasses. "Agreed!"

"Well, then," Mrs. Beabots said, "Cate made half the dishes you're enjoying. She shouldn't have to clean, either."

"Cate, too!" Trent led the cheers.

"And Gina is having us all to her house for the dessert. Gina should be exempt as well!" Maddie exclaimed.

Cheers went around the table again as Gabe stood and refilled wineglasses.

Trent turned to Cate. "Fortuitous."

"What is?"

"I need time alone with you, Cate. Is there somewhere we can talk before I drive us out to the Barzonni villa?"

"Yes." She settled her eyes on his. "The gazebo at the back of the garden. I'll meet you there after dinner."

"Thank you."

CATE WHIRLED THE aqua throw around her shoulders and felt a trifle guilty about not cleaning up with the others as she walked down the flagstone path to Mrs. Beabots's gazebo. Pools of golden light from the huge Victorian house formed lacy patterns on the frozen ground. Chrysanthemums bloomed in the beds around the carriage house as if defying the coming winter.

She saw Trent standing in the framework of the opening, tall, broad shouldered and strong. Amazing. If she saw him a dozen times a day, she knew she'd always catch her breath. She'd want to stop and stare, to question if he was real.

He reached for her hand to help her up the steps.

So gentlemanly. So mannered.

"I'm sorry I took so long. I had to make sure Danny put some things together in his overnight bag."

"Where's he going?"

"To Sarah's to spend the night with Timmy."

Trent hesitated, though he still held her hand. She could tell he liked touching her. However, she felt his apprehension.

"What's wrong?" she asked.

"I have so much I want to talk to you about. But since you brought up Danny, we should start there."

She pulled the throw around her and folded her arms over her chest. "Okay."

"Let's sit." He gestured to the bench.

His physical presence was a buffer against the coming storm. And there was going to be storm. That part she knew.

"There have been some developments in our case. We had thought that once Le Grande discovered your existence here in Indian Lake, he'd make a grab for you."

"And it hasn't worked."

"Not yet. I can't tell you all the particulars, but we're setting up a sting. I am confident that we'll arrest him while he attempts a drug deal."

"So, what about Danny?"

"Until the bust goes down, I don't want you

and Danny separated any more than is necessary."

"Oh." She heaved out the word with so much dread, she felt her ribs contract.

"I need you to tell me every single plan you have each day. Because it's the holidays, I know that you'll want to shop and decorate. All those things that moms do for their kids."

"Yes, I do. Christmas is Danny's favorite time of year. We're going to get our tree on Sunday."

"Where?"

"The tree farm just north of town."

"We'll go together."

"Together? The three of us?"

His eyes were penetrating. "Cate, it goes further than that. I'm never going to be more than a few feet away from you."

"What? How will you manage that?"

"I'm moving in with you," he said bluntly.

"Whoa! Wait a minute!" She held up her palms. As if she could actually stop this train wreck. She'd asked for this, hadn't she? By wanting Brad out of their lives, she'd forced Trent to come in. "I don't think—"

"I didn't say that right." He chuckled. "What I'm going to do is rent the couch downstairs at

Mrs. Beabots's. If anything happens, I'll be on the premises."

"This is serious."

Trent flung his head back and took a deep breath. When he lowered his head, his lips were nearly on hers. Nearly. "Frankly, I thought we would have apprehended Le Grande by now. We have the best man on the inside. Recently, one of his gang members became an informant for us. But whenever a buy goes down, Le Grande disappears. He's like a ghost. At the same time, he's become more greedy and aggressive." He paused for a long moment.

"In fact, Cate, I wish I could move you out of Indian Lake altogether and put you in witness protection—"

"You want me to run?"

"But we can't. We're so close."

This time she took his hand in hers. Held it between her palms, feeling the calluses. "I told you," she said firmly. "I'm done with running. I have a life here and I'm not going to give it up. I don't want Danny to think I was a coward. I want him to see his mom as brave. Just like you said I was earlier."

"You are brave, Cate." He placed his forehead against hers. "I've never met anyone like you."

"Then don't ask me to leave."

Silence.

He touched his nose to hers, but didn't kiss her. He put both his hands on her cheeks and slid his thumb along her jawline. Splayed his fingers across her temples and into her hair. "You make me nuts. You know that, don't you?"

"No."

"Well, you do. I vowed to keep you safe—"

"Trent. You said that Brad has become more aggressive. What are you not telling me?"

She felt his fingers tense.

"Trent? What has he done?"

"Murder. He's murdered one of his gang members."

"Here?"

"No, in Chicago."

The marrow in Cate's bones seemed to freeze. She was numb. She was stone. Her emotions withered inside her. Panic, fear and the terror she'd lived with for weeks fizzled. She felt her heart slow. Reality fell into place.

Cate didn't care if she survived any of this anymore. She wanted only two things. Danny's safety. And revenge.

She wanted Brad behind bars with two life sentences. She wanted him to pay for every second of pain he'd caused her and Danny.

And she wanted Trent to be the cop who put him away.

Facts sifted into a bullet list in her brain. "And that's why you've been hovering so close?"

"Yes."

"But that's not enough now." She scarcely recognized her own voice it was so devoid of emotion.

"No. It's not."

"So, your plan is to accompany me and Danny wherever we go until Brad shows up?"

"Yes. I'll be by your side until it's over."

She took his hands from her face. "And what about after that?" she asked, her voice still cold as the coming December snow.

"After that?"

"Where will you be after you catch Brad?"

Trent lowered his eyes. Inhaled deeply and retracted his hands. "That's the other thing I have to talk to you about, Cate."

"So, talk to me." She nearly bit her tongue. Her future happiness rested with Trent's every word. She had to listen carefully.

"You have to know that I care about you, Cate. I can't stop thinking about you."

"And that's why you don't answer my texts or phone calls? Or if you do it's a one-word reply? Come on. I may not know much about men and relationships, but I do know that even being a good friend requires effort."

"It's not like that for me. I wanted to call you a dozen times. A thousand times. But I can't."

"Because I'm just a case to you—"

He grasped her shoulders and pulled her close to him. "I'm in love with you, Cate, and nothing could be worse."

"You're what?"

"I'm in with love you."

She didn't understand. Why was loving her a bad thing? Why did it scare him so much? Then it hit her like a wrecking ball. "There's someone else."

He shook his head. "There's no one else. Not for six years. I was engaged once. In Afghanistan. She was American. Military. But she broke it off."

"I'm sorry, Trent," she said.

"You see, Cate, I couldn't be with her any more than I can be with you. Or anyone. I'm not marriage material."

"Whatever it is, Trent, you can tell me. Please." She put her hand on his strong jaw and forced him to look into her eyes. "We can work through anything, but we have to be honest with each other. I've told you everything.

A drug-dealing, now homicidal, ex-husband." She tried to laugh, but failed. "I'm doing this to put Brad in jail where he belongs—where he can't hurt anyone else. But you also have to know I'd do anything for you, Trent."

"I know that, Cate. That's why I don't want to hurt you." He swallowed hard. "When I was on a mission in Afghanistan, my best buddy got blown up right in front of me. I went into shock. We completed our mission, of course, and I got the rest of the men out safely. But the incident—it messed me up. I have flashbacks and nightmares. I kick and scream at night. I fall out of bed. If you were in bed with me, I could strangle you in your sleep. That's why I can't be with you."

Of all the confessions she'd expected, this wasn't it. This was real and frightening. All this time, his PTSD had kept him from living his life. From loving. Cate felt her heart stretch. She wanted him to have safe harbor with her.

"Don't you see? We can never be together."

Cate's heart tripped, fell and stopped. Never? Cate didn't believe in never. She couldn't let Trent think like this. He looked lost. She wanted desperately to help.

"Lots of people have post-traumatic stress. Including me."

"What?"

"You don't think I could go through what I did with Brad and come out of it as normal as one of Mrs. Beabots's apple pies, do you? I got professional help. That's what you have to do. Once you have therapy—"

He backed away and crossed his arms over his chest. "You really don't understand. I had the best shrinks the military could provide. Overseas and stateside. I went through all kinds of programs. Even medications. Nothing worked. I talked until I was empty. None of it did any good. In some ways, it's gotten worse."

Cate was afraid to ask, but she plunged ahead. "How?"

"The flashbacks. I can't tell anyone about them. I especially can't tell my chief or my team. I've never breathed a word about it... except now, to you. I feel I can trust you." His eyes were filled with intensity.

"Yes. You can trust me."

He exhaled deeply, withering breaths fading into the chilled night air. "It sounds like nothing. Flashbacks. How much harm can they do? Right? That's what most people think. But they come, and they cause problems. Big, big problems." He placed his elbows on his knees and stared at the gazebo floorboards. "It was my fault that we didn't capture Le Grande on that sting."

"Your fault?"

"In the middle of the fracas, he'd started to escape and just as I pulled my gun on him, I had a flashback. I was back in Afghanistan. I felt the dry, sandy air on my skin, and smelled lamb being grilled. I heard their voices speaking in Pashto and some Dari. The warehouse had faded away. I saw my friend being blown to pieces. It was only a few seconds, but it was enough. And because of my flashback, my hesitation, Le Grande is a threat to you. To Danny. Even to me."

When he lifted his head, his eyes were flooded with tears. Cate ached for him. Trent. So immovable and sure of himself. Certain of his plan and his ability to save them all. Trent, upon whom she'd relied since that moment when he asked her to join forces with him to bring Brad to justice. It was because of his commanding qualities, his leadership and his unshakable commitment that she agreed to become his bait.

All this time she'd felt a closeness to Trent so unprecedented, it had both exhilarated and frightened her. Though she'd been wary because he was a cop, she'd found it harder to sustain her fears the more she'd come to know him.

She loved him, and she knew it now more than ever. He'd been reluctant to tell her the truth about himself, which was understandable since he was her protector. But what was he really saying?

She had to know the truth. All of it.

"Danny worships you, Trent," she said, though her throat had constricted with emotion. The tension inside her had built like flood-water behind a dam.

She managed to continue. "When this is all over, Danny's not going to understand if you just vanish."

"I feel the same about him, Cate. I do," he replied. "If he was my own, I couldn't love him more. Or want more for him. But I'm not so naive as to believe that just because we care for each other, everything will be smooth—and, well, right—for us." He fumbled the words, and she could tell he was holding on just as much as she was.

"PTSD is a terrifying thing to live with, Trent," she said, taking a step closer to him. "I had no idea you were going through this." She reached out, feeling that if she could touch him, somehow her empathy would give him hope. Even a cure, though she, of all people, knew that wasn't possible. For too many soldiers, war victims, refugees, trauma victims, the night terrors never died. They might disappear from time to time, but they were always there, lurking, and seeking a new tunnel, a perfect time to reign again.

She'd been there. That was one reason she'd agreed to help Trent. If she did this, helped to lock Brad away, she would finally be safe. She'd have closure. She could move on. She'd be free to love again.

"Trent, listen to me. Psychiatry is making breakthroughs all the time. You should at least give it a try."

"I want there to be a cure. I do. But nothing worked in the past. I don't know, Cate. I just don't know."

Her heart broke for him. She slid her hand up his arm and felt his heat through the tweed jacket. It felt like centuries since his strong arms had encircled her. She wanted to help him, but all she felt was resistance. "I know it's scary. You're probably thinking that if you hope for real results and then don't get them, you'll be right back at square one."

His sharp intake of breath told her she'd hit the truth. "Exactly. Then I would have pulled you and Danny along with me, dreaming of something that could happen for us. And then doesn't."

His eyes were uncharacteristically deadened. He was defeated, and she didn't know how to bring him to the surface of the abyss that had swallowed him. He was focused on saving her. Saving Danny. But he wouldn't save himself.

"Trent, I've never seen you like this."

"Yeah?"

"I mean it. This isn't like you. You're always the one to take charge—"

"This is the real me." His words were so sharp she felt as if she'd been bitten. "Got it?"

She pulled away. "Got it."

"You can't help me, Cate. No one can," he said angrily.

She stood and looked at the back of his head.

"If you don't try, then there's nothing I can say, is there?"

"No. Not really," he said under his breath, and slowly lifted his head to look at her. She could have sworn she was looking at a stranger. Maybe he was right. She didn't know him at all.

"Then I guess we're done here."

"I guess so."

Cate wrapped her throw tightly around her shoulders and walked toward the sound of happy voices and laughter coming from the house. She left Trent behind and told herself that he was part of her past. Just like Brad.

CHAPTER TWENTY-TWO

CATE'S NEW KNOWLEDGE about Trent lodged in her brain like a well-read encyclopedia volume. But this one seemed full of questions, not answers. *If you love me, why won't you fight this syndrome for me? What happens to us once you capture Brad? Will you be in court when I have to testify against him? Will you still want to see Danny? How do I explain to Danny that you don't want to be his new father? How can you live without me? How can I live my life without you in it?*

"He needs more blankets," Mrs. Beabots said, coming out of the linen closet and handing a down pillow to her.

"Who does?"

"Trent, of course," she said, piling a set of sheets and a Hudson's Bay wool blanket on Cate's outstretched arms. "I told him he could stay in the library. I could get one of those blow-up beds. But he insists on sleeping in that drafty parlor." She shut the linen closet door.

"Oh, it's fine in the summer, I quite enjoy it, but in winter, he'll freeze."

Cate followed Mrs. Beabots to the parlor. Outside the windows, the porch furniture was covered for the season, though Mrs. Beabots decorated everything for Christmas.

Cate looked at the Victorian red velvet settee. "There's no way Trent can sleep on that. It's too short."

"That's what I said!" Mrs. Beabots stated, plopping two blankets on the settee. "I suppose he could pull the ottoman up and use that for his feet. But he insisted."

"I don't understand," Cate said, handing the rest of the linens to Mrs. Beabots.

"He said he has to watch the street." She harrumphed.

"Oh," Cate replied, feeling the magnitude of Trent's plan. "I know what he's thinking. He's not planning to sleep."

"Apparently not. But the least I can do is keep the boy warm." Mrs. Beabots walked around Cate and motioned with her arm. "Come along. I'm making hot cocoa for our trip, and Trent is meeting us in twenty-five minutes."

"Trent is doing what?"

Mrs. Beabots whirled around and faced Cate with a look of shock. "You can't have forgotten? Danny has talked of nothing else since Thanksgiving."

Thanksgiving.

Cate hadn't thought of anything except Trent. She'd gone through the motions of helping clean up after the Thanksgiving party. She'd packed up Mrs. Beabots's Thanksgiving decorations and ordered Christmas presents online. She'd phoned her clients and checked in with her boss. She purposefully had not left the house... Trent's orders. He'd been across the street at the police station for the past day and a half. She hadn't seen him once.

Tonight she would. He would be sleeping here. In the same house.

"But it's hours till Trent finishes at the station," Cate said, looking at her watch.

"He's not there anyway, dear. He said he's on his way here. He's taking us to buy our Christmas tree. Like he promised Danny." Mrs. Beabots leaned closer and peered at Cate. "You did forget, didn't you?"

"The tree. Right. Today. Ten thirty."

"That's right. Now go up and get Danny. I'll make a thermos of cocoa, and when Trent gets here, we'll be on our way."

Cate felt as if she were tethered in place. These were familiar fears. The ones that held her back. Kept her from living her life. Brad had created them and used them to seduce her into marrying him. Used them to make her think she needed him. They were the fears all abusers used to trap prey. All this time with Trent, she'd never felt those fears. She'd felt like Cate. Independent. A survivor. An accomplished woman.

She'd clipped those fears from her life once before. She could do it again. Right now. This minute. She wasn't going to let Trent's stubbornness stop her. After all, if you loved someone, weren't you supposed to help them? Show them new possibilities?

"I'll get Danny, and we'll both help you," Cate said brightly. "Some marshmallows would be fun."

"THIS IS A really cool car, Trent," Danny said for the third time as they pulled up to Jarod's Tree Farm. "I'm really glad you got it."

Trent parked the SUV and turned off the engine. "Like I said, Danny. It's a rental. Just like the other cars I'll be driving from time to time. It's not mine to keep. Besides, I like my car better anyway."

"That's right, Danny," Cate said, opening

the passenger door. "Trent's own car is very special."

Cate opened the back door for Mrs. Beabots.

Danny unhooked the seat belt on his booster seat by himself. "What makes your car so special?" He waited for Trent to open the door and then climbed out. He stood looking up at Trent with mischievous anticipation. "Does it have wings?"

"Close." Trent chuckled. "It has a Mercedes engine. It can go nearly 200 miles an hour."

"Awesome sauce!"

"Come on." Cate laughed. "Let's find the perfect tree for Mrs. Beabots."

"Oh, good heavens," Mrs. Beabots said, twirling her Burberry scarf around her neck. "I chose my tree months ago. I'm just here to pick it up."

"What?" Cate asked.

"I do it every year. Once I decide exactly what theme I'm going to use for my decorations, I select the right kind of tree."

"Theme?" Trent cocked his eyebrow. "You mean you don't put all your memorabilia on the tree? Little ornaments made of popsicle sticks and pipe cleaners?"

"Bite your tongue, young man. Haven't you seen that great big carriage house of mine?"

"Sure," Cate and Trent replied in unison.

"Well, it's packed with ornaments, and all are different themes. One year I did a Harlequin theme. Black, gold and white, with masks and clowns and feathers. One year was all angels and Renaissance musical instruments. But this year I want to do my Jackie tree."

"Jackie?" Danny asked.

"Kennedy. When she was First Lady, her Christmas trees for the White House were pink, turquoise and gold. I bought all my ornaments to match hers exactly."

"And you still have them?"

"Certainly. Enough to fill a twelve-foot Douglas fir." She walked proudly ahead of them. "Oh, Jarod! There you are, dear. Is my tree ready?"

Jarod Hart was forty-three years old, tall, broad shouldered and claimed to anyone who asked that he had a major crush on Mrs. Beabots. He rushed up to her with open arms and hugged her, lifting her off the ground.

"Jarod, my goodness! You'll give Trent and Cate the wrong impression," Mrs. Beabots said as he set her on the frozen ground.

"Don't you go teasin' me." Jarod laughed and kissed her cheek.

Mrs. Beabots smacked his arm playfully and smiled up at him.

It was the first time Cate had ever seen Mrs. Beabots flirt with a man. Jarod didn't take his eyes off her. Cate couldn't help thinking she needed to spend more time with Mrs. Beabots. She was learning all kinds of things from the older woman.

Jarod leaned over with an outstretched hand toward Trent. "Jarod Hart. How'd ya do?"

"Great," Trent said with a smile. "Trent Davis. This is Cate Sullivan and her son, Danny. They'd like a tree for their apartment, as well."

"No problem. I've got Mrs. B's tree all bundled up for her." Jarod looked over Mrs. Beabots's head toward the SUV. "That your car?"

"It is," Trent replied.

"We can just tie it to the roof. No biggie." He rubbed his hands together to ward off the cold, then lifted them to his mouth and blew on them. "Now, what kind of tree do you want, Mrs. Sullivan?"

Cate's eyes roamed over the rows of uncut trees. "I'm not sure. I heard you had trees that were only ten dollars."

"That would be the Scotch pines. They're only four feet tall…"

"That's plenty for us," Cate said. "My decorations are still at my hou— Uh…in storage. Danny and I were going to make cookies and hang them on the tree."

"Yeah," Danny said delightedly, "and string cranberries and popcorn. We already bought three boxes of candy canes." Danny grinned widely. "I like candy canes."

"Can we get both trees on top of the SUV?" Trent asked.

"I don't think it's a problem at all," Jarod answered. "Mrs. B's tree is nearly thirteen feet this year. I put the stand on it myself. It's a beauty. Just like she likes it."

Cate leaned down and said, "Do I want to know how much your tree cost?"

"More than yours, dear," was all Mrs. Beabots said. "I gave him my credit card over the phone."

"Oh," Cate said, digging in her purse for the ten-dollar bill she'd put aside. "Is it extra for you to put the wood stand on mine for me?"

Jarod glanced at Mrs. Beabots and then back at Cate. "Since you're a good friend of Mrs. B's, no charge."

"Thanks," Cate said, and held out her hand to Danny. "C'mon, sweetie. Let's find the best one."

Trent stood back as Cate and Danny went down the row of pine trees.

They'd inspected six or seven trees when a light snow began to fall.

"Look, Mom!" Danny lifted his face to the snow. In moments, the snowfall grew heavier, the flakes looking like feathers floating down to earth. "The angels are shaking their wings," Danny said, closing his eyes.

Innocence. Purity. Trust.

Danny was the embodiment of all these to Cate.

"You're my angel," she whispered.

Danny opened his eyes. A snowflake landed on his eyelashes. He closed his eyes.

This was a moment Cate knew she'd lock in her heart forever. She looked up and saw Trent watching them. Gone was his stern and interrogating stance. His shoulders had softened. A smile bloomed slowly across his lips, and his eyes twinkled at her like stars. It was the look she remembered from those frightening nights when Brad had first appeared and Trent had been there to hold her. Comfort her.

Trent didn't move, but his eyes carried a thousand messages to her, and all of them spoke of love.

He loved her. She knew it, and no matter how much he protested that he wasn't good for her, she knew otherwise.

Danny opened his eyes, righted his head and stretched out his hand. "This one has magic, Mom. Let's buy it."

Cate didn't take her eyes off Trent. His gaze was unswerving. "Yes," she said. "Magic."

CHAPTER TWENTY-THREE

TRENT HAD HELPED Jarod tie two Christmas trees to the roof of the SUV. Just as they started toward town, the pewter-gray skies sifted fat snowflakes across the rolling farmland and divided highway. As they passed a two-story white clapboard farmhouse with green shutters, Trent noticed the couple on the wraparound porch hanging a wreath on the front door. Adjacent to the house, two black-as-night horses bent over a stash of hay just inside a fenced-in corral, oblivious to the snow.

"Mom, look at the horses!" Danny exclaimed. "Just like the song. Dashing through the snow."

"That's right," Cate said, and suggested they all sing Christmas songs.

It had been a long time since Trent had felt like singing or paying the least attention to holidays. If it weren't for his mother's pleading, he'd miss Christmas altogether. He liked the way Danny substituted words he didn't know for the song. He especially liked the sound of

Cate's voice and the way that she glanced at him from time to time, making sure he was joining in the fun. He almost felt he was a part of their...

Life?

No. Impossible, Trent. Get your head where it belongs.

They all kept singing. Trent couldn't help dreaming and asking himself, *what if?*

Trent had gone along with "Jingle Bells," but by the time Mrs. Beabots started singing "Winter Wonderland," Trent glanced in the rearview mirror and realized that the red Jeep Cherokee behind them hadn't passed them when several other cars had. Trent was driving five miles under the speed limit due to the trees on the roof.

Danny sang in a voice so clear, Trent encouraged him to try out for the children's choir. This set off a new round of discussion and kept Cate and Mrs. Beabots busy conversing with Danny, giving Trent a chance to scope out the driver.

He could see two men in the front seats and a third in the back. They were young. The driver wore a hoodie and had the hood pulled down so far that Trent had a hard time making out any of his features, though he thought he saw black hair falling over the man's forehead. He couldn't make out the man in the backseat at all.

They'd entered the city limits, and Trent slowed the SUV. He thought seriously of taking a page from Cate's playbook when she'd circled Indian Lake when Le Grande was following her. The difference was that she'd been alone. He had three passengers. He couldn't risk their safety.

Trent drove down Main Street and stopped at the light to Maple Boulevard. He eased into the left-turn lane.

The snow was coming down in full force. He turned on the wipers. The headlights were already on. He watched for the Jeep. It was six cars back in the through lane. He wasn't being followed.

He exhaled. When the green arrow lit up, he turned left. It was only four blocks to Mrs. Beabots's house.

Trent parked at the curb so that he could untie the trees and take them through the front door.

Trent used his pocketknife to cut the twine that held the trees. He hoisted Cate's short pine tree off the SUV roof and placed it on the ground.

"Our tree! Now it's really like Christmas!"

Danny said, clapping his hands as Cate grabbed the tree and started up the walk.

"If you'll hang on a minute, I'll help with that," Trent said.

"Should I call Luke next door to see if he can help you with Mrs. Beabots's tree? It's awfully big," Cate said with a smile that warmed Trent more than a mug of hot cocoa.

"Nah, I've got it," he assured her, and walked around to the side of the SUV. He grabbed the tree, hauled it off the roof and held it over his head.

Just as he did, he heard a car driving toward them. It was going fast. Too fast. Trent's inner alarms jangled. He looked up at the red Jeep.

This time, all three men were staring at him as if they knew him.

Le Grande's gang! Trent instantly recognized the driver from the mug shots Richard Schmitz had sent him.

Trent pitched the Christmas tree to the ground with no more effort than if the Douglas fir were a toothpick.

"I'll be back!" he shouted at Cate and Mrs. Beabots, and shot across the street, over the boulevard, across the other side of the street and to the police station parking lot. He took his car keys out of his pocket and hit the remote before he got to his vehicle. He jumped in the car, turned the engine and peeled out of the lot.

At the crosswalk, he turned the car in the opposite direction and sped past Cate, Danny and Mrs. Beabots, who stared wide-eyed at him.

He turned on his siren and lights.

"This time, I gotcha."

The Jeep was no match for Trent's Mercedes engine. In seconds he was right on their tail as they hit the southbound highway out of town. There was little traffic, but the snow was coming down thick and heavy.

Trent wasn't about to let even a whiteout stop him.

The Jeep driver hit the gas rather than slow down.

It was just as Trent predicted—criminals made mistakes. An illegal car chase with police would land these yahoos in the can for a month.

He reported to dispatch his location and asked for backup.

The Jeep increased its speed, and so did Trent. They careened around a pickup truck and a Prius, but kept going. The snow made the highway slick, but the greater danger was the fact that it was becoming nearly impossible to see any vehicles ahead.

"Add reckless driving. Keep it up, boys."

Before the Jeep topped 90 miles an hour, Trent overtook them doing 110. He rolled down his window and motioned for them to pull over.

The Jeep tried to lunge ahead.

Trent heard sirens in the distance.

He pressed his foot to the gas and sped ahead, then wove just close enough to them to let the driver know he intended to force them off the road if he needed.

The Jeep slowed. Trent kept pace. It was possible they could brake hard and spin. Crash both cars. Kill them all. If they were high on the heroin they sold, there was no telling what they would do. They were loose cannons. Unpredictable and a hundred times more dangerous than sober perps.

The sirens behind him grew louder. Trent could see the flashing lights through the snowfall, making everything look like a winter wonderland.

Before the three backup cops arrived, the Jeep had slowed and pulled off to the shoulder. Trent stopped behind them. By the time he got out of his car, one of the backup cops had shot around to the front of the Jeep and parked his car so that the Jeep driver couldn't take off. The other two cars parked behind Trent.

He was glad to see Sal Paluzzi and shook his hand. "One of these guys is wanted by CPD. Check out the others. I'm betting they're all Le Grande's men."

"Good work, Detective."

"Not really. Apparently, they were on to me. I don't like it." He looked up at the Jeep and watched as the other officers handcuffed the three men.

"What are my marching orders?" Sal asked.

"For now, take these guys to the station and book them. I'll be there in half an hour to fill out my report."

"Where you goin'?" Sal asked.

"I left a Christmas tree on the sidewalk. Once I get it taken care of, I'll meet you at the station."

Sal smiled. "A Christmas tree? Never thought I'd see the day."

Trent playfully socked him in his bicep. "Funny."

Trent got back in his car, buckled up and drove to the U-turn in the median. He topped the speed limit getting to town.

These men had surely called Le Grande and told him that Trent was hiding Cate at Mrs. Beabots's house. Trent took a measure of comfort in the fact that he'd be sleeping in the parlor at Mrs. Beabots's tonight.

He gripped the steering wheel and straightened his back. He was determined to keep them all safe. He had promised Cate.

CATE'S HEAD WAS filled with a constant replay of Trent tossing Mrs. Beabots's monstrous tree onto the sidewalk and bolting across the street to his car. She hadn't seen anything that would cause her to worry or be on alert. But Trent had. Before she'd dragged her little tree to the front steps, four police cars had shot out of the police station lot and raced past the house, lights flashing, sirens screaming. Danny had covered his ears. Mrs. Beabots had looked unfazed. She'd turned to Cate, adjusted her vintage Chanel purse on her shoulder and said, "Trent is taking care of business, I see. Let's go inside and worry about the trees later."

Cate had yanked the tree another few feet, but Mrs. Beabots was already walking quickly toward them both with her hands out to her sides as if herding geese.

"Inside."

Mrs. Beabots had ushered them into the kitchen where they hung their coats on the white wooden pegs in the back entryway. "I'll make us some tea," she said, hustling to the sink to fill the painted kettle. "Danny, would you like a cookie? After all that work picking out a tree, I should think you're famished."

Danny's eyes grew wide and wary as he shot a glance at Cate. "Can I, Mom?"

Cate didn't miss the wink Mrs. Beabots gave her. "Sure. But just one."

"I'll make a large pot of strong tea. Trent will want some when he gets back," Mrs. Beabots said, turning on the gas stove.

"Did he tell you that? He just took off so strangely..."

Cate hadn't known what to think of his actions. Her first thought was that he'd gotten some kind of text from the dispatcher. Obviously, he was still on duty, though he'd told her that she and Danny were his primary case.

"He didn't have to. I know my way around police fairly well," Mrs. Beabots replied with mixed tones of assuredness and vagueness. She was forever dropping hints about things that could only relate to her past.

"You do?" Cate wasn't about to let this one go. For one thing she wanted to know if Mrs. Beabots knew aspects of Trent's character that Cate had missed or overlooked. Secondly, there was the woman herself who was one of the most interesting mysteries in town. Perhaps it was because Cate had told so many lies about her own past that she was curious about Mrs. Beabots. Cate had seen too many tap dances instead of direct answers to questions from the elderly woman. No, there was something here. She knew something.

"Of course, dear. I've been on the board for their Widows and Orphans Fund for decades. That's only the beginning." Then she busied herself with the tea, cookies and lemon slices.

"I'm sure," Cate said, and helped carry the tray to the front parlor where they could watch for Trent's return.

Within twenty minutes, the snow stopped and Cate could easily see his car as he pulled in to the police station lot. He sprinted across the street, picked up the huge Christmas tree and rang the bell.

Danny abandoned his cookie, and raced to the door to welcome Trent with a huge hug.

"Hey, buddy. Now, Mrs. Beabots," he said as Cate and Mrs. Beabots had walked into the foyer, "just exactly where is the tree going?" He smiled brilliantly at Cate, never taking his eyes from her face.

She felt herself blushing. And putting her hand to her cheek. And looking away as if his stare would turn her to jelly or dust or something unpleasant. She wondered if Mrs. Beabots could see that, too, with her finely tuned sensitivities.

Cate took her cue from Trent who obviously was not about to tell her anything. "I've placed a plastic tarp in the library where Mrs. Beabots wants the tree this year."

"In the corner next to the fireplace," Mrs. Beabots added.

Danny scrambled past Trent and Cate, shot down the main hall to the library and flung open the huge mahogany pocket doors. "In here! This is where Santa will come down the chimney!"

She and Trent placed the tree and righted it. He wired the trunk with some fishing line to a hook screw he'd placed in the wall next to a gilt-framed portrait of Raymond Beabots, with permission from Mrs. Beabots.

When they'd finished stringing the lights, it was dinnertime. Mrs. Beabots, who gave the impression that every meal was a culinary extravaganza, ordered pizza. They sat on the library sofa, eating and talking about the position of lights.

"After we finish our pizza," Trent said, "I'll

get your tree upstairs for you, Danny. You can put the lights on tomorrow."

"Thank you, Trent," Cate replied, reaching for another piece of pizza at the same time as Trent. Their hands skimmed each other. The zing she felt was familiar but still stunning. She dropped the slice. "Sorry."

"Did you want that one? It has more sausage."

Heaven help her, she looked into his eyes and melted faster than snow on a spring day. He quickly turned his head and asked Danny a question about Christmas, and Danny launched into his near-delirium over the upcoming school pageant.

All Cate's thoughts focused on Trent. Tonight he would be sleeping in the front parlor. He was downstairs. Right beneath her bedroom. Yet, he could have been a million miles away.

She knew now the wall he continued to build between them was due to his PTSD. She wished she could show him how wrong he was—allowing himself to be a slave to a disorder that was treatable. She wanted to help him, but he allowed barely any conversation between them. Every topic was inane and shallow. Polite chatter. And heartbreaking for her because she wanted so much more.

True to his word, Trent put up the little tree, said good-night to her, hugged Danny fiercely, then ruffled his hair. "Go have your bath and say your prayers," Trent said. "I'll be right downstairs." He looked at Cate meaningfully. "I'll be working on my report on my laptop so that I don't have to go to the station to file it. I can just email it in."

In that space of mere seconds, she believed she could hear his thoughts. He wanted to say more to her, be more to her, give more to her. But it was as if barbed wire and trenches had been erected between them. Things were what they were. She was his charge, and as such she was his duty he had to perform. For some reason he didn't believe that he could find treatment, even a cure. He'd been wounded so long he was used to it. It was his comfort zone.

What he didn't know was that Cate was determined to wrench him out of that place and show him that maybe he could have a different life. A better life.

"See you in the morning." Danny waved as Trent left the apartment.

"Mom? Earth to Mom?" Danny poked her cheek with his forefinger. "Do you think Trent will really be there to see me in the Christmas

pageant? I beat out four kids to be the angel."
He puffed out his chest. "He just has to see
me!"

"I know for a fact that he wouldn't miss it."

"But what if he has to go away? Like today?
You know, on an emergency?"

"Then I'll video your performance on my
phone."

"He just has to see me," Danny said with a
sigh that only a six-year-old could expel, filled
with expectation and devastation over promises
not kept by adults.

Cate enfolded him and held him close, smell-
ing baby shampoo and the vanilla shower gel
he loved so much. "Trent would do anything
for you, Danny."

Danny hugged her back. "Then can we ask
him for Christmas dinner, too?"

"Sure." She released him and finished but-
toning the top button of his pajamas.

"What about asking him to come on the Candlelight House Tour with us?"

"Uh-huh."

"And what about Christmas Eve? He could
go to church with us. And open a present with
us. I got him something, you know."

Cate sat back on her heels and held Danny by
the shoulders. "When did you do this?"

"Mrs. Beabots and I went shopping. She helped me," he said proudly. "I bought yours, too."

"And where did you get the money for this?"

"Piggy bank." He rolled his eyes like she was clueless. "Where else?"

"My goodness. You're way ahead of me."

He nodded as he climbed into bed. "I know. But you have to work, and that takes up too much time."

"It does." Cate and Danny recited his prayers.

"And God bless Mom, Mrs. Beabots, Annie, Timmy, Mr. Luke and Miss Sarah and my friends and especially Trent." Danny smiled at her, held out his arms and hugged her.

"Now close your eyes," she said as she shut the bedroom door and went to her room.

She showered, washed her hair and dried it. She slipped on a pair of flannel pajamas she'd bought on sale at the discount store. They were thin and would never keep her warm enough, but she was too tired to put on a cardigan. Instead, she climbed into bed and drew her knees to her chest.

She wondered if Trent was warm on the sofa. Did he sleep soundly after that car pursuit, which he couldn't or wouldn't tell her about? Did he think about her even half as much as she thought about him? And if he did, what were his thoughts?

Did he think of what Christmas would be like if he spent it with a little boy who adored him and a woman who'd come to love him?

Did he believe in Christmas miracles?

Cate knew she did. She expected miracles.

CHAPTER TWENTY-FOUR

THE BULLET PIERCED the window, spiderwebbed the antique glass and entered the wall three and half feet from Trent's head. Only half-asleep, his adrenaline and training slammed him into high alert. He rolled off the sofa, pulling his gun off the ridiculously tiny table he'd moved closer to the sofa, where he'd also placed his cell phone in case Cate needed him.

He crawled to the window just as a second bullet pierced the window at the far end of the room and penetrated the plaster wall. Trent peered down Maple Boulevard.

"Drive-by," he grumbled as he grabbed his cell and dashed through the door to the hallway, unlocked the front door and raced down the steps and out to the street. The motion lights went on. He knew the cameras were rolling. Maybe they got a shot of the car. He saw enough of the taillights to know the vehicle was a dark sedan. He would bet it was Le Grande. Or one of his minions.

Trent lowered his gun and looked at the house. He'd heard three shots. Two he'd seen— at a distance that was much too close for comfort. He couldn't see where the third had gone.

He punched in the station number on his cell and got Ned. He reported the shooting and asked for Forensics to come by…

Ned told him he'd call back with an ETA.

Trent looked upstairs. Cate's bedroom light illuminated. "Cate!" *That third bullet.* His heart sank and his breath froze in his lungs. If she'd been shot— If anything happened to her, to Danny—

Trent's only family was his mother, but at this moment, the love he felt for Cate and Danny overtook him like a tidal wave. Black thoughts swept through his head.

If these goons injured Cate or Danny…

He raced into the house and took the back stairs to her apartment two at a time. When he got to the door, he tapped lightly, not wanting to wake Danny if he was asleep.

Anxious and breathing rapidly from the exertion, he tried the door. It was locked. The one time he wished she wasn't so careful. He knocked again. "Cate. Are you okay?" he said loud enough to be heard—if she was conscious. Not bleeding on the floor…

He heard footsteps. Soft and muted. She was wearing slippers, he thought.

Cate flung open the door. "Trent, what's going on? I heard something that…was it gunshots?"

"Yes."

"Are you okay?" She scanned him head to toe, her eyes lingering on his chest; then traveled up to his face—hypnotizing him. She was all right. He wanted to pull her into his arms and hold her there next to his heart—forever.

"Trent?"

"Huh?" He glanced down and realized he was wearing only a T-shirt, sweatpants and he was barefoot. He'd gone outside in the snow barefoot and hadn't noticed.

"Is Danny awake?" he asked.

"He slept through it. What's going on?"

He reached for her hand. "Come downstairs. Let's talk in the kitchen. I don't want him to hear."

In the kitchen, Trent sat on a stool at the island. Cate stood. He put a hand on her shoulder and then let it run the length of her arm. Then back up. For some reason he needed to touch her.

"Cate, the police are going to be here in a

few minutes. I believe Le Grande or one of his men shot up the house just now."

"They shot at the house?" she asked incredulously. Her hands flew to her mouth as if to take the words back and somehow make the nightmare vanish. She stared at him.

"It's happening. He's come for me."

"I believe so."

She started shaking and sank onto the stool opposite him. "Cate, I know this has been your fear, but I think it's more than that. He knows the cops have fifty grand of his money. Not to mention the fact that we have even more of his heroin. We've put a real chink in his business. That's a lot of incentive."

She shook her head. "Did he really try to shoot me?"

"No. The shots were random. A drive-by. Gangs use them for intimidation. They want you, er, us, to be afraid."

Her eyes bore into his like searing irons. He flinched, nearly feeling a sharp pain. "Well, it worked," she said. "I'm terrified. I want to go somewhere safer."

He understood her feelings perfectly. In her position, he'd want the same thing. But if she left now, he might lose the edge on Le Grande that he'd spent all these weeks building. Trent believed that Le Grande shot up the house not only to scare Cate, but also to give Trent a warning. True, Le Grande probably didn't know where Trent was sleeping—exactly. But Le Grande's men would have told him that Trent was hanging around Mrs. Beabots's house. Trent would never forgive himself if any harm came to Cate or Danny. Ever. At the same time, he was as certain as he could be that Le Grande was falling for their sting operation.

This drive-by was a tip-off that Le Grande was getting desperate. Le Grande was planning something, but Trent didn't know what. He might be trying to make a grab for Cate.

Trent had a choice. Cate wanted to leave and she should. It was her right and duty to protect her son.

Or he could talk her into staying and helping him. She'd been willing before, but bullets raised the stakes.

"Cate. You're right. I should get you out of here," Trent said, taking her hand.

Just then, he heard the door to the stairwell creak open. Danny stood in his pajamas, robe and slippers, wide awake.

"How long have you been standing there?"

"I just got here," he said sheepishly. Then as he moved toward them, his voice grew stronger.

"You just said you wanted to go away. Mom, we can't do that. Monday is my pageant." He put a hand first on Cate's knee, then on Trent's. He raised pleading eyes to them one by one. "The kids are counting on me. Especially Annie. She rehearsed with me. I know all my lines." His voice cracked in the heartbreaking way of a child facing broken promises.

"Oh, Danny." Cate pulled him into her arms.

Trent watched them, remembering the night when Le Grande had invaded their backyard. They'd been terrified, and Trent had been their savior. He'd held them both, and it had been like coming home. He knew that now. He cared deeply about them. Loved them. He couldn't believe what he was feeling was make-believe. He had to protect them—somehow. Some way.

"Okay. Here's how it will go. You'll have your play and be the star you know you are. I'll be there, and I'll have my entire team there. Undercover, but present. But right after the play, I'll have things set up so that we can leave town." This time he looked directly at Cate. "I can't risk either of you any longer."

"Thank you," she said, and reached for his hand.

When she squeezed his fingers, he felt the warmth all the way to his soul.

"No-go on my detectives sitting at some kid's play. Not with what we know now," Chief Stan Williams said to Trent.

"What do we know?"

"Here," he said, handing Trent a printout of an email from the Chicago Bureau of Organized Crime.

"This is from their chief." Trent read the lengthy email. "They believe Le Grande has fallen for my trap. He's wants to sell a hundred thousand dollars' worth of heroin. Intel expects them to set this up anytime. Le Grande will name the place and time. You can bet it won't be in the warehouse district like the last one."

"No. It won't." Chief Williams pointed to the door. "Targeting the location is your job."

"Yes, sir." Trent rose and left the chief's office.

CATE HELPED DANNY slip his arms through the shoulder braces that hooked to the angel wings she and Mrs. Beabots had made. The white tunic he wore was edged in gold-and-white braid that Mrs. Beabots pulled out of a drawer filled with what looked like forty-year-old beaded belts, corded braids and tassels. She'd told Cate they were remnants from her days in

Paris. Cate had turned over one of the gorgeous braids and found a tag that read: Coco Chanel 31 Rue Cambon. Cate didn't know much about designers, but she believed she was looking at the genuine article.

Someone had been more than an angel to Cate and Danny. That someone was named Mrs. Beabots.

"How do I look, Mom?"

Cate assessed him and tried to be objective. "The cutest angel I've ever seen."

"Aw, Mom. Couldn't you just say I was handsome?" Danny looked over her shoulder just as Annie walked up.

Annie was dressed in a white tunic with a swirl of sky-blue fabric wound around her head and tied at her waist. She had a gold rope and tassel at her waist. Annie, with her riotous red hair and blue eyes, looked beautiful. Cate glanced at Danny. He was beaming at Annie.

No wonder he'd insisted they not leave until after the play. This was more than just a role. Cate stood and put her hand on Annie's shoulder. "Is your mom here, sweetie?"

"Yes. And my dad, too. He's helping Timmy with his costume. They changed it up a bit this year. They added a shepherd's hook."

Danny adjusted his bell sleeves. "Okay. I'll see you after the performance, Mom."

Cate knew when she was being dismissed. As she walked away, she noticed that Annie reached her hand to Danny and they skipped away toward the stage.

Cate opened the side door to the auditorium and gasped. Had the mayor proclaimed a holiday so that just about every person she knew in town could come to the play? Nearly every seat was taken. There were three rows filled with familiar faces: Sarah and Luke; Nate and Maddie; Gabe and Liz; Rafe and Olivia along with her mother, Julia; Mica sat next to his mother, Gina, who was holding hands with Sam; Austin and Katia; Jack and Sophie.

But no Trent Davis.

Mrs. Beabots waved to her. "Over here, Cate!" She patted the empty seat next to her. "I saved you a seat."

Cate greeted all her friends as she made her way down the aisle.

Just as she was about to sit, she saw Trent slip through the door, his eyes scanning the room like a surveillance camera. His face was devoid of any expression. If he saw her, he didn't acknowledge her. He walked up the aisle to the back of the room and as he did, she noticed a white coil coming from his ear. He lifted his wrist and spoke into it.

She should have been used to seeing him working, but in that instant, she was acutely aware of the danger he faced. He, and other officers like him, were the shields of protection not just for her but everyone in Indian Lake. Pride for him jolted through her, yet she braced herself. He was prepared for something. She needed to take her cue from him.

A Christmas carol played from the stereo. A child's voice came over the microphone. Cate could feel Trent's eyes on her, and every nerve in her body exploded.

Her fingers dug into her thighs in the hope of holding herself in her chair. The only thing she wanted to do now was grab Danny and run like the wind.

But she didn't.

Ever since the night of his disclosure about his PTSD, their actions toward each other had become distant; professional and heartbreaking. But what she felt now was different. She glanced again at Trent as he spoke into his wrist microphone.

She felt as if Trent was hiding her from something. If she or Danny were in greater danger than they'd already been in, Trent should confide in her. But he acted as if she were on another planet.

The heavy maroon stage curtains opened and the music increased in volume as the children paraded on stage singing "It Came Upon a Midnight Clear."

Timmy walked onstage, and with a handheld microphone he read the familiar Bible passage.

Cate didn't hear a word. She saw Trent leave. Then another man, also wearing a white coil earpiece, followed him. Something was happening.

In an instant, she felt alone and abandoned by Trent. A wave of dread came over her.

Brad.

Suddenly, Danny was onstage, standing on a riser higher than the rest of the children. He shouted his lines rather than spoke them.

"Joy to the World!" Danny yelled to the very back of the room.

Cate heard Luke behind her. "That kid's got presence."

"He's fantastic!" Gabe leaned over and whispered in Cate's ear.

She was torn between pride for her son and rising fear.

Danny continued with his lines and didn't falter. His enthusiasm brought applause from the audience. As everyone cheered and clapped for Danny, Cate noticed that Trent had returned to the assembly hall. He was applauding, too.

How had he appeared so instantaneously, as if he walked through walls? He stopped clapping before others had. He said something into his wrist again. Then he motioned to a man who walked down the aisle from the other side and eased his way in front of the others. He said something to the man sitting next to her. Her neighbor got up and left and Trent's cop sat.

"Who are you?" she demanded, her heart thundering in her chest. She'd been in this place before—the place where danger gathered strength.

"Sal Paluzzi." He offered his hand.

She took it. "What's going on?"

"When the play is over, I'm to escort you out."

"Is there a problem?"

"Just being cautious, ma'am."

Mrs. Beabots, who was sitting on the other side of Cate, took her hand.

Now Cate was truly frightened. Mrs. Beabots never held anyone's hand. She patted a hand. Or patted a knee. She hugged, very gently. But she never held a hand—or squeezed one as if to reassure. Mrs. Beabots was always assured. She was seldom afraid.

Cate exhaled through her nose as if to release the fear she'd been holding on to for the past twenty minutes. Her eyes flew to the stage. The children were singing "Hark! The Herald Angels Sing." They filed off the stage still singing. The pageant was over, and Cate barely remembered it.

The audience rose with thundering applause, demanding an encore. Some of the kids skipped back on stage. Annie was the lead actress, and she took a separate bow. Luke sprinted to the stage and handed a bouquet of flowers to his daughter. She bent to kiss her father.

The whistles and shouts were deafening. Mrs. Beabots was clapping. Cate was certain she was applauding, but whatever she did was rote. She felt numb.

The kids left the stage, but still, she didn't see Danny.

The man, Sal, took her elbow. "We need to make our way to the parking lot."

"Where's Danny? I didn't see Danny!" Cate said. "Where's my son?"

"He's with Detective Davis."

"Why?"

"For his protection."

Trent had received the report directly from Richard Schmitz, since he was part of the elite core of the CPD who were helping with the Le Grande gang sting.

For nearly a year, all of Indian Lake Police had known that the most active drug dealers conducted business in close vicinity to the area schools.

Richard's report stated that the Le Grande gang had rented a house on the south side of St. Mark's school yard. They'd been onsite less than four hours. Indian Lake PD had immediately started surveillance. Little had been moved into the house—duffel bags, food and folding chairs.

Trent believed this was a temporary site for Le Grande.

At 9:16 a.m., a white Cadillac Escalade with an Illinois license plate drove up.

Fourteen minutes prior to Danny's school pageant, Le Grande entered the rental house.

Throughout the play, Trent had been in constant communication with his team. Because Trent had been ordered to watch Cate Sullivan and her son, he would take point on the sting.

His palms itched with the desire to be the one to apprehend Le Grande.

When Trent went outside to take the call

from Chief Williams, he watched as a stream of cars pulled into St. Mark's school yard. He was amazed. It was a kid's Christmas play. A quick count told Trent there were nearly three hundred people, and they were still arriving.

"Code Purple," Ned had radioed all the team members.

The Indian Lake PD was prepared for a possible kidnapping attempt. Trent knew that Sal was inside the auditorium, assigned to Cate. Once the play ended, Sal would walk Cate to the station, and there, he and Cate would wait in a Honda minivan until Trent met them with Danny. From the station, they would drive downstate to Carmel, Indiana, where a safe house had been prepared for Cate and Danny until Le Grande was apprehended and permanently behind bars. Trent hadn't told Cate how long that process would be, but he hoped it wouldn't be more than six months—for their sakes.

Trent felt they'd prepared a viable strategy. He'd been up most of the night making the necessary relocation plans. He'd even arranged to have the Christmas tree moved for them. And Cate's favorite aqua throw.

As the play was ending, Trent couldn't help being caught up in the praise for the kids.

They'd all done a great job, and Danny had stolen the show with his exuberant innocence. If ever there was child to make one believe in angels, it was Danny Sullivan.

The children had gone offstage, and Trent gave Sal the sign to escort Cate to the station. Sal's unmarked car was parked in the parking lot only six vehicles from the back door. Cate would be fine.

Parents, friends, family members and the other schoolchildren formed a riptide of humanity that Trent hadn't calculated into his equation. Getting backstage to Danny took several minutes longer than he'd planned.

As he'd promised Cate, he purposefully didn't explain any of the details of his plan, of their moving after the play to Danny. Neither of them wanted Danny to be unduly frightened, especially if Le Grande didn't show up.

Now that he had, a new layer of concern landed on Trent's shoulders. He needed to get to Danny. If only to ease his own tensions.

The kids were taking off their choir robes and tossing them at each other playfully, to the dismay of Mary Catherine Cook, who laughed along with them as much as she scolded them.

Recognizing her from the time he'd made a presentation to her third-grade class, he went over to her. "Have you seen Danny Sullivan? The little angel?"

"He is, isn't he?" She chuckled. "But no, I haven't." She leaned over and whispered, "If you find Annie Bosworth, you'll find Danny. Look for her mother."

"Good tip," he said, and scanned the room, which, from his height, was easy. The heads of the children bobbed as they giggled and whispered to their friends.

He walked past shepherds removing their tunics and a wise man gingerly removing his paper crown.

The audience had dispersed, and many had gone outside. Trent couldn't find Danny. A terror's jagged edge sliced through him. It was the first time in his life he knew what it felt like to lose the most precious thing. A child.

Danny wasn't even his, yet his heart thundered and his feet moved with incredible speed. "Danny!" he shouted as he made his way up the aisle. He jumped on a chair and scanned the entire room. "Danny Sullivan!"

People looked at him like he was crazy.

He jumped down and slammed his palms against the door handle, shoving the door against the outside brick wall.

"Danny!" he shouted into the frigid morning.

It was Annie's red hair he saw first. Luke and Sarah were belting themselves into their SUV, which was on the far south side of the playground.

Annie was standing outside the red SUV talking to Danny. She laughed and touched his wings.

Trent started toward Danny. The boy was still in costume. No coat. No hat. No mittens.

People milled about and crossed in front of Trent as he made his way toward Danny. Astounding how many relatives and friends a little kid could have and how many of them wanted to be part of their Christmas.

Annie kissed Danny on the cheek and got in the car. She buckled up and waved to him. He waved back. The Bosworths drove away.

"Danny!"

Danny looked up. His eyes met Trent's.

But Trent hadn't called Danny's name. Not at that moment.

Le Grande stepped away from a family of three who cut to the left and went to their car.

Le Grande grinned defiantly at Trent and then dropped his eyes.

Trent stopped breathing. Time altered as it always did when he went back there. But this time, something was different. The scene didn't change. He was still in the moment and as horrifying as it was to watch Le Grande take two strides, reach out his arm and grab Danny by his angel wings, Trent had not flashed back.

"Danny!" Trent shouted with so much force, he thought he'd ripped a vocal cord.

Danny screamed. "Trent! Trent!"

Trent didn't know what happened. His legs felt like iron had replaced his bones and muscles. He lunged toward Le Grande, who'd hoisted Danny under his arm. Le Grande turned and quickly shot away.

"Danny!" Trent shouted.

"Help!" Danny cried. "Help me, Trent!"

Trent forced his legs to run. He lifted his wrist and shouted. "Two-oh-seven in progress. Kidnapping. Send backup."

CATE SAT IN Sal's unmarked car watching her only son, the light of her life, being kidnapped by her psychotic ex-husband.

Chills raced down her spine. Her blood turned to ice, and she opened the door, unbuckled her seat belt and took off running.

The one thing Cate could do was run.

Brad had Danny.

Fear spread wide, menacing wings over her and then drew them in, strangling her. As incredulous and horrific as this was, Cate had known it could happen.

It was inconceivable to imagine a single day in her life without Danny. She pushed away the vision as it sailed toward her like a whorl of black smoke, a funnel of possibilities, sinister and deadly.

Sheer will pumped her legs—faster. She had to save Danny. The jarring up her spine as she pounded against the cold asphalt was the only thing telling her that what she was doing was right.

She should never have let Trent talk her into this insanity. She'd succumbed to altruism and community pride. As much as she'd believed that Brad would stop at nothing to get her back, she'd trusted Trent to keep them safe. She'd believed more in Trent and his promises than her own gut instincts. She should have insisted they leave town sooner. She should have run.

The cold air froze Cate's ears and muted all sound.

The world around her fell away. Her vision was focused solely on Brad. Danny had freed an arm and was pounding on Brad's back. He screamed for her, but she didn't hear his voice.

She watched his lips moving as if they were in slow motion.

She ran faster. Adrenaline sang through her body like smashing cymbals. The rush of energy catapulted her toward the street without looking for traffic. Oncoming cars didn't dare stop her.

Shouting Danny's name was impossible. No sound came from her throat, but she felt the fire of anger surge through her veins.

What was she going to do once she reached Brad? Shoot him? She didn't have a gun. Strangle him? He still had Danny. Brad was big and strong—just like Danny dreamed of being. How sweet Danny had been all autumn wanting anything and everything that would mark his passing from a little kid to a bigger kid. Danny wanted so much to be grown up, and she did everything she could to hold him in place. Making time stand still hadn't worked.

Her face burned with emotion. Sadness. Terror. Dread and above all, determination.

Brad would never have Danny. She'd rather die first.

She focused on Brad. What was he planning to do with Danny, now that he'd snatched him?

Her peripheral vision scanned the curb along

the street. She didn't see a vehicle. No paneled SUV in which to abscond with Danny.

She realized that Brad was running toward a house with peeling white paint and broken shutters. She saw faces behind the windows. Evil faces. Men with guns.

Guns. Instruments of death.

She had no weapon. She wasn't wearing protective clothing or a Kevlar vest. These men could kill her. They could kill Danny.

Her ears had cleared along with another hot surge of adrenaline. She could hear Sal calling her name. She heard his heavy shoes hammer the pavement as he chased her, but she would beat him.

Even though Trent was nearing the street crossing ahead of her, she was more than half-way across the parking lot.

Trent. She'd been wrong to let herself fall in love with him. He didn't care about her or Danny. He was a cop apprehending a criminal. Doing his duty.

If she'd been so much the fool that she lost Danny because of Trent, there was nowhere on Earth far enough away for her to run.

"Mom!" Danny screamed.

Cate pumped her arms and ran faster. The cops couldn't save Danny, but she would. Even if those evil men shot her, even if Brad beat her, she would save her son.

POLICE SIRENS SLICED the brittle December air. The cars exiting the school parking lot stopped. Cops on foot thundered down the sidewalk toward the school. Orders were being shouted, but Trent couldn't make them out. Didn't want to hear them. He had to save Danny.

Trent hurdled over the curb, crossed the street and just as Le Grande was about to hit the steps to the house, Trent lunged at him, grabbed him by the heels and brought him down.

Danny screamed as he hit the sidewalk.

Trent grabbed Le Grande by the shoulders and yanked his arms back. "No, you don't. You're mine."

"Get off me, pig!" Le Grande spat and tried to wrench out from Trent's hold.

Trent reached in his pocket and pulled out a regulation zip tie and snapped Le Grande's wrists together. Then he leaned very close to Le Grande's ear. "And now I've got you for kidnapping."

Le Grande spewed a string of obscenities like venom.

Trent ignored him as his eyes flew to Danny. "Danny..." His reassuring smile died on his lips as he saw the painful grimace on the boy's face. "Danny... I'm so sorry."

The child's face was slick with tears as he held his left arm with his right. Danny looked up as Cate ran to him and scooped him off the pavement. "Danny, darling. Are you hurt?"

Danny's expression was stoic, but his eyes swam with tears. "My arm. Mom, I think I broke it."

The action around Trent increased in tempo like a film on fast-forward.

Sal rushed up and already had his cell phone out. "I need an ambulance."

Sal took out his gun as he bounded up the steps and kicked down the front door. "Police! Freeze!"

A melee of uniformed policeman overran the house and hustled to assist Sal indoors. Police cars skidded to a halt at the curb.

Trent hauled Le Grande to his feet. He had a raspberry on his nose where Trent had pressed his face against the pavement.

"Danny, you're going to be all right," Trent said. "An ambulance is on the way."

He looked at Cate. Her aqua eyes were unforgiving.

CHAPTER TWENTY-FIVE

CATE KISSED THE top of Danny's head for the hundredth time in the past two hours. Already, the pandemonium of police officers arresting the drug dealers, Trent and Sal dragging a very resistant Brad to a squad car and the EMTs who strapped Danny onto a gurney seemed surreal.

Trent had held her hand as she climbed into the back of the ambulance. "Cate, forgive me." Then he'd shut the doors.

She hadn't answered him. All she could think of at that moment was Danny. She'd sat on the narrow bench along the ambulance wall and placed her hand on the top of Danny's head. "You're going to be all right, sweetheart."

But was she?

A thousand recriminations swirled like a tornado inside her. Cate knew she was at a crossroads in her life. Danny had been saved. Yes. But at what cost? Would he be traumatized—like Trent? Would he shut down his innocence and high-spirited friendliness that drew people to him like the magnetized force he was? All through these days of semi-hiding, under Trent's promised protection, Danny had blossomed. He'd always been precocious, but she now saw leadership qualities in him. He wasn't the least afraid to show his affection for Annie.

That was more than she could say for herself. She'd jumped out there, kissed Trent and he'd recoiled like a turtle into its shell. She'd backed away, too.

Her choices from here could determine whether Danny went on being the Danny he was born to be, full of a sense of adventure and willingness to learn new things and most importantly, to go on trusting people to do what they say they're going to do.

Cate was afraid that if she revealed one trace of her own fears and paranoia, she would stifle him more than all the shock and panic he'd been through today.

"I love you, Danny," she whispered, but the EMTs were talking on radios to the hospital and drowned out her voice.

His tears had dried, and the EMTs had stabilized his arm with a splint and a sling. Ice packs had helped to numb his pain. As the ambulance pulled away from the curb, rocking slightly as it hit a pothole, Danny had winced.

The one-mile trip to the hospital was over in a blink. The EMTs wheeled Danny into an ER bay that had been made ready for him.

"THE BREAK IS MINOR. A fracture of the ulna," Dr. Hill, the emergency-room doctor, said. "But we still have to cast it. Fortunately, the EMTs did a good job stabilizing it and I don't have to reset it." He leaned close to Danny. "Resetting can be painful. This way, you don't have to go through that. The worst is over, sport."

"Thank you," Danny said politely. "So, does this mean I don't have to have any shots?"

"Shots?" Cate asked.

"Yeah. I was thinking I'd have to have shots. That's why I was crying."

Cate dropped her jaw in amazement. "You weren't crying from the pain?"

He gave her a crooked grin. "No way. I'm big now. Tough like Trent. It's just a broken arm."

Cate rolled her eyes.

A nurse came in with an assortment of materials. Soft cotton pads and gauze were applied to the skin. "Danny," he said, "you have to choose the color of fiberglass."

"Yes!"

Danny mulled over the choices from checkerboard patterns, pink, yellow, blue and finally chose neon green.

Once the arm was cast, Danny was released.

As they walked out the hospital doors into the December afternoon, Cate realized her car was at the school.

"Trent!" Danny yelled. "Look, Mom, he came for us!"

The afternoon sun, as harsh and precise as a diamond-cutting blade, blinded her. She raised her hand to shield her eyes. Trent was standing in front of his car, arms folded across his chest. He'd been looking down at the pavement, but at the sound of Danny's voice, his head jerked up and he smiled so broadly, Cate felt the warmth of it.

Danny raced toward him before she could stop him with warnings about possible dizzy spells from his earlier fall.

Trent squatted and opened his arms to Danny, who flung his arms around Trent's neck.

"Ouch!" Trent laughed, lifting his hand to Danny's small, cast-covered arm. "Green, huh?"

"Yeah, they didn't have dark green, but they had Grinch green, I call it. You can sign it. The nurse gave me a special pen for my friends to use." Danny looked at his arm. "I'm gonna ask Annie to sign it next."

"What about your mom?" Trent asked, finally looking at Cate as she crossed the driveway.

"Oh, she can sign it anytime," Danny replied.

Trent rose slowly, not taking his eyes off her. She wondered if he could see her trepidation.

She pulled the lapels of her long red wool coat over the black turtleneck and black pants she wore. Her black boots crunched against the piles of dirty, plowed snow.

She pointed to his car. "Is that another Christmas tree tied to your car?"

"No. Actually, it's yours," he said, stumbling a bit over his words.

She wondered if he was nervous. Impossible. The man was a hero. He'd just rid the town of the largest drug cartel in its history. In the ER, the nurses had talked of nothing else. The news of the bust was being reported by the local radio station.

"I thought I'd drive you home."

"Home?" She moved closer, still thinking about that invisible crossroads. His eyes were glittering blue pools—serious, searching and hope filled. For much of their time together, he'd trained himself to shut her out. He'd built a wall so strong and permanent, she was convinced he'd never let her through. But here was a door, and she knew it was up to her to turn the knob. Take a chance. See what was behind the door.

"I want to take you to your home. Where you and Danny belong."

"Really?" Danny asked. "I liked it at Mrs. Beabots's house. She was always making cookies for me."

Trent's mouth turned up into a half smile. His eyes twinkled. "My mother taught me how to make sugar cookies. A Christmas tradition I still keep," Trent said, his gaze on Cate.

She tilted her head to the side. "Christmas tree and cookies? Are you trying to wrangle an invitation from us?" She wasn't quite sure what he wanted, an evening with them? Did he want to be their companion for the holidays? Or was this part of his processing to assuage whatever guilt he harbored over the fact that Danny had nearly been kidnapped and suffered a broken arm.

"No, it's more than that." He shook his head sheepishly. "I just thought that after I got you settled at home, put the tree up, that I could help out—in the kitchen."

"The kitchen," she repeated. Disappointment wrapped sinewy fingers around her heart. He was being cordial. Performing his duty as he'd always done. That was all, she was certain.

"Sure." She went to stand behind Danny and put her hands on his shoulders. "You can drive us home, yes." She nodded toward the tree. "And it would be very kind of you to bring the tree in. But we can take it from there."

Before he said another word, she walked to the passenger door and waited for him to unlock the car.

Danny was thrilled to be in the backseat of a real police car with no child protective seat to hinder his movement or his animated conversation. The cast notwithstanding, Danny couldn't wait to rehash every detail of his own near-miss with tragedy.

Cate noticed that Trent's responses were monosyllabic. And that his eyes tracked to her nearly every other second.

Once at home, Cate was surprised at the flood of relief she felt in the simple act of inserting her key in the door. Danny pressed past her and pushed his way between her and Trent.

"We're home! Home for Christmas!" He whirled around. "Isn't this the best Christmas ever?"

"It is, sweetheart," Cate answered, not believing it.

"I gotta check out my room. See if everything's still there. You're not going away, are you, Trent?"

"No, buddy. I'm not," he replied, casting a doubtful look at Cate. "I grabbed a few things at Mrs. Beabots's for you," Trent said. "I'll go back to get more once we get the tree up...for Danny."

"Yes," she said, putting her keys in the shell-shaped dish on the table near the door. "I'll help you with the tree."

"No need," he said. "It's small." He slipped out the door without looking at her.

Cate took off her coat and hung it neatly in the front closet.

"Where do you want it?" Trent asked, standing just outside the front door, waiting for permission as if he'd never crossed the threshold before.

"In the corner by the fireplace."

"Just like Mrs. Beabots. You two have a lot in common," he said with a wan smile, walking past her.

She watched as he stood the tree up and moved a box of firewood and starters out of the way.

"That's where we put it every year, and I've always thought it looked so homey..."

He turned, and his face was filled with determination as he took three strides toward her. He reached out to hold her shoulders. "Cate. I can't stand another minute of being in the same room with you and not telling you..."

"Tell me what?" She'd tilted her head to take in his handsome face. His eyes spilled over with all the sparkling emotion she'd hoped to see. It was love in all its glory. She was back at that fork. Hovering. Panting with anticipation, praying that the road before her would be filled with joy.

"I love—I love you," he said with a hitch. "But that's not enough."

"Trent—"

He placed two fingers on her lips and pulled her closer with his other arm. "Don't say anything. I owe you so much, and none of it has to do with what happened today. Although, I hope you can forgive me for Danny. I miscalculated the flood of people backstage and Danny got away so quickly. Before I knew it, Le Grande had him… I'm so sorry." He paused. "But that's not really what I want to say."

She took his fingers from her lips and kissed them. She curled her hand around his, protectively. "Tell me, then."

"Because of you, I want… I mean, I need to try to put the past behind me. For good. I'm willing to do anything, Cate. Therapy. Counseling. I've done some research, and there are a number of new therapies out there for PTSD. Virtual reality treatments. Cognitive restructuring is supposed to help my sense of bad memories. I've already started with some stress inoculation training. I saw it online, and it's amazing. In just one session it's helped me to look at my past in a much healthier way." He took a deep breath. "Cate, I want you to know I've contacted a psychologist in Chicago. Richard Schmitz says the CPD highly recommends him. But all this is to say that I've realized, Cate, I now have a purpose for wanting to be healed. And that purpose is you."

Awe for the magnitude of the love she had for him nearly buckled her knees. Nearly. She sagged against him, putting her arms around his massive chest and placing her cheek against his heart. She'd opened the golden door—the door to her own heart—and walked into her new life.

"I'll help you in every way I can. Attitude and determination are so important."

He lifted her chin with his fingers. "So is love. Everything I want in life is right here with you and Danny. From the little Christmas tree to the prayers you say with Danny at bedtime. I don't think I can spend another day of my life without you in it. You and Danny have come to mean everything to me. Tell me you forgive me," he said pleadingly.

"Oh, Trent. There's nothing to forgive. I knew what I was getting into. I was afraid, but deep down, I think I always believed you were the only person who could stop Brad— for good. And I was right. You did protect us. You saved Danny."

He touched her nose with his as he rested his forehead against hers. "Now you're saving me."

"I'm saving us, Trent. We'll do this together. I promise."

"Then will you make me another promise?" he asked.

Cate couldn't help the smile and giggle. She felt light and free as she never had. People were wrong when they said love tied a person down.

She felt as if she were filled with helium and could float to the stars. "Getting greedy, are we?" she teased and kissed him softly.

"Promise me you'll never stop doing that, for one. And for another, marry me, Cate. Marry me and let me be part of your life."

Cate eased her arms around his neck. This time when she kissed him she held nothing back. She let him know that hers was a heart meant for loving. Releasing him was the hardest thing she'd ever done.

"Well?" he asked, staring at her with anxiety all over his face.

"What?" She blinked.

He stood stock-still, not even taking a breath. She gasped. "Didn't I say yes?"

"No." He laughed. "You didn't."

"Yes! Yes."

"Thank God." He exhaled and crushed her in his arms.

Effervescent happiness filled Cate. Out of the corner of her eye, she saw Danny had tiptoed down the hall and watched them.

"I told you, Mom, this is the best Christmas of all."

Danny raced into their open arms.

Trent kissed Danny's cheek and beamed at

Cate. "We are the Christmas miracle I never thought could happen."

Cate kissed them both, believing for the first time there was joy in the world.

* * * * *

*If you enjoyed this story by
Catherine Lanigan, check out
SOPHIE'S PATH,
FEAR OF FALLING and
KATIA'S PROMISE.*

*And come back to Indian Lake in
Lanigan's next book,
coming in July 2017
from Harlequin Heartwarming!
Available at harlequin.com.*

Get 2 Free Books,
Plus 2 Free Gifts—
just for trying the Reader Service!

Get 2 Free Books,
Plus 2 Free Gifts—
just for trying the Reader Service!

HOMETOWN HEARTS ♡

YES! Please send me **The Hometown Hearts Collection** in Larger Print. This collection begins with 3 FREE books and 2 FREE gifts in the first shipment. Along with my 3 free books, I'll also get the next 4 books from the Hometown Hearts Collection, in LARGER PRINT, which I may either return and owe nothing, or keep for the low price of $4.99 U.S./ $5.89 CDN each plus $2.99 for shipping and handling per shipment*. If I decide to continue, about once a month for 8 months I will get 6 or 7 more books, but will only need to pay for 4. That means 2 or 3 books in every shipment will be FREE! If I decide to keep the entire collection, I'll have paid for only 32 books because 19 books are FREE! I understand that accepting the 3 free books and gifts places me under no obligation to buy anything. I can always return a shipment and cancel at any time. My free books and gifts are mine to keep no matter what I decide.

262 HCN 3432 462 HCN 3432

Name	(PLEASE PRINT)	
Address		Apt. #
City	State/Prov.	Zip/Postal Code

Signature (if under 18, a parent or guardian must sign)

Mail to the **Reader Service:**
IN U.S.A.: P.O. Box 1867, Buffalo, NY. 14240-1867
IN CANADA: P.O. Box 609, Fort Erie, Ontario L2A 5X3

* Terms and prices subject to change without notice. Prices do not include applicable taxes. Sales tax applicable in NY. Canadian residents will be charged applicable taxes. This offer is limited to one order per household. All orders subject to approval. Credit or debit balances in a customer's account(s) may be offset by any other outstanding balance owed by or to the customer. Please allow 4 to 6 weeks for delivery. Offer available while quantities last. Offer not available to Quebec residents.

Your Privacy—The Reader Service is committed to protecting your privacy. Our Privacy Policy is available online at www.ReaderService.com or upon request from the Reader Service.

We make a portion of our mailing list available to reputable third parties that offer products we believe may interest you. If you prefer that we not exchange your name with third parties, or if you wish to clarify or modify your communication preferences, please visit us at www.ReaderService.com/consumerschoice or write to us at Reader Service Preference Service, P.O. Box 9062, Buffalo, NY. 14240-9062. Include your complete name and address.

Get 2 Free Books,
Plus 2 Free Gifts—
just for trying the Reader Service!

YES! Please send me 2 FREE LARGER-PRINT Harlequin® Superromance® novels and my 2 FREE gifts (gifts are worth about $10 retail). After receiving them, if I don't wish to receive any more books, I can return the shipping statement marked "cancel." If I don't cancel, I will receive 4 brand-new novels every month and be billed just $6.19 per book in the U.S. or $6.49 per book in Canada. That's a savings of at least 11% off the cover price! It's quite a bargain! Shipping and handling is just 50¢ per book in the U.S. or 75¢ per book in Canada.* I understand that accepting the 2 free books and gifts places me under no obligation to buy anything. I can always return a shipment and cancel at any time. Even if I never buy another book, the 2 free books and gifts are mine to keep forever.

132/332 HDN GLQN

Name _____ (PLEASE PRINT)

Address _____ Apt. # _____

City _____ State/Prov. _____ Zip/Postal Code _____

Signature (if under 18, a parent or guardian must sign)

Mail to the **Reader Service**:
IN U.S.A.: P.O. Box 1867, Buffalo, NY 14240-1867
IN CANADA: P.O. Box 611, Fort Erie, Ontario L2A 9Z9

Want to try two free books from another line?
Call 1-800-873-8635 today or visit www.ReaderService.com.

* Terms and prices subject to change without notice. Prices do not include applicable taxes. Sales tax applicable in N.Y. Canadian residents will be charged applicable taxes. Offer not valid in Quebec. This offer is limited to one order per household. Books received may not be as shown. Not valid for current subscribers to Harlequin Superromance Larger-Print books. All orders subject to credit approval. Credit or debit balances in a customer's account(s) may be offset by any other outstanding balance owed by or to the customer. Please allow 4 to 6 weeks for delivery. Offer available while quantities last.

Your Privacy—The Reader Service is committed to protecting your privacy. Our Privacy Policy is available online at www.ReaderService.com or upon request from the Reader Service.

We make a portion of our mailing list available to reputable third parties that offer products we believe may interest you. If you prefer that we not exchange your name with third parties, or if you wish to clarify or modify your communication preferences, please visit us at www.ReaderService.com/consumerschoice or write to us at Reader Service Preference Service, P.O. Box 9062, Buffalo, NY 14240-9062. Include your complete name and address.